Journalist, story-writer, play... Evans (1878-1945) became the ... *My People,* a collection of ... Wales, was published in 191... the outstanding narrative and satirical write... ...

John Harris is a lecturer at the College of Librarianship, Aberystwyth. He is well-known for his bibliographic work, and has edited *My People* and *Fury Never Leaves Us* by Caradoc Evans.

CW00395143

CARADOC EVANS

Nothing to Pay

with an afterword
by John Harris

CARDINAL

A CARDINAL BOOK

This edition presents the text of the novel as published by W. W. Norton (New York) in 1930. There are small differences between this and the British edition (Faber and Faber, 1930): the American edition corrects a few misprints and offers some slight revision. The main change is a reversal of the order of the first two chapters. The Faber edition begins with what in the present edition is chapter 2; that is, with Amos being lifted above his grandfather's coffin.

Published in Great Britain by Carcanet Press Ltd 1989
This edition published in Cardinal by Sphere Books Ltd 1990

Text copyright © The Estate of Caradoc Evans 1989
Afterword copyright © John Harris 1989

All characters in this publication are fictitious
and any resemblance to real persons, living or dead
is purely coincidental.

All rights reserved.
No part of this publication may be reproduced,
stored in a retrieval system, or transmitted, in any
form or by any means without the prior
permission in writing of the publisher, nor be
otherwise circulated in any form of binding or
cover other than that in which it is published and
without a similar condition including this
condition being imposed on the subsequent purchaser.

Printed and bound in Great Britain by
The Guernsey Press Co Ltd, Guernsey, Channel Islands

ISBN 0 7474 0717 7

Sphere Books Ltd
A Division of
Macdonald & Co (Publishers) Ltd
Orbit House
1 New Fetter Lane
London EC4A 1AR

A member of Maxwell Macmillan Pergamon Publishing Corporation

NOTHING TO PAY

CHAPTER I

AMOS MORGAN was the son of Ianto the son of Shacki the son of Bensha Wedding Bidder.

In the spring of her years Bensha's wife Matilda bore the child Shacki, and she was consumed by a burning malady. Wherefore Bensha departed from God; he chewed tobacco, drank strong beer, scambled at fairs and ploughing matches, and wenched with women in their beds. He was a head over every man in Breoc; this is the plain of arable and pasture and moor on the broad way which comes up from Cardigan and goes to Aberystwyth and at the stretch where tracts went to the limekilns of New Quay and Llangranog on Cardigan Bay. He had great strength: he enticed a bull to the sea shore and into Caranoc's Cave and wrestled with it and brought it to its knees and he carried a calf in his arms through the twenty-five miles of heath and hill and valley to the inland town of Castle Owain. He had great daring: he entangled in a fishing-net the merman who wrecked a vessel in New Quay and dashed him against the lighthouse rock, and of all the people he alone remained in the streets at Castle Owain during the visitation of the flying serpent.

Furthermore he had much skill in the making of hedges; whereas the life of a hedge is the life of three men, it was said that the life of a hedge by Bensha would be that of six men. A certain farmer in Breoc, knowing that he loved hedging more than he loved woman, hired Bensha to fence his land and gave him and the lad Shacki a bed in his stable loft and food and small beer and nine shillings a week. Bensha laboured constantly, except on the uncommon occasions that he journeyed to announce a coming wedding and to bid gifts in money and kind for the bride and bridegroom; and on these occasions folk were glad to see him in his gay attire: azure cutaway coat with brass buttons, waistcoat of patches of many colours, corduroy knee breeches, grey woollen stockings, a staff hung with scarlet ribbons; and he sang songs of his own making and they were lewd songs and he told jests that were carnal jests.

Hence Bensha Bidder, it being a Welsh custom to join the name of a man's calling or of his house to his name.

One day he was bidding presents for his master's daughter. When he was come to the edge of the moor a ram charged him. He seized the animal and threw it from him. Immediately he had done so he was disquieted, inasmuch as he thought that the ram was possessed by God or Satan and was urging him forward for good or evil. He called the ram to him that he might read its eyes, but it scampered off.

Three miles below him was Avon Ceri. Like window-panes were the small fields on the hillside and like the white smoke from God's nostrils was the mist over the valley. There was a house here and a house there, but Bensha could not see a house of God. He spat out a quid of tobacco and with a handful of heather wiped his bushy beard of its yellow stains; and he waved his garlanded staff into the Sign of the Cross. Then he went on the cart lane the toes of which are in the valley, the desire of his soul having changed. He heard the sharpening of scythes and he entered into a field and made the Sign of the Cross. The men who were cutting hay and the women who were scattering it saw him.

'Bensha Bidder!'

'Ben—sha!'

'A song of the love night!'

'And a frothy jest!'

Bensha spoke and his voice was rich past their understanding:

'Thatch the head of your rick you will with straw. But you have no thatch for God's head.'

The owner of the field was confounded that such a saying should issue from such ribald lips. He marked Bensha's mouth

8

and he knew that the man was not drunk.

'Nearest capel is in Castle Owain,' he said. 'Ten miles and over.'

'Has God then,' cried Bensha, 'forgotten Ceri?'

He reached the tramping road that brings you into Ceri from the Well of the Cross which is to the south of Breoc. Perhaps this road was once the path by which pilgrims went to the Well. He passed over the bridge where the Ceri winds, his back and his left hand on the sheltering hills and his right on the river. At Big Pistil the road forks, one prong going upward to meet the highway for Castle Owain and one continuing in the valley. He climbed upward that his body should be wearied in well doing. In house and field he recited pieces from the Bible and chanted little prayers; and in many breasts that day there was conceived a longing for a chapel in which the true God could be worshipped in the true language. Many of the people knew that the God of the Church was a heathen, they having had this declared unto them from the pulpits of Cardigan and Castle Owain and by preachers passing through Ceri.

Night fell and Bensha was again at Big Pistil. He went on the lower prong and came to the end of the valley, being nearly three miles from Pont Ceri. It is here that the Parish Church hides her steeple in a cluster of trees.

A husbandman was folding his cattle and he asked Bensha:

'Bidder, what you carry?'

Upon Bensha delivering his message, the man took him into his house.

'Rest you awhile,' said Daniel, 'for weary you must be. And eat a bowl of uwd.'

Bensha supped of the flummery oatmeal and milk; and Daniel's wife Sal brought a loaf of bread which had not been broken and she broke it and the first piece she gave to him; and under the wide, low open chimney he gazed at the stars and spoke of the Welsh God.

'Parson Church is a dam,' said Daniel.

'He cannot talk the Welsh,' said Sal.

'Come you, Bidder,' said Daniel, 'to our abodes on Sabbaths

9

with your gentle prayers and thunderous preaches.'

'Yes,' said Sal; 'come you now your tongue is whitewashed of badness.'

'Breoc is far from Ceri,' Bensha answered.

'Jasto!' exclaimed Daniel, using a word the significance of which has been lost. 'Pitch a house on the moor.'

'How can one pitch a house in a night?'

The moor was common land, and it was an ancient law that any man who built a house thereon in a night and unseen by human eye could not be removed, and the same law stood by the man who fenced a piece of moorland. But he had no redress if one seeing him destroyed his walls and his fence.

'Take a night or ten nights to pitch your house,' said Daniel. 'My hands shall help you and my gun shall shoot the man who says nay.'

The morning was the Sabbath and Parson, having put his horse to graze among the graves, tolled his bell. Only his four women servants obeyed the call and within twenty minutes they were going homeward; and young men were playing at kicking the black ball and their goal was the eastern forehead of the church and Parson was on a tombstone shouting the orders of the game.

'Look you, Bidder,' said Daniel, 'how he can hardly keep his legs for drink.'

'And hearken,' said Sal, 'there is no other burial place in Ceri.'

'This,' said Bensha, 'would silence an angel's harp.'

'And he puts us down in the thin English language,' Sal wailed. 'And in the Big Waking hap the Angel will mistake us for the English and close against us the door of the Mansion.'

Bensha turned to the sea; and answering his master he said that he had been bidding for God. The master sent him and the boy Shacki out of his sight, denying them the stable loft even for a night.

Bensha came back to the moor and he fixed stakes around an acre in which he made a quarry and digged stones. He also fixed poles around fifteen acres of land, and in this, at the place

10

where the ram had charged him, he began to build a house. A man whose sheep fed on the moor was jealous of his rights, and he spied on Bensha and seeing him started to tear down the walls, as the law had it. But Daniel shot at him and blinded an eye, and when he had ceased his hullaballooing, Bensha said to him: 'Bear you your brand for God's sake.' The mud and stone house was called Tyrhos, which is the House on the Moor, and it was a quarter of a mile from the quarry.

The people were more glad of Bensha Preacher than they had been of Bensha Bidder. On the Sabbath they came to Tyrhos to hear him pray and preach and to sing hymns in his company. He was often sought to go and comfort the dying, and every night a candle burnt at his window that no messenger should lose his way and howsoever black or stormy the time none asked him in vain. The cart lane was trodden into a road and unto this day it is called Road Saints.

Bensha made his fifteen acres as fruitful as he could. He died and was buried in the Church burial-ground. His memorials are the hedges at Tyrhos and in the land as you go down to New Quay.

Houses were put up on the hillside and on the tramping road both sides of Pont Ceri. Jonathan the father of Ben opened a shop, and David the father of Deio made a wooden shed for carpentry, and Luke the father of Simon Schoolin set up as a stonemason. They three had their houses on the tramping road and they made a treaty, saying to the people: 'Let us build a Capel Moriah.' They chose a parcel of ground at the rise of the prong against Big Pistil; and men and women, hungry for spiritual refreshment and in the certainty of a God other than the God of the jocose Parson, brought stones from Bensha's quarry and timber from their fields; and so that the doors of the finished Moriah should be opened they made sacrifices in money that Jonathan and David and Luke were paid for the building and the furnishing of Moriah.

Shacki Bensha's son pulled down Tyrhos and on its place he built a house which had a stall for a horse and two stalls for cows and a sty for pigs, and on the slope a few feet below it he built another and this he portioned out into a dairy, a dwellingplace, and a smithy, and each portion had a door, and the house looked like three houses. The number of Shacki's children was two: Ianto Tall, so named for his height, and Abel Robber, so named for his thievings. Abel ran away in the fear of the law. Ianto married Silah Harelip, and she was the mother of the child Amos.

CHAPTER II

AMOS was in his sixth year when on a winter afternoon the hefty, red-haired Katrin lifted him above a coffin which rested on six chairs.

'There,' she said, placing the child's body on the body which was in the coffin, 'is the perished corpse of your grandfather.'

'The little boolin,' said Deio Carpenter, calling the child by a childish name, 'can't get flat for the knees of the corpse are crook.'

'For why, Deio, you didn't pull them straight?' asked Simon Schoolin, cantankerously closing his squint eye as was his manner when setting a problem.

'Your work is summing, Schoolin,' said Deio. 'Mine is doing.'

'Because the coffin,' said Schoolin, 'would need more timber and more nails and more yellow varnish yes.'

Amos had scrambled out and was on the floor drawing traces with spittle-moistened fingers on the name-plate.

'A clatch I'll give you on the backhead,' Katrin cried, dragging him to his feet, 'for your huff to the corpse.'

'Odd for sure me,' said Deio, 'that crook knees don't stiffen in the dead.' He spread out his wide long, beard on his chest and looked at it as if he was measuring the mystery.

Ben Shop touched the crook knee and then drawing his fingers from the nape of his neck over his bald pate to the tip of his nose, as if he also was trying to measure the mystery, he said: 'Death is a great stiffener.' He pressed his nostrils to hide the meaning of his mouth.

Schoolin struck his tuning fork and with unassuming cow-like lips led in a doleful hymn the people who stood on the uneven flagstones of the small, moulded parlour of Tyrhos; and the hard voices of the singers sent the fowls scuttling and clucking from the dung-heap in the close.

The hymn ended and Richard Preacher Capel Moriah spoke: 'I'm going to do a prayer, being prayer number one. Prayer number two will be in the capel and prayer number three at the graveside – at the side of the yawning grave.' He closed his eyes and lifted his husky voice: 'O Big Man, death is in this house. The house Tyrhos. House Shacki Morgan. We knew death was coming. Enoch Gravedigger smelt him and what did Enoch do for not to waste time? He put a new edge on his pickaxe and an edge on his shovel and an edge on his spade. And where death is, O Big Man, there must also be a very religious preacher. If he is not there where will go the perished? Parson Church will steal him. Be with us from here to Moriah. Your little servant will ride in Deio's cart for nothing. Iss, for nothing, Deio Carpenter, and don't you make your face as awful as it is. Big Man, keep at the side of Deio's mare, for slippy is Road Saints and the mare is a madam. For now then, amen.'

Deio tapped the coffin with his screw-driver, and said:

'Any more peepers?'

Ianto Tall stepped to the coffin, and stood thereat with Amos wedged between his legs. He bowed his head and bit his moustaches which were like a horse's mane, and he uttered the sounds of anguish that are expected from a man at his father's funeral:

'A widower am I and an orphan. The orphan father of an orphan boy. Dear me. Farwell, father bach.' (The Welsh people say bach for a male and fach for a female and they both mean dear.)

Carpenter drove screws through the lid; and as four men seized the four handles of the ornaments, Ben Shop cried out sharply:

'You'll break the trimmings, boys! What's the matter with a rope I don't know!'

14

'Deio Carpenter,' said Ianto solemnly, 'cheats with the timber. And there's only one coat of varnish. Ask Schoolin if I tell lies. Ben Shop, for shame. The handles of the trimmings are no good for carrying. Why you are such forgers?'

On the way to Ceri, where white-washed Moriah stands lovelily on the tramping road, the people who were come to bury Shacki spoke of Shacki as they walked in the rain and through the melting snow. Man very frisky was Shacki, as frisky as the stallion which he took up and down the land. There was none like him in shoeing a horse or repairing a plough. There was none like him in building a hay rick; even when he built on a slope his ricks never fell. On rick tops between the loads he frolicked with the wenches. Hay harvest is in July and the wenches' harvest is in March. He buried three wives. Ianto was by the first and two days before he was born the woman trespassed, whereupon Shacki punished her, holding her by her feet and with her head down from the straw-thatched roof of Tyrhos and swinging her as if she were the pendulum of a clock. Abel was by his third wife. Yet each year his children were as numerous as the hay ricks he built. How will fare Katrin, the lusty woman he brought from the land about New Quay? He was stricken in the middle of the night, so she said, at a moment that his strength was as the strength of his stallion. Well-well, he killed three and the fourth killed him. Number four always kills. Shacki will not lower his trousers again.

The congregation sang in Moriah and Richard Preacher prayed and preached; and in the burial ground, while the rain was falling upon the coffin in its grave, Preacher said these words:

'O Big Man, Shacki was up here now just; and now just he is down there. Give thanks, persons, we are up here.'

'Amen,' said the people. 'So be it always.'

Preacher also said:

'A tidy house Gravedigger has made. Plenty of room to turn in it. A grave too narrow is as useless as a house with a door you cannot take a coffin in and out. No landlord will disturb you, Shacki bach, for rent, and no parson will come for his old tithes. You will have not to struggle Sabbath and Sabbath for a rag of shirt and a morsel of bread and cheese like certain preachers Gospel have to. Ho, no. Happy Shacki. The Big Man sent you to Moriah and Moriah will keep you freely until the trumpet wrenches the lid of the earth and chases the clouds with his breath and opens the highway to the Mansion. Cry, Ianto Tall. It is meet to cry. Cry double for your brother Abel Robber, and when he comes from distant Merica make him cry three times three. Cry you, Amos bach, for if there was no Shacki there would be no Ianto and no you. Big Man, be with your son who starves for your sake in Moriah's pulpit and cause the congregation to show him more charity. In your name I plead. Amen.'

CHAPTER III

AT the death of Shacki Tyrhos, the fifteen acres of stony land, the quarry, and the stallion and two cows and twenty-five sheep and two pigs and many heads of poultry became Ianto's. Katrin did not complain that Shacki had left her nothing, although on her marriage day she brought to Tyrhos her cow, which was in calf, and two suckling pigs. She held her peace. She toiled as if her mind was Ianto's mind; and she accounted to Ianto for everything that she sold.

Ianto was religious and thrifty. He observed the Sabbath with a black coat over his shoulders and an indiarubber collar around his neck, but after each service he laid aside his coat and his collar until the time came for him again to repair to Moriah; he shaved his chin and cleaned his hands with gravel and water on the eve of the Sabbath, thereby keeping the day sacred. Katrin was vain. On her way to Moriah she had delight in lifting her skirt and showing her scarlet petticoat and firm ankles. Moreover Ben Shop said that she sometimes washed her feet and legs and thighs with soap and water.

Ianto was learned. He could count without pencil and paper, dispute with Richard Preacher, haggle in the thin language with English cattle dealers, and he could nonplus tramping paddies who boasted about their travels in foreign parts. He wrote love-letters for young men and women. Maids sought his advice as to trapping confessions from men who had been bad with them, and men sought his advice as to circumventing the maids. Some paid him with stolen eggs, some with a handful of meal or of seed, and some with a penny or two. Among the people who were refreshed with his speech was Ben Shop.

On a Sunday afternoon Ben came up to the moor, having been summoned by the Big Man to meet an angel. On his way back he paused at Tyrhos to have a religious talk with Ianto, and while the two were talking Ben brought forth a silk handkerchief of gaudy colours.

'There now,' Katrin exclaimed. 'How grand indeed!'

'Iss-iss,' said Shop. 'So-so.'

'Tut-tut!' Ianto remarked. 'No fancy have I for things silk. They are for the lazy in the land. Queens use them in their little back houses.'

Amos asked:

'How, father bach, do queens wipe their noses?'

'The noses of queens,' replied Ianto, 'don't run.'

Presently Ben remarked the time of day.

'Off we must to Moriah,' he said.

Ianto went for his collar and coat and when he was gone, Ben gave Amos a halfpenny, saying to him:

'Set off now, boy bach. None can be too early in Moriah.'

The boy obeyed; then Ben put his face against Katrin's and the handkerchief in her hand.

'Perished,' he said, 'is the male husband. Half a year in his grave. Does not the night stir you, wench fach?'

'Shut your sound, Shop,' said Katrin coyly. 'Soon Ianto will be here.'

'A collar is a poser to put on and takes long.'

'Indeed then!'

'Shonk is your body. There's legs, dear me! And smooth are your thighs. Come you to the shop for stockings. Fashionable they are.'

Amos showed his halfpenny to Ianto, and he turning to Katrin observed:

'Shop will come to want for throwing money away.'

'Man stingy is Ben Shop,' Katrin returned. 'Behold, his old silk napkin is on the ground.'

'Keep that I will,' said Ianto. 'When he comes for it, well-well, is it not written that every lost sheep is not found? Tell me, Amos of your large buyings with the half a penny.'

'Hold it I will,' the boy replied.

'Two marbles you can buy,' said Ianto temptingly. 'Or spanish for to make spanish-water.'

'Half the penny is better in the pocket trowsers,' Amos declared, 'than in pocket Shop.'

That night Amos could not rest across the foot of Ianto's bed because of the heaviness of his riches, and he was much pleased when he heard his father praising his thrift to Katrin.

Ben Shop came to Tyrhos every Sunday until the early spring. Then one Sunday he did not come, and Amos was grieved and he asked Katrin the reason thereof.

'Breathless is the hill,' she replied, 'for a male with a jobbin to do quickly.'

Amos said that he had not seen Ben doing any job at Tyrhos; besides one does not labour on that day or even whistle, for whistling is speaking to Satan.

But the next night at the prayer meeting in Moriah, Ben knelt on his knees and lifted his eyes to the roof and he informed against a certain woman who lived in the house of a certain man on the moor and who for six weeks had sold him cluck eggs which had chickens in them and the chickens were of no use because they were dead.

The people in Ceri talked, one saying: 'If Ianto put ten eggs a day in his belly he won't get his fat back,' and another: 'She killed Shacki and she's killing Ianto Tall,' and yet another: 'Ianto, poor dab, is losing his shonkness.'

These sayings and many that were not said were carried to Ianto, and he spoke to himself: 'Not losing the shonkness am I. No-no. Very sprightly am I.' He looked at his face in a mirror, but he could not see beneath the grime of several days.

'You rob me,' he said to Katrin.

'Foolish is your spoutings,' she answered.

'Give me the money for the cluck eggs.'

The woman laughed merrily and she brought the silk hand-kerchief in which was tied two shillings and two pennies.

Ianto took the money and was overjoyed.

'An old black is Shop,' he said. 'Only two and two and only

twelve halfpennies for Amos bach.'

But he could not rid himself of his concern for his fat; it stayed the cunning of his hand at the mating of the stallion and slackened his arm at the anvil. His anxiety made him cough.

'As I told,' one said. 'Poor dab Ianto is in deep decline.'

Enoch Gravedigger, who was a round man with bandy legs, came to Tyrhos to learn the truth.

'How you was?' he asked.

'Very hearty,' replied Ianto; and then the man's mission caused him to cough.

'Bad is your cackle,' said Enoch. 'Like this it sounds,' and he scraped with his clog the rocky ground through the slush that was gathered at the door of the dairy.

He came again with his implements.

'Put a sharp on these,' he said.

'Who's perishing shall I know?' asked Ianto.

'Asking you are when there's no answer to your ask. Be you quick. Have them ready next tomorrow. Work, Ianto Tall, for the night cometh and perished men shrink.'

Ianto saw death in Enoch. But death without his implements is harmless. On the morrow he said to Enoch:

'An old accident there's been. The poles of shovel and pick-axe and spade are broken. Go to Carpenter for new poles.'

'You don't say!' Enoch cried. 'You can't say like that.' He spat on the palms of his hands, closed them, and struck Ianto a blow.

'Why you hit me, Enoch bach?'

'Why for you break poles when you are perishing? I don't know, but there's mean you are.'

Enoch struck Ianto again. Then Ianto called in a loud voice upon his son and when his son was come he told him to blow up the fire in the smithy, and he placed the poles in the middle of the fire. Enoch seeing this took off his coat and pranced about, waving his fists. But Ianto seized him and put him on the fire as if he were putting a child on a stool, chanting in the meanwhile:

'Blow, Amos, blow.'

Gravedigger related to the people how he had beaten Ianto and how he would demand not sixteen shillings for digging his grave but two sovereigns.

People therefore spoke slightingly to Amos about his father, and Amos answered as he had been told to answer:

'Only when Gravedigger's trowsers are down can you see what the father did to him.'

CHAPTER IV

IANTO TALL asked himself this question: 'If Katrin can rob cluck eggs can she not rob good eggs?' So he made a bed in the house of his stallion and his cows and his pigs; and he and Amos slept in it. Thus two years passed; years of toil and thrift, and of prayer and going to Moriah. Ianto was become a man of repute in the chapel: he was a Big Head and sat in the Big Seat below the pulpit. He was great in prayer and howsoever long were his prayers, such was their sweetness and fierceness that none of the congregation even shuffled his feet while he was counselling God.

He bore with Katrin's oddness. In the middle of one night she came to him and shouted and screamed, and when she saw that he would have none of her, she tore the door from its hinges. He made peace with Ben Shop and asked his help.

'Talk softly to her of religion,' he said to Ben.

'Religion is not good if you're not on the knees.'

'Grand is your tone, Shop. And religious your spirit. Come you to the moor to see the angel bach.'

At the end of the third day Ben heard a voice saying: 'Go you to the moor, Ben Shop, every Sabbath till I tell you to stop.' He obeyed, and every Sunday afternoon he talked about religion to Katrin while Ianto was putting on his collar.

Once while Ianto was away with his stallion a short, thick bearded, brown skinned man came to Tyrhos. He had a sailor's cap on the side of his head, a belt over his waist from which hung about fifteen rabbits, and a rabbit trap in his hand.

'Is your mam in the abode?' he asked Amos, speaking with pulpit solemnity.

Katrin was on the threshold before Amos could answer, and her lips were parted in astonishment. She brushed the hair from her eyes as if she were gazing at a treasure which had been lost and found again.

'Well?' she said wonderingly. She added quickly: 'The step-grandson is the boy bach.'

'And who is the husband shall I say?'

'He was Shacki. O you heard of Shacki – Shacki Stallion.'

'I have been in ships,' said the man. 'I have been with black heathens and whites in Holy Sherusalem. The sea is a stormy place. Have you rabbits to sell?'

Amos made this pronouncement:

'There are no rabbits on tidy farms.'

'Out of the mouths of babans and sucklers,' said the stranger.

He showed how to set his rabbit trap.

'All iobs know that,' said Amos.

'Young youth, call me not a fool of a iob. This trap was made in foreign parts. It was made for me. And my name is on it – Robert. Ten weeks ago I was Robert Sailor. Today I am Robert Rabbits. Young youth, the rabbits come into this trap without asking.'

Amos listened, marvelling.

'Go and put it,' said Robert. 'Whistle for half an hour and the first will come. The others will follow the first and when you can't carry any more bring them hither.'

'Iss,' said Katrin, 'take it to the quarry in your father's moor.'

Amos ran.

'Boy sharp is the boy,' Robert remarked, removing his belt. 'How then and how now, Katrin?'

'Come you in, sailor bach, with your dracht of buttermilk.'

Amos came back with the trap.

'Trap no good whatever is she,' he announced.

'Afraid am I,' said Robert; 'you're a bit of a toop.'

'For serious I'm not a dolt,' Amos cried.

Robert buckled on his belt and strode down Road Saints, swinging his trap and his rabbits and humming the Old Hundredth.

They told Ianto about Robert Rabbits and he made a trap, which Amos bach set every evening; and once a week Robert came to buy the rabbits which were caught. The oddness lifted from Katrin and she laboured with good will, turning her shouts and screams into laughter and song.

Amos was in his twelfth year when as he was climbing home from Schoolin's School he saw Katrin standing on a mound on the moor. Her strong legs were set apart, her head was upright, and her face was on the rise. He walked up to her; and soon Robert appeared in the distance and hailed them with a wave of his cap.

'Fair day, Katrin and step-boy bach,' he said when he was with them. 'In a sail am I. This hour tomorrow – yea, the very next tomorrow – I'll be in a ship on the mighty ocean. Here is the medcing for the tooth.'

Soon he was waddling briskly and lightly on the road as if the road were a ship.

'The black!' Katrin muttered. 'He's a pranker.'

She looked at the medicine, which was some white powder, and placed a little of it on her tongue. She spat it out and threw all the powder on the dung-heap.

'He's a cunning slitterer,' she said angrily.

The twilight deepened. Ianto stabled his horse and he and his son went to their bed.

'Father,' said Amos, 'a religious boy bach am I.'

'The little Jesus bach was born in an old stable,' said the father.

'Well-well,' said Amos, 'Katrin is in the family way.'

He was going to say more, but he was told that he who sleeps early also awakes early.

In the morning a chicken was dead on the dung-heap and Ianto picked it up and was stricken with grief at his loss; and he addressed it in the following words:

'Why didn't you grow into a big hen, hen fach? Tell me that. You would give me eggs – very costly eggs. And then the Fowler would come to buy you. How much? Two shillings. No, Fowler; half one crown. Two and three. O-rait, Fowler.

Fair day for now.'

Amos then told him what he had tried to tell him in bed, and Ianto moved about that day as if he were carrying a cartload of blackness he knew not whither. At milking time he leaned against the door-post of the cowhouse.

'Katrin,' he said, 'go you off.'

The rill of the milk was louder than his voice. He passed in and repeated that which he had said.

Katrin interrupted him:

'Hold the tail of the old cow, man, from whisking.'

He did so.

'You must go away from here,' he said.

She finished her second milking and rose, a bucket in each hand.

'Am I not your father's widow woman?' were her first words.

'Sorry am I, Katrin fach. Much money is your keep.'

'You give me nothing for my labour.'

'The bed I need.'

'What's the matter with the bed? You can't tell. You had to-do with me in the bed.'

'You cannot name me, for no to-do I've had with you.'

'What an old liar you are! A better man was your father. He plucked my flower but he wedded me. Ask you Amos what he saw.'

Amos, who was listening at the door, showed himself and answered cleverly:

'Can you then, Katrin, see in the dark? Father has had no to-do with you.'

During the next day she wept and cajoled.

'Ianto son of Shacki,' she cried, 'where is my coffer and my bed? And the cow in calf, and suckling pigs?'

'What for you need another cow in calf?' Ianto answered quietly. 'And more suckling pigs?'

'Ho, iss,' Katrin cried, shamelessly resting her hands upon her broad thighs. 'This is your misdeed, Ianto Shacki. What a black to go with his father's mournful widow?'

Ianto went to Shop.

'Ben Shop,' he said, 'a small word in your old ear now.'

'Word your words, Tyrhos.'

'Sorrow follows love's delights.'

'Open you your head and speak.'

'Katrin is going to live in your house against Pont Ceri. And you have a few chattels in it. Quite enough for a poor widow fach. The next tomorrow she will be there. And don't you put in the door an old key that doesn't turn. That's all for now, Ben Shop.'

But Katrin would not leave Tyrhos. She pleaded for a little time, for a mishap might befall her on the way.

Ianto took her in his arms and carried her, in spite of her strugglings, as far as Catti's Lane, which is about half-way down Road Saints.

In due course she bore a male child, and with the child in her arms, whether sitting at her door or parading the village, she told everybody that Ianto was the father.

'There is much clonk about you, Ianto Tyrhos,' said Richard Preacher at the Seiat, the solemn monthly meeting at which we testify our godliness.

'There's no bad gossip of me,' said Ianto. 'Is not Amos bach here? Cross him with cross-questions.'

Amos was summoned to the Big Seat to be examined by Preacher and Big Heads, the Big Heads present being: Deio Carpenter, Ben Shop, Simon Schoolin.

'Where, Amos Ianto, do sinners go?' asked Preacher.

'Religious Preacher,' Amos answered, 'I have learnt your pulpit lesson.'

'Sensible. Sensible. Where do preachers go and Big Heads?'

'The Big Capel of the Big Man.'

'Who was the first man, Amos?'

'Adam.'

'And the first murderer, Amos?'

'Cain the black.'

'The first sinner now, Amos?'

'Eva.'

26

'The youth is a knowing scholar,' remarked Schoolin.

'Who is the sponer who was bad with Katrin?' asked Deio Carpenter.

'Innocent is the youth,' said Schoolin. 'A sponer, Amos Morgan, is a man who goes courting.'

Amos was silent.

'How many lengths of my footrule is his tallness?' Deio persisted, opening his footrule.

Amos looked at Ben Shop as if he expected him to answer.

'Half one minute,' said Ben, scratching his bald pate.

'Say,' interposed Schoolin, 'was the bad man hairy on the head?'

'Ben Shop –' Amos began to say.

'Cute is the boy bach,' said Ben in a loud voice. 'O iss, cute he is – though he goes to Schoolin's School. Take you this threepenny piece – a silver piece. Think you. If you don't know, how can you tell?'

Amos tested the silver with he teeth and replied at once:

'Katrin was bad with Robert Rabbits.'

Ben rose to his feet.

'Congregation,' he said, 'congregation and Schoolin, the man is named. Preacher Richard will now tell God about him.'

CHAPTER V

GOD made the darkness on earth and under the earth that He shall perform His miracles. Seeds stir under a blanket of earth and the rocks are pregnant with water. God does not reveal His workings. Amos asked his father why not? Because if He did He would cease to be God. He swung the sun that man shall labour by its light. But the night and the dark places and the secrets thereof are the Lord's; hence it is not lawful to light the darkness. Amos said that there were lamps oil in Moriah. 'My houses you shall light (said the Lord) and none other.'

In that fashion Ianto explained to his son why Tyrhos was not lit by candle or lamp wick.

'Put your think on my roobob,' he said. 'There's a miracle. It's the glory of Ceri.'

He spoke the truth, but nothing other than rhubarb would flourish in his garden.

'Father!' Amos exclaimed, clapping his hands. 'I will sell the roobob.'

Ianto killed a pig, and he cut up the carcase and put the pieces into two baskets, and in each basket he also put some sticks of rhubarb; and father and son went to hawk the meat and the rhubarb, Ianto going beyond the moor and Amos down into Ceri.

Between Shop Ben and Pont Ceri Amos saw Katrin. Her child, folded in a shawl, was at her breast. The youth made to pass her civilly, but she seized the handle of his basket.

'Tasty,' she said, 'is pig's flesh. Very tasty. Nice bit is this, and toothsome is this bit and that.'

She dropped three pieces into the breast of her garment.

'Pay you,' said Amos, 'three shillings and four pennies.'

'Jawch!' she cried, swearing in a word the meaning of which nobody knows. 'What's the frog braying about? The flesh is for your brother bach. The child of Ianto Tall.'

People came out of their houses, and she bade them witness the likeness between her child and Amos.

'Katrin fach,' said Amos, 'give you the money and roobob you shall have to make a tart.'

'Ho-ho!' she cried, sniffing her nose. 'Where's the old smell from? Go before I catch the fever. Why is the roobob so big? You and your father make your businesses on the bed.'

Amos tried to go away, but the woman held his basket, saying that Ianto ate uncooked carrots and turnips, that he had starved his stallion into dryness, and that the pig had perished of a disease.

On hearing this Ianto's heart was wounded, and he resolved to display his wastefulness. The next day he was on Catti's hearth.

'Large is my favour to you,' he said.

'What is your want?' asked Catti humbly.

'Man very generous am I. Very generous indeed. Brew two bowls of mess broth every day for me and the son bach and I'll give you one penny every day. One penny a day, Catti fach, is three hundred and sixty-five pennies in a year. What a mountain of pennies in a pile! What a solemn pile!'

Catti was compassionate because few showed her compassion. Ten years before she had lain with a tramping paddy in a barn and the barn went on fire and she and the paddy were put in Carmarthen Jail. There is no forgiveness for the sinner who destroys one's possessions. After her term in jail none in Ceri would give her shelter. Now Parson Church – this being the parson who prayed every Sunday morning and evening for his horse Peter and whose spirit always reached the Rectory fifteen minutes before it fleshly covering and warned the servant women to dismiss their lovers by slamming the stable door – heard of Catti's plight and in his pity for her and his hatred of Moriah he gave her at a rental of a shilling a year the zinc-roofed cottage and three acres of land which are aside Road Saints. So she became a Church woman, but ready-made prayers and short sermons were unsatisfying, and she longed for the sour prayers and the incantating eloquence of Moriah. As she longed for Moriah so did many a man of Moriah hanker after her strong slim thighs and her breasts which trembled like rosebuds. But howsoever great her need she remembered the past and she would not be tempted to go with any man into ditch or barn or behind haystack or headstone.

Several days went by and as the gossipers made no clonk of his generosity, Ianto broke two cluck eggs into his pigs' trough and scattered the shells on the road outside Tyrhos. But the clonkers remained silent. One day Cockler came by, shouting: 'Cockles!'

'Well, iss,' Ianto said to him. 'It's a large sin, but there's fond am I of the belly. See you the egg shells? Eight eggs me and the son eat every morning. Two pennies of cockles now, Cockler. Fat cockles. And let your measure overflow.'

The shells of the cockles were also strewn on the road.

In about an hour's time Catti brought up the mess of water and potatoes and carrots and cabbages and leeks and potatoes. Ianto was at his anvil.

'There's a bit of clonk,' she said, resting her arms on the top of the half door.

'What's the old clonk, Catti fach?'

'Twelve eggs a day you gobble.'

'And cockles,' Ianto added.

'Two pennies a day I want for the mess.'

'I'm only a poor dab.'

Catti turned to depart, but Ianto called upon her.

'My poorness is wordless,' he declared, lifting his leathern apron and displaying his nakedness. 'Too poor am I to wear the trowsers.'

Life went on, Ianto milking his declining cows and churning their thin cream, and baking his bread and tending his straggling flocks. Every morning Amos scattered the shells and every evening he gathered them in.

30

Evil fell upon man Tyrhos. The stallion was a burden, he not earning any money. 'Frisker,' said the people, 'is a gelded mule than Ianto's stallion.' Moreover the animal was a big feeder. Had he not eaten much of his manger? Ianto must take him to the next fair and sell him. But he will put him out to graze for a week or so that he may recover his prance. The stallion was brought from the stable and when he was in the close he gave a tumultuous heave and fell upon the ground, splashing Ianto with the slush. Although Ianto coaxed him with words and beat him with a stick and poured water on his head, he died.

Evil follows evil. Catti demanded fifteen shillings which he owed her for the messes.

'Hard you press me,' said Ianto. 'Wherein have I sinned that ills hit me?'

'You have eaten the messes,' said Catti.

'A cheater you are, Catti. Where are the slices of bread you promised with the messes? Amos bach, did you have bread?'

'No, little father. And the bitch vowed a slice with every bowl.'

'No quarreller am I,' said Catti. 'But Parson Church will know.'

Ianto sorrowed. Fifteen shillings! Nearly one sovereign. As a cow spends half the night in chewing her cud, so he spent half the night in meditation. What has Catti got? Four pigs, two goats, and hens. The stallion would have fetched twenty sovereigns if it had lived another twelve days. The next night he stole into Catti's pigsty. 'Pigs very good. They will be ready for Pigger in six weeks. About eighteen score they each weigh and pigs are nine and six a score. Stop you now. The goats have tidy udders. Goats can feed on moorland.'

He was again on Catti's hearth, saying:

'Man born of woman is lonely with no woman.'

Catti did not know how to answer.

'No mam fach has the son Amos,' he went on. 'Sons should have mams. Quite handy you would be about Tyrhos.'

'What is in your gabble?' Catti asked quietly.

Ianto sat upon a low stool, nodding his head as in prayer. But he was not praying; he was debating whether he should do that which he had purposed to do. He made up his mind.

'Three should sit at the table of food,' he said, 'in honour of the Godly Three.'

'Putting your cap on your thoughts you are, Ianto Tyrhos.'

'Cracked the shell of life I have with the teeth, Catti fach, and inside I found you.'

'Well-well?'

'Wed you I will for sure me.'

The woman laughed outright.

'Better for me to lie wedless on my straw bed.'

'Come will I with you.'

'No boy bach shall fire my sin, Tyrhos.'

'Don't you snuff my flame,' he said. 'The rain, Catti fach, is falling. It's beating on your roof as if the Big Man was beating His fingers on the dome of the universe bidding creation awake.'

'Speak you do, Ianto Shacki, like a preacher.'

'You have winnowed my heart fach.'

'No, indeed, I will not wed you, Ianto Shacki.'

The light from the small window made his dusky face almost white.

'I comforted a tramping paddy,' said Catti.

'A sin was the old fire.' Then Ianto eloquented: 'You are in the fire, Catti fach. Let me now take you out of the fire and hammer you into such saintliness that even Moriah will hosanna to the Big Man.'

'Grand are preaches Moriah and soundful your words.'

'Through the day and night I shall solace you with speeches better than speeches in Moriah. Come and let me be your guide. I will feed your wan pigs. I will make them fatter than their skins can hold and for nothing to pay. And I will nourish your sickly goats into the staff of life. We shall sow seed together and together we shall reap the abundant harvests.'

Catti wept with joy, and she cried and shouted as her people do when they are under the spell of a sermon.

'Amen! Don't stop! Amen! Go on, man bach!'

CHAPTER VI

CATTI adorned the windows of Tyrhos with her curtains, the rooms with her furniture, and the ceiling with two sides of cured bacon which she brought with her. She enlivened her husband's heart with the money which her pigs fetched and his stomach with meals of bacon. Ianto was as happy as he could be. Sometimes he sing-songed 'The Lamentation of the Black Pig': 'Very sweet is a slicen of pig's flesh with a taten'; sometimes he greeted Amos with: 'How now, fat calf?'

Catti was industrious. She cut into the close a ditch which carried the running sludge into a field below the house; and she removed the dung-heap into the garden. She built a hedge to separate the close from the road and in the gap she set a gate which she contrived from other gates that had fallen to pieces. She did her utmost to make Shacki's clothes fit Amos, but she could not mock Ianto into wearing trousers while he was in the smithy. Men who watched her at her work – her short skirt coiled around her waist, her shorter petticoat waving about her bare thighs, her hair fluttering over her temples, her arms tanned and darkly downed – were jealous that Ianto possessed such exciting loveliness.

She was contented; at night her spirit was never too broken to feast on Ianto's bedside eloquence or her body too wearisome to be stirred by the sounding lashes and the sweetening honey of the perfect prayer.

'Tidy are affairs now,' Ianto said to Amos one day. 'Pigs and fowls that go from me come back in money. And for the things that come in there is nothing to pay.'

The boy cherished his father's wisdom. He took to coming

33

home from Schoolin's School through the fields and often on his way he collected an egg or two from the hedge nests of straying hens. Of this Catti was told nothing.

Once he set his father a puzzle. It was this: he went to school with nothing in his pockets and returned with the blade of a pocket knife. How came he by it? Ianto could not guess. He raced a boy for it and when he saw that the other was winning he shouted after him: 'You are losing your marbles glass.' The boy stopped and Amos passed him. Amos was cute and his ways were a joy to his father. Schoolin said: 'A tuneful singer is the boy bach.' But Amos only fashioned his lips to the words of the song because he could not sing.

The bacon finished and Ianto would not have another pig killed. But Catti trapped rabbits and hares and she did not sell them, and so food fell before Ianto like manna, for which the only payment was a word of thanksgiving.

On a windy, rainy afternoon in the month of November, about four months after they had been married, Ianto was engaged in a religious task: he was binding in one book the two Bibles and the Hymnal, and inside the first cover he was making a box.

'What for is the box?' Catti wanted to know.

Ianto thought for a moment and then answered:

'When strangers preach in Moriah I write the best bits on paper and the box is for the wisdom.'

'Father,' said Amos, 'Schoolin tells you are a saint and sinner in prayer.'

He spoke so knowingly that Ianto was startled.

'Iss,' he said, 'useful are bits and pieces when the tongue doesn't know how to go on when there's going on to be.'

'The Word,' said Amos, 'should be locked against peeping Schoolins who are fond of tellings.'

Catti put a shawl over her shoulders and went to bring the cows in; and the two cows were pressed against each other, their hindquarters tottering against the wind; and the sheep were flocked together like fearsome sheep in a slaughterer's yard. She drove them into the cowhouse, wondering as she

34

did so how the lean creatures had not been swept away by the wind.

She entreated Ianto to make a shelter for the animals.

'What they want shelter for I don't know,' he answered.

Catti cried out in great scorn:

'A piece of a man you are! Niggards are always lazers.'

She built a shelter; and on stormy days she also tethered her goats within that shelter.

The month was hard. Milch cows are drained of their strength every morning and evening and be they never so prodigal they cannot give by grass alone, and moorland hay is thin and wispy and without nourishment. But Ianto proves that Bible Nebuchadnezzar lived by grass. Pigs need more than potatoes and cabbages, and fowls more than dung-hill pickings. But Ianto proves that the Big Man provides manna for man and beast.

Thereafter Catti caught more rabbits and hares than her husband knew and these she sold for cake for the cows and meal for the pigs and fowls.

One day Ianto said to her:

'Very soon Schoolin will have no more to teach Amos. He tells what a grand scholar he is. And he's great in counting. "Make him a preacher." That's what Schoolin told.'

He paused and then added:

'Counting is good to preachers for they are the only men with money to count.'

'Don't you mock the Big Man,' cried Catti in alarm.

'College Preachers is costly. And he may perish before he is called to a capel and that would be wasteful. Handy will he be here.'

'Handy! His hands are handless.'

'My apron – my father Shacki's apron – shall be his apron.'

'And then will you forever walk in your smithy with no cover for your legs?'

'In the Beybile there is nothing about old trowsers. And in the Beybile Pictures there is no picture of trowsers – not trowsers corduroy or trowsers cloth. If nakedness is a sin, Catti,

35

dear me what a sinner you are in the night! Ho, iss, my hammer shall be his hammer.'

'The boy bach has no notion for the hammer.'

'And there's the land.'

'Ianto bach, talker you are. Your land is like a pauper – all ribs and bones and no flesh. Strew the dung of the ages on it and nothing you get.'

She also might have said that of all peoples the Welsh and the Jews are the worst farmers. The land on the banks of Avon Ceri is as slovenly and disorderly as are the dawdling tillers thereof, and the houses are as shiftless and tortuous as the lolling woman within them; life is lived in and out of next-door, ill-aired cowsheds, hence young men and women decline and die.

'Thin is the English speech,' said Ianto to Amos. 'But she must be known. How much do you know?'

'Father bach,' Amos replied, 'I know the piece.'

He backed his hands schoolwise, and recited:

> River is 'Avon',
> Brook is 'Nant',
> Twenty is 'Ugain',
> Hundred is 'Cant'.

> Hands is 'Dwylaw',
> Gloves is 'Menig',
> Gentlemen is 'Gwrboneddig'.

> Ash is 'Onen',
> Oak is 'Derwen',
> Holly-tree is 'Pren-Calinen'.

'Neat scholar bach,' commented Ianto. 'The two first verses will take you into palaces. What are you going to be?'

'Preacher religion,' announced Amos. 'The Big Man on His washing day makes His rain pelt the stones down Road Saints. I shall be His washerman and pelt sinners down to Hell.'

The words were those of a preacher and Ianto vowed to fashion a padlock for his Box-Bible.

'Boys shops make money,' he said. 'Ben Shop is rich.'

'Schoolins make money too,' Amos responded. 'Schoolin wears the indiarubber Sabbath cuffs every day.'

'In the shop,' said Catti, 'the coat is ever dry. And the little feet are never wet.'

'Thinking am I,' said Ianto, 'of the shop draper. Large profits they make.'

'Preachers make money on the Sabbath,' said Amos. 'Holy is Sabbath money. I'll be a preacher and shopman, and there will be seven days of money.'

Amos was wise. Whence came his wisdom?

'Prayed have I respectable in Moriah,' said Amos. 'And scared crows with the imitation preaches.'

'When you are a shopman, boolin bach,' said Ianto, 'you will know there is praying time and money time, but the praying time is not money time.'

Light dawned upon Amos. He said:

'Good are your thinks, father bach. You can't pray and take money at the same time.'

CHAPTER VII

WINTER ended his chastening of man and beast and earth, and Spring chased away the gloom and cleansed the slab and ooze. Amos was in his fifteenth year and had left Schoolin's School. When he addressed God in Moriah his brown hair wagged over his forehead with religious fervour; and there was the religious gripe in the movements of his lips and the colour of angels in his face. Though he was endowed with such blessings, he decided to be apprenticed to a draper. So Ianto sent letters to shops in Cardigan and Aberystwyth and Carmarthen, but none answered. The boy fretted.

'Why no answers, Twm bach,' he asked Twm Good News, who brought the post up the hillside.

Twm was on a settle in his cottage, which is between Shop Ben and House Katrin; and he was groaning from a poisoned foot.

'Many days have darkened,' said Amos, 'since Tyrhos has seen you.'

'As pangful is the foot,' said Twm, 'as a poison snake. Wait you now and don't happen to be here.'

He opened the letters of that day and read them; and those which contained bad news and no news he put on his fire and those which contained good news he put aside. Having finished his hard labour, he hobbled to the low wall before his house and leaned against it and waved an umbrella, which was almost as high as himself, to passers by, telling them to acquaint this man or that man that Twm Good News had a letter for him.

There came a letter for Ianto. Twm gazed at the stamp and

read the letter, and such was his wonder that he did not speak for some time.

'Why stand you like that?' he cried to Amos. 'You stand like a cow's tickling pole.'

'Tickled you are with news,' said Amos. 'Rub against me.'

'Ho, no. Am I not called Postman Good News? Hurry and tickle your father's curiosity.'

The youth was beside himself with eagerness; and he put his cap in his pocket and ran off.

Before they reached the foot of Hill Saints, Ianto and his son met Deio Carpenter and he congratulated the father that Abel was returning from America. In their progress men and women also congratulated them. A fortune Abel had made in America. Millionaires live in America. Hap he will buy a farm. Hap a mansion. None had anything but good to say of Abel.

Ianto read that on such and such a day Abel would be at Holyhead, on his way to Ireland, and that he would like to meet his people. Well-well. Abel had always been close about his business. His deeds were done in secret and when he went away none knew for two years whither he had gone, and none had heard from him for five years. What did he want in Ireland – the land of paddies? Abel Millionaire was coming to buy Ireland. Ianto sobbed dolefully that Shacki was in his grave, and cried joyfully that his brother who was thought poor was rich.

CHAPTER VIII

'Clip my hair with clippers.'

'Then is your hair a patch of bracken?' said Catti for a joke.

'Laugh you do at nothing.'

'With scissors, little husband, will I lop your hair and straighten the gaps in your moustache.'

She made his head as neat as a well thatched roof and the moustaches as trim as the edge thereof.

Ben Shop sold small cards, each bearing a Biblical picture and a text, and the price was a shilling for fifty. Ianto bought six hundred of them. What did he want them for? That was a puzzle. But his tidy head caused men and women to guess that he was going on a journey and that the purpose of the journey was to meet Abel Millionaire, and so these people of Ceri behaved like other peoples: they took gifts to princes. Deio Carpenter placed Amos against the wall of the smithy and measured him with a foot rule, and at the height of five feet he made a notch, saying: 'Take the ruler, boolin bach, and show it to Nooncool Abel.' Richard Preacher toiled up Road Saints for the first time since Shacki's funeral, carrying the most precious thing in Ceri: himself. 'Bring Abel home, Ianto,' he sang in his pulpit manner. 'Bring Abel the wanderer home. Tell him I didn't believe he thieved. Liars are polisses. Tell him I'll have a religious memorial service to his father Shacki with two very specially made sermons, and there will be tea and bread currants in House Capel. Pity was Abel's inside companion. When he sees my crumbling abode his shout will be redder than lightning. Paint it needs, and paper on walls, and handles on doors.' Schoolin gave Amos a slate and a pencil that he could help to count Abel's money; and Ben Shop gave Ianto a pair of yellow leather gloves that he be accorded pious respect at strange prayer meetings. Others sacrificed unto Ianto tins of sardines and of salmon, shop biscuits and loaves of bread and chunks of cheese, and such like. Ianto promised all to report their givings to Abel.

He fixed iron shoes on the soles of his clogs and on those of Amos, and he wrote in his Box-Bible as follows: 'This is the beloved Bible of Jesus this is the right-hand gift of God presented to Ianto Morgan our beloved Big Head by preacher and big heads of congregation Capel Moriah in Ceri in Shire Cardigan a nobler Christian no man can know.'

In the full of the dew father and son set out on their journey: the father with his corduroy trousers strung by stout ropes and with the Box-Bible caught inside his coat by a rope drawn around his waist, the son with a sack over his shoulders containing the slate and a loaf of bread and some cheese and with strings tied under his knees to hinder his grandfather's trousers from trailing on the ground.

They were on the moor with their faces towards the sea before Catti knew that they had gone. She ran to the door and shouted: 'Farwell for now!'

They went on as if she had not spoken. On the plain Ianto paused and gazed upon the valley; and he sneered at Ceri.

'Foolish,' he said, 'is the flatterer who takes away nothing for his praises.'

'We had a lot for nothing to pay,' said Amos.

'Much shall we want for nothing.'

'O Big Man, make little holes in their purses.'

'Amen,' said Ianto. 'And bring us back with pockets filled with soverens. Pockets running over with soverens like a brimming butter cask.'

'Why for you gorge the throat with thinks of losings, little father?'

'Better have soverens to lose than no soverens.'

'Sinful it is to lose money.'

They meditated in silence, a newly awakened melancholy

upon them. Rabbits and dogs squealed in the teeth of traps, disturbed ewes bleated to their lambs, crows croaked dismal salutation to the morning. They left the moor for field paths. The cattle were just arisen and the spring had not returned to the grass upon which they had laid. But the hour of labour was nearing and by the time they were at Breoc women were driving home their cows and men their horses.

Father and son walked from ditch to ditch and with the stooping slouch of peasants.

Amos gave utterance to the end of his meditation.

'Father,' he said, 'our too full soverens we can put in Box-Bible.'

'There is a proverb in the thin language,' said Ianto. 'It is "Waste not, want not." Fools Ceri don't understand the thin language.'

'Useful will Box-Bible be, father.'

Ianto quoted another proverb from the thin language: 'Like father, like son.'

They talked little, not even when they rested to eat a morsel of bread and cheese or when searching for barn or cattle shelter in which to sleep. On the third day, being in a strange land, Ianto swung his Box-Bible from his neck and peddled the cards to passers-by and at the houses.

It was on the road which glides down into Dolgelly, and the hedges of which were clothed with spring life, that they heard one singing in a tangled voice:

> A pilgrim in a desert land,
>   Both near and far I roam,
> Awaiting every hour to see
>   My Father's glorious home.

The singer, a tall man with a straggling red beard and a tattered frock coat buttoned around his slim body, was beating time with a crooked stick.

'An old paddy,' remarked Amos, 'in a pulpit coat.'

Amos began to sing the hymn, whereon the man came to them quickly, saying:

42

'You bray like an ass locked in a swamp.'

The youth was abashed, for the other had spoken truly.

'Where shall I say is your pulpit?' Ianto asked.

'Man, you are Tomos Doubtful. Why you are doubtful? The pulpit is me and where I am there also is the pulpit. Collecting am I for Afric's blacks and China's yellows and Greenland's icy mountains and India's coral strand.'

'Silver and gold have I none,' said Ianto. 'But in religion the pocket is full.'

'No one penny,' the man asked, 'for to light dark hearts with religion?'

'Peace to you, stranger. Long is the road for me and orphan.'

'And I'm the lonely orphan,' said Amos.

'I go,' said the man, speeding his stride.

Ianto seized his coat so suddenly that the man stumbled and nearly fell.

'Greasy is the way,' said Ianto, 'for runners off from religion.'

Amos peeped through his half-closed hand as if through a spy glass.

'Tramping paddy I see,' he cried playfully, 'and his stick has the wriggle of the snake.'

'Glib is your tongue, young youth,' paddy cried hotly. 'For clatches you ask and clatches you'll get.'

But Amos, heedless that the stick was raised up against him, searched in Box–Bible for a certain card, and when he had found it, he slanted his head, declaiming softly:

'"And unto him that smiteth thee on the one cheek offer also the other." Read, paddy.'

'Large thanks,' said paddy, grinning impudently.

'Northman,' Ianto cried. 'North Welsh, your religion is very bad.'

'And the religious card,' said Amos, 'is in his pocket.'

'Three pennies, paddy,' said Ianto. 'Don't say you are a robber.'

'Take you the old card,' said paddy, throwing it on the ground.

'Dirt is your inside, bad paddy,' said Ianto with much concern. 'You dirty the Big Man's name. Change you your think. If this day you fall into a quarry of sharp stones or a lake of deep water, people will say you were an atheist – yea, an atheist. But if they find this in your pocket, what a funeral you'll have. Forgiving am I. Two pennies I paid for the text. Keep you it and it will take you to the Palace when you perish and give me one penny. One small penny for the Big Man.'

Paddy relented and he gave Ianto a penny and he went humbly before them wiping the tears from his eyes.

Then Ianto offered this comment: 'Braggers are the North Welsh and they throat their words like cuckoos.'

The wayfarers moved on, the land on all sides of them seeming to be without form and void as it was in the beginning. Once they sat down to eat and before them there was a road which wound around a mountain like a rope; and as they were champing with their jaws they saw a woman coming strangely towards them. Her garments were black and now and again she stopped and gazed at the winding road. Amos likened her to a cow parting from her calf.

'Fair day, woman,' Ianto mumbled through the food in his mouth.

'To a funeral you've been?' asked Amos.

'Iss,' said the woman. 'A funeral.'

'Shall I say funerals hereabouts are healthy?' asked Ianto. 'In Shire Cardigan they are nice and long.'

The woman answered: 'Iss. Very long. Five years is the length of the funeral. And it's time for my son to wake from his dead sleep.'

'Well now!' said Ianto. 'Here's an accident. A little text. "Blessed is he that cometh in the name of the Lord." Two pennies is the cost of the text for to make you glad.'

Amos folded his arms and recited:

> Sweet soul, the cold and swollen waves
> Of the deep Jordan are at hand,
> And Sion, holy city, now
> Rises upon the farther strand.

'Two small pennies,' said Ianto, 'for a big message. Two pennies in the name of the Lord.'

The woman's eyes were on the road that was strangling the mountain.

'He's coming!' she shrieked. 'See you him! He's skipping with the hangman's rope!'

'Because of that affair,' said Ianto, 'I give you two texts for two pennies.'

The woman was so glad that she gave him three pennies, and Ianto and his son went onward, and after they had gone some distance Amos remarked that she had not moved from where they left her, and he said:

'She noised like an old sheep.'

'And her bleats are as senseless,' said Ianto, 'as an old sheep for her killed lamb.'

They proceeded northward. Mountains heaving in divine anger and torrents yelling horror down the clefts of awesome rocks witnessed the Lord's way with sin; well timbered nants and green meadows, fat kine and fruitful gardens, and farmhouses and chapels witnessed the Lord's goodness to those who believe in Him.

On a morning Ianto looked at the face of the sky and it was red and lowering, and he said: 'Come to the valley, for the old rain is on us.' The wind and rain caught them in the hollows, and their path became a carpet of mud.

'Is it storming on the sea, father?' Amos asked.

'Shut your lips, iob!' Ianto cried angrily. 'What for you mean to put bad thinks in the Big Man's head with Abel Millionaire on top of a ship?'

One Sunday evening they were in Capel Bethel, which is in the valley of the Ogwen, and they stayed for the Seiat; and after many had spoken, the preacher said that there was a strange man among them.

'Open your mouth, stranger.'

'No, indeed,' said Ianto, 'me and boy bach are too full of your sayings.'

'Is the youth your son?'

45

'The orphan.'

'The youth's voice I heard in song,' said the preacher.

'Iss,' said Amos. 'Young am I but a sweet praiser in song.'

Ianto drew on his hands his yellow gloves and rose in his pew and delivered himself in this wise:

'The Big Man's voice you heard; the Big Singer was playing on the harp of my son Amos. Pretty is His voice. We harped our journey here. We were walking through a patch of bluebells. Do you know, people, the Big Man's song is like a peal of bluebells! Off we are to Holyhead – what a very saintly name! – to meet my brother Abel – Abel who was thought to be drowned under the sea. How do I know he is not drowned? Well, people, we live on a moor. A cloud came and hid the sun. The beloved wife Catti was afraid. The cloud fell upon me, like Catti's petticoat over her head. And a voice said: "Ianto Morgan, Abel is not under the sea but on the sea. Sending him from Merica am I. Go and greet him. He is now Abel Millionaire!"'.

'Amen!' many cried.

'Not riches I want, people. I will fall on his neck and say to him: "Abel bach, my brother! Come you with me, for you must be weary. Not a red penny of your money I need." And I shall tell him of Capel Bethel in Ogwen Valley, and we will come this way and tarry in your midst.'

'Amen!' many cried. 'Forget me not.'

Ianto opened the Box-Bible and showed the congregation the writing therein.

'And the box? That is for the text cards. A text in the pocket drives away the snake.'

He sold all the cards, and he and his son were given refreshment and a bed in the House of the Capel; and when they were alone, Amos admonished his father:

'The snake was my think first.'

'Great is the maker of wisdom,' said Ianto, 'but still greater is the crier of it.'

'Little father, we saw no bluebells.'

'Amos, my son, a lie is only a lie when it sounds a lie.'

It was not until they were in Bethesda – that sacred town in which the houses are like headstones in a grave yard – that they bought more cards; and as they were passing out of the town a policeman charged Ianto with unlawful peddling.

'Show your licence,' said the man in the thin language.

'Lishens!' Ianto repeated in dismay. 'Do a nobleman want lishens to bring off revivals? I am a convertationalist. Polissman! Polissman! Your words are talky flakes of snow that burn. No more nonsense. You inshult the One up on top – farther from you than the highest star and nearer than the small shirt under your heavy shirt. Here a text. "The Lord have mercy upon me". Six pennies and be soon to pay.'

The policeman obeyed.

'Now pray on the knees,' said Ianto.

The man realized that he had erred and he fell upon his knees and such was his remorse that he covered his face with his hands.

'Polissmen North Wales,' remarked Ianto as they went on, 'are buttons and bellies.'

Now a rich squire had recently come to live in a mansion about five miles from Bethesda. He was a Roman Catholic and his deeds were an abomination; and people said that his breakfast was fried in brimstone. Ianto and his son reached the rich man's mansion and they passed through the gateway; and they beheld the man. He was a large man with a red nose and a gruff voice; and Ianto seeing that he was giving meat to four or five dogs knew at once that he was in the presence of evil.

'What the hell do you want?' the squire shouted in the thin language.

'Curserer and swearerer, whitewash your tongue,' was Ianto's quiet reproof.

'This is private property. Get out! Quick!'

'Father,' said Amos in the Big Man's language, 'smell do I the fire of Hell.'

'What did he say?' asked the squire.

'The orphan say Satan is burning you with Hell's hot coals.'

The squire found that his lighted pipe was burning a hole

47

through a pocket of his breeches.

'Dammit!' he cried. 'Blast!'

'Satan,' said Ianto, 'blasts in the place where bad breeds. A text will drive him off. I have sanctimoniously texts. Take six gratis. Two for trowsers, two for coat, and two the waistcoat. Give two shillings for them.'

'If they're so dam useful,' said the squire, 'why the hell don't they keep you out of mischief?'

Ianto lifted his forefinger and warned the squire.

'In twice or thrice minutes I'll pray for you. Now you know I am no joker at a joke.'

The squire guffawed.

'I told you,' said Ianto, 'thrice times once before to the flat of your face and the straight of your eyeball you are in peril. I know because I am Nonconformist.'

'Noncon!' exclaimed the squire. 'Good God, that means you believe in nothing.'

Ianto made a show of his gloves, and said:

'Entice me not to leave you in peril.'

The squire's anger cooled and he examined the Box–Bible and the cards.

'Come into the hall and pray,' he said. 'I'll get some of my servants to listen to you.'

'Rich man, how much?'

'Here's a shilling. Convert me.'

'The shilling is for God. Come you, Amos bach,' and Ianto pretended to go away.

'But the prayer?' cried the squire.

'In Welsh or English you want her?'

'Welsh, of course. No one will understand you, because they're all English here.'

'Then the cost is five shillings,' said Ianto.

There was a table in the hall and Ianto put his ragged hat on it, but the gloves he held between his knees in the fear that they would be stolen; and on his knees he told the Big Man of the huge concourse of men and women who had come from far distant places to hear the message and of the Welsh chapels that there are in all foreign lands and in the North Pole; he counselled Him to give no ear to the book prayers of Church parsons or to the lying plaints of cattle dealers; he told Him of the iniquity of squires and landowners and tax-gatherers; he asked Him to keep the sea dry until Abel was safe home at last. For these things and more he prayed. His ignorant congregation copied their master, as servants do, and giggled at his antics, whereupon he paused and without opening his eyes, said in English: 'Where are my yellow gloves? I don't know. O yes, I speak the English as well. Amen. And amen.'

Man and youth pressed on, the richer by six shillings and a parcel of food.

'Father bach,' observed Amos, 'we don't get much in the North for nothing to pay.'

In the South when they had asked for a dracht of water they were given a bowl of buttermilk and often if it were at the mid-day meal hour a boiled potato or two to mash with the milk, and often also Ianto would debate the meaning of the Word while he and Amos were sharing a meal with some field workers. But in the North they had to buy food. Churlish are the North Welsh: to cross the bridge at Menai Straits cost them two pennies; yea, even on this Sabbath evening.

The burial place set in the sea gave Amos a new thought: in Hell there will be not only burning, but also boiling.

'Hap they are capellers,' said Ianto.

'How can they be capellers with old crosses on their graves?'

Their doubts were put to flight when they saw a parson tolling his church bell.

'Iss,' said the boy, 'people Church are down there. Think they do to cheat the fire. But Satan is not a oner to be cheated. Boil will the sea. Ho-ho.'

They were on the arrogant Holyhead Road, passing between low hedges and wire fences, by crooked villages and straying sheep, by trees which looked like tramping hunchbacks and fields which shamelessly flaunted their sterility. Short dark people in black clothes, the hopelessness of impotency in their

49

gait, were shuffling to their chapels; chapels which are memorials to the ages of toilers who cast their sweat upon the desolation around them.

'The capels,' remarked Amos, 'are not big enough for large collections.'

Father and son walked throughout the night and in the infinite silence of the wilderness. The father recalled Abel and his doings, and all his doings were praiseworthy. He was a brother among brothers. Far is America, but not land or sea can divide the love of brothers. Abel shall be greeted as the Bible father greeted his Prodigal Son and as the Widow of Nain the boy who rose from the dead. 'Well-well, Abel bach, big is my gladness in seeing you.'

Amos reminded his father:

'And this is the orphan son.'

'Indeed, iss.'

Amos again reminded his father:

'Bigger you are in Ceri than the preacher.'

'Shut your sound about that,' said Ianto. 'Not a red penny shall he give iobs Ceri.'

Amos fancied this talk:

'The likeness of you am I, Nooncool Abel.' 'Why, iss. The spit of me you are, nephew bach.'

Ianto fancied this:

'Hire we will a cart to carry your money, Abel. Robbers there are in Bethesda and Ogwen and everywhere. Don't you take them to Ireland. Robbers are the old Irelands.'

At the going into Holyhead Ianto put on his hands the gloves and Amos on his bosom the slate; and Ianto saw Abel leaning against a certain wall, and the man's body was bent and there was no health in it. Ianto lifted his eyes to the smoke which was rising straightly from the chimneys of the houses, and he said:

'There will be heat.'

Then he and his son turned their faces to the South.

50

CHAPTER IX

IANTO howled on Pont Ceri:

'Drowned under the sea is the brother Abel. Terrible was the going down of the ship. Put thinks in your thinks, people. A pipe comes from sky to water. What is the pipe? One day it is the Big Man's gold fountain pen writing His pledges on the breast of the waves. The next day Satan breathes through it and the sea is ink and the wind a whirl. There's weeping in Anglesea. Island Mona is bowed down. The sea is thundery with the mournings of the people under the sea. Poor dabs bach.'

Some of the people doubted and some listened and did not stagger.

Schoolin covered his squinting eye with two fingers and bent his head and his unassuming lips were closed like a miser's purse; and like a miserly haggler at a bargain he suddenly threw up his head and spoke.

'Tyrhos,' he said, as if he were questioning a lying scholar, 'who went down with the old ship?'

'Mean you,' said Ianto slowly and in the manner of a thoughtful witness.

'Drowned?'

'Boys from everywhere. Boys from foreign parts. Ship and boys are under the sea. Schoolin, you have knowledge. Is a man drowned on land? Very fond am I of herrings. Large money have I spent on herrings – fresh and salted. But no herring fresh or salted shall go into the belly bach again. For in eating him shall I not be eating the brother Abel?'

Ianto spat to make known his disgust.

'But the salt,' said Ben Shop, 'eats up the taste of the drowned. I have tasty salted herrings in the shop.'

'Salted herrings hardened Pharoah's heart,' said Ianto. 'I keep my heart tender.'

Katrin laughed maliciously, a spiteful idea brewing in her mind.

'Male Tyrhos,' she asked, 'who told you of the drowns?'

The men of Ceri were surprised that such a wise question should come from a woman.

'Iss,' said Shop, 'if all the boys, old and young, fell in the pool of the sea, who swam up to tell you?'

'Tyrhos,' said Schoolin, 'your hand is hot meaning your heart is on hell.'

'Bad men like you,' said Carpenter, 'don't perish on the Sabbath. Look you out.'

Ianto smiled as if he were in the presence of little children; and he was inspired to say:

'The news of the drownings travelled beside the carriage of the wind.'

'O jawch!' exclaimed Carpenter.

'I have seen books,' declared Schoolin, 'and no account there is of anyone seeing the wind. Fill your apron with wind, Katrin. Well, you can't for you can't.'

'Your tellings are as unseemly,' said Shop, 'as a funeral that goes too fast.'

'Ask you Amos bach then,' said Ianto. 'Is he a liar? Did you teach him liarings, Schoolin? But wait you a while. For he is in a fever. When we got to Tyrhos last night the weary one fell in the close. Bad is his fever. Make you prayers for him. Bearing women, weep for him. Sterile women, lament for him. Frolickers, pray for his like. Shop and Katrin, remember your little shop-child.'

'Stop you at once!' Ben interrupted. 'Say you again what you didn't say and my anger will be like the anger of Jonah after the whale's belly.'

The people followed Ianto up Road Saints, clamouring for the return of their presents. They would not leave him though he said that of the three graces the most godly is charity; and he told them of the sorrowful widow he succoured with money, of the ribald singer whose bawdiness he changed into praise, of the policeman who laid hands upon his Bible and was paralysed by lightning; and he related the miracle of the five hundred English atheists who at his behest were made to pray in Welsh, and of the rich man whose tongue God tied because he scoffed. Of these he spoke gravely, for there is no difference between the voice of truth and the voice of deceit. But the people were not appeased.

'Say you to me,' said Schoolin, 'why do you mourn Abel?'

With his arms outstretched Ianto declaimed that the only sorrow is the loss of brother or father, they being of the same flesh, but Schoolin broke his speech with:

'Why is Island Mona – Anglesea in the thin language, people – why does Mona weep for boys from foreign parts?'

'The squint in your eye, Schoolin,' Ianto answered derisively, 'has knotted your gut compassion.'

Like a man who is bowed down by his enemies he went into the smithy, but he came out in bare hairy arms which were as black as his anvil, and he had with him a great hammer; and he strode with long, high steps to the gate and he stood thereby with the hammer raised to strike.

'Come you, boys bach,' he said softly, his hammer slanting on the gap. 'Come you and take off your mean little presents. Come you one by one in the words of the religious hymn. Or in two and twos. Come you in threes.'

The people jostled one another away from the gate and when they were beyond the length of Ianto's arm they made excuses and ran beyond the length of Ianto's throw.

Then Ianto went into the road and he shouted in a voice that made them tremble:

'Boys Ceri, I am a savage!'

But man's ecstasy of victory over man stays but a little time. The morning and evening mists lifted and the sun washed away the frost which gleamed on the grass and the ploughed earth. Yet Ianto found no joy. His heart was as lonely as a dead

53

man's heart. In Moriah and at eisteddfod and in mart and fair he was forlorn. The inhabited places were desolate, for he merged his mind in no one's. God's promise was unfulfilled, and he was discontented with the discontent which is begotten of money and which nothing can lull to sleep.

He sat on the moor, striking two white stones against each other.

'Fire is life,' he remarked to Amos. 'Dead is the stone, but with fire it sparks. The little sparks give life to the dead.'

'Not many,' said Amos, 'of the white stones there are here.'

'Few for sure me! Worth gathering they are. Rare are costly things. Bulls and stallions and stones gold that glitter like angels' eyes and stones diamonds that shine like angels' wings.'

These precious words provoked Amos to say that he wanted to go to a shop draper.

'Look you,' he said, 'the life outside sends me into a sickness and who can find angels' eyes and angels' wings in an old bed?'

Ianto sent out letters and he received an answer from Powell, Manchester House, Carmarthen, saying that Powell would take Amos as an apprentice for three years if Ianto would send him testimonials from Schoolin and Preacher. Ianto wrote the testimonials and sent them.

'Husband bach!' exclaimed Catti. 'The boy is like an old paddy. A sorry old paddy. His coat, his trowsers, his shoes.'

'The shopman is inside not outside,' Ianto replied.

'No sense you talk. Boys tidy are boys shops. Clothes he must have.'

'Woman! Woman! Don't you pain the pangs I got already. Powell Shop Carmarthen must give him clothes. I give him the son – the only son of my flesh. I will send a kind but sensible letter to the shopman.'

But Catti moved him and with the money of two pigs she had clothes made for Amos; and on a night she washed him of the smell of stubble, earth, manure, and the sweat and breath of animals; and the next day, the day being the first in the year, she had him and his wooden trunk taken to Castle Owain, from which the trains go to Carmarthen.

CHAPTER X

AMOS did not leave the train at Station Carmarthen until he was sure that it had stopped and that he could step forth without fear. His father had told him how to find his box; he found it and sat on it. He was timid of going alone into the big town. On their journey Northward he and his father had passed through towns with lowered gaze; for gazeful men, according to Ianto, have their money stolen by thieves and painted harlots who lurk and loiter in the streets. He heard a whistle and saw a man waving a flag, and he saw the engine dragging her long wriggling tail.

People huddled against one another on the platform; they spoke in strident voices, ending every sentence on a high note. Men and youths and matrons and maids moved slowly towards the gate, their progress being hindered by the wide baskets which swayed from the women's elbows and the coops of poultry and tubs of butter which littered the floor. They were black-garbed – for funerals are often – and as noisy and talkative as if they were going to a burial instead of to market. Two or three farmers, sticks caught under their arms and tongues bulging their cheeks, dawdled near the gate, bandying sly words with the collector in the hope of passing through without giving over their tickets. A preacher who had placed a penny in the slot of the water-closet was admitting thereunto, one by one, his six sons. A few men were bantering some women at whose drooping breasts were suckling infants. A youth kept on blaring: 'Trots Manchester House! Trots Manchester House! Trots Manchester House!' Presently the youth, whose rat-like hair was sooted, stood before Amos.

'Prentice Manchester House?' he asked.

'Well now, iss,' answered Amos.

'Damo! What ears you have for not hearing. Where is your box?'

'Just now it was just here.'

'Under your backside is the box.'

Trots had lived his sixteen years in the town and therefore he disdained the loutishness of country folk. He stepped away from Amos and regarded him as if he were in a mind to return him to the place from which he had come. Other trot boys joined them and they grimaced and walked around Amos.

'Where's your address tag?' asked Tom.

'Manchester House is my going,' replied Amos.

'Calves, man, are tagged for trains.'

Two trots put their hands in Amos's pockets and under his trousers, but they could neither anger nor perplex him.

'Where's the wegen?' one asked.

'No sweetheart have I,' said Amos.

'Court in bed we do in Manchester House,' said Tom.

In a few minutes Amos and Tom were crossing the bridge which is over the Towy, the box between them and the other trots at their heels, and while they were climbing the short hill on the top of which is the deformed castle which was a jail, Tom said to the lads: 'Stop at the shail'; and they passed on. 'Big fair there is on Tuesday,' he remarked to Amos. 'Damo, busy we'll be! If you're no good then, Boss will give you a bucket of bullets to blow yourself with.' They went up, and of the jail Tom said: 'This is Manchester House. Knock the door.'

Amos knocked lightly at the door.

'Kick it, man,' Trots urged. 'Kick as if you're kicking a dog. Tell Boss you'll be o-rait on Tuesday.'

The door was opened by a jailor.

'What do you want?' he asked, rubbing Amos's nose with the bristles of his savage moustache.

'Though only a prentice am I,' Amos answered him, 'o-rait I'll be on the Tuesday morning.'

The man growled and closed the door with a great clatter.

Amos was nonplussed. Then he saw the trot boys grinning at him.

'Come on, Cardi Cardigan,' said Trots. 'That's the shail.'

They went on, Tom striking the box against the slow-going folk and answering their fretful protests with: 'I thought your old bum was a house.'

But he shed his swagger upon entering Guildhall Square.

'Ho-ho, Tom Trots,' cried Amos. 'I see Manchester House.'

'Fancy a Cardi can read!'

Amos did not know that Cardi is a disparaging term, even among the Welsh, and he said nothing.

But the silence was foreboding to Trots, who uttered this plea:

'Don't you clap on me. A joke fach was the shail.'

The front of the shop was hung with bundles of towels and stockings, blouses and shirts, braces and ties, scarves and shawls, and rolls of oilcloth and calico and printed cotton and flannelette rested against the windows. A slender man walked backward and forwards, speaking to the people who were examining the wares, leading them by the arm into the shop, and returning again to the pavement. His square-crown hat, grey with dust, did not tally with skin that might have been tanned on the shore of the Red Sea and with high cheek bones and half-closed eyes that might have been designed in Egypt. He was nearly blind, but he knew every footstep in the town and every voice, and he could feel the colours of materials.

'So you're going to be a draper,' said Boss. He spoke quickly and in English, and scarcely parting his lips.

'The shop,' remarked Amos in Welsh, 'is full of persons. Start I will to sell the sellings.'

'Today,' said Boss, 'you'll help Tom.'

So on the first day of his apprenticeship, that being a Saturday, Amos took parcels to the station for home-going farmers, watched over horses while their owners were shopping, gathered refuse from the floor, and at night put up the window-shutters. He slept with Slim Jones, who served through but whose department was that of men's hats, in a room which overlooked the Square; and in the morning Slim took him to the gallery of Capel Lammas Street. Even on that morning Slim manifested his irreligious mind by singing to a hymn tune the poem which tells of a woman who had too many children and which begins:

> One cries for breads and one for cheeses
> And one, 'I've messed my breeches!'

At the dinner table he was shy of the company. They spoke the Carmarthen language, this language being a leavening of English and Welsh. Slim's red hair was drawn down to his eyebrows from where it rose upwards in a curl; Davies Haberdashery's high stiff collar rested over a broad ready-made black tie; Thomas Manchester's face was freckled like the skin of a trout. There was also Miss Owen Showroom who lived with her mother in Plumber's Lane but who came in for the most important meals to save the cost thereof.

Amos was so shy that he could not eat.

'The Boss will be angry,' said Rachel Housekeeper, who lost her temper only at the times that the staff would not eat. 'The Boss will be angry if you don't eat.'

She was right. Boss had been a prentice bach in Carmarthen and had gone to Manchester, where the food was thin, and on opening Manchester House he said: 'I'll feed my flock.'

'I always leave a bit for manners,' observed Davies Haby. 'Students College do so.'

'Old students College!' cried Rachel, with a hoity-toity laugh. 'What good are they? No preachers are they and no prayers. What good are they?'

'O-rait with girls in fields,' said Slim.

'Mr Jones,' said Miss Owen, 'I beg you remember your habits. This is Sunday and you're mocking preachers to be.'

'O-rait they are,' Rachel added, 'when a young lady wants filling.'

'You converse for yourself,' said Miss Owen. 'Ach y fy! Scuse the Welsh.'

Thomas Manchester placed a yellow watch at his ear, and shook it to make it go.

58

They finished their meal and went to their several Sunday schools.

The next day Boss said to Amos:

'The draper who can't eat can't sell.'

On Tuesday Amos rose early and joined the multitude of town and country people who were gathered in the streets about the jail and when the clock in Guildhall Square had struck the hour of eight and a black flag had announced that the justice of the Lord had been executed, Amos felt small and he did not recover until he said to Trots:

'One jokan again, Trots, and a kick I'll give you so you can't trot once more.'

Thus ended his fourth day in Manchester House.

The days were short and the nights were long, and in the darkness of the mornings Amos was restless to be up and to take down the shutters, to sprinkle water on the floor of the shop and sweep it, to rub the counters and the bannister, to remove the dust sheets which protected the ladies' hats and gowns in the showroom, and to put the chairs back to back alongside the counters; and when his labour was over to stand like Boss stood throughout the day, his hands behind his back, gazing bliss-fully on the shops in the Square – the druggist's, the clothier's, the grocer's with its coffee pot sign, the stationer's – which were only then showing signs of waking, and at the doors of which sleepy owners or sleepy apprentices were gingerly handling brooms. Amos did his work gladly and alone, for crafty Trots arrived always late, his collar in his pocket, his face unwashed, his shoelaces trailing in the dirt. Trots was lazy, but there's a bustler he was when Boss was looking on.

Amos found a sixpenny piece on the floor. At once he laid aside his broom and ran into the house.

'Where's Boss, Rachel fach?' he cried.

'What's the matter?' cried Rachel. 'You wink like a light-house sweethearting a ship.'

He rushed into the Boss's bedroom.

'Boss bach,' he said, 'piece sixpence I picked under counter. Put him under the pillow now or lose him again you will.'

So he passed the test by which every apprentice was tested.

'How often do you write home?' Boss asked him at dinner.

'No letter yet.'

'And you've been here five months.'

'Ho, they are o-rait. Penny stamps cost one penny each.'

'Send a letter to-night,' said Boss. 'And tell them I'm very pleased with you. Here's a shilling.'

Boss did not wait to be thanked. He never did, because his givings were never charity givings.

Amos's industry and honesty were further rewarded. Thomas Manchester made his second step to London, London being the ambition of every apprentice's heart, and went to Ben's Swansea. Davies Haby became Davies Manchester, and Amos was put in the haberdashery which is the department of trifles: pins and safety pins, needles and thimbles, tapes and shoe-laces, cotton and silk reels and silk braid, shirt buttons and trouser buttons, and so forth. Moreover he was allowed to serve through, whereas in shops in big towns you are confined to your department. Also, in common with every assistant in Manchester House, he received a penny halfpenny for every pound's worth of goods that he sold. At other shops you were paid a commission – 'spiff' they called it – only on remnants and damaged materials.

O iss, Boss was o-rait. He held no trade secrets from his assistants; they knew the wholesale cost of everything and where everything came from. He spoke to them not in Carmarthen English but in plain English, thus familiarizing them with the language of the draper in Swansea and Cardiff, in Bristol and Liverpool, and in Manchester and London. Most tradesmen in the town kept their doors open as long as there was a customer about, but Boss at five minutes before the clock marked the closing hour went about jingling his bunch of keys in their ears of shoppers. Every fair night he gave his apprentices half-a-crown each, screwed up in a piece of paper, in order that they might go and taste the glittering offers of the fair. O iss, Boss was a bit of o-rait. He was not like Jim Evans the wholesale grocer in London. When Jim was holidaying in Carmarthen he used to give away pennies and then say that the pennies were half-crowns and used comfort the poor with self-pattern talk and a handclasp.

Davies bought fairings for a girl in Golden Fleece.

'Davies bach,' Amos said, 'wasteful you are.'

'She will be Mrs Davies when I begin a shop.'

'Spendthrifts can't begin shops. And what is an old wife for? Boss is not wedded.'

Amos was wise. He spent no money on vanities. If he smoked a cigarette it was one given to him by Slim Jones or Williams Cloth Hall or Hughes Shop Big Hat, or by some other boy shop. He kept his money in crowns, because it is harder to part from a big coin than it is from a small coin. 'Little money is big temptation. Half-penny in collection plate (why do capels want collections for I don't know!), half a penny on this and half a penny on that. Penny and a half a penny gone.'

Slim Jones was a good draper and his salary was twenty-five pounds a year living in; that is, twenty-five pounds and all his eating and lodging. He had been in the trade for five years. When a man came to buy a hat, Slim would examine the head in the light and shade and feel all over it with his hands, and the first hat he would bring forth would become the man's head 'like a wreath of flowers glass on a grave.' Amos learnt from him. The term 'miss' annoys many ladies but the term 'madam' pleases every lady. Impudence is the privilege of every lady customer. Upon meeting a lady you raise your hat. 'If the hat is not on the head, how then?' asked Amos. 'Then your front hair is your hat,' Slim answered. In walking abroad with a lady the lady walks on the inside of the pavement. A clumsy action should be followed by lift of your hat and a 'Beg pardon, madam,' and a 'Beg pardon' from a lady should be followed by 'Granted I'm sure' or 'Don't mention it, madam.'

In the sight of other shop assistants Slim was a blade and a piece, and they said that Amos was greatly favoured to sleep in his bed. Assistants copied his curl and his brown hat, the billowy sides of which were like neat little gutter-pipes and which was set in such a fashion as to show the glory of the curl, and they also made their right shoulders higher than their left because that was the way in which God had made Slim. Slim saw a commercial traveller cleaning his ear with a matchstick and did likewise and likewise also youths shops. When on an evening they loafed beneath Coffee Pot, Slim would lean against the wall and tell the secrets of the town: Satan spat on the forehead of the corpse of Price Buffalo Inn, Mrs Isaac Shop Stationer took a wreath from her husband's coffin and laid it on her dog's grave, a deacon in Baptist Tabernacle stutters because a white cat climbed out of an open grave while he was having a to-do with Nell Capel Keeper. What ho!

In some such manner Amos learnt the ways of the town, of men and women and of his trade. He was at the end of the second year of his apprenticeship. He was six inches taller than he was when Carpenter measured him and he was as fair to the eye as the fairest preacher. He was in the Manchester, Davies having gone to Ben's Swansea, and there was another apprentice in the haby. He could cut, fold, and pack a dozen yards of calico with amazing quickness; he knew the quantity of flannelette for a shirt, of material for a gown, of print for a blouse, of corduroy for a pair of trousers, of cloth for a man's suit of clothes. His ways were winsome and he could sell to a woman the things that she did not need. His stock under the counter was as prim and tidy as that which was on the shelves behind the counter. The haggling woman who wanted a penny off this and a halfpenny off that, he circum-vented by putting a penny on this and a halfpenny on that and then bringing down the prices to agree with those in code on the labels. So haggling women were humoured into the belief that they were robbing Boss. He measured accurately, neither stretching nor using the flat of his thumb falsely, and yet he could make his customer believe that she was receiving a few inches over that which she was paying for.

Boss saw that his mind was nimble and his understanding swift, and he said to him: 'I will pay you a salary of ten pounds for your third year.'

CHAPTER XI

In the month of May a company of play actors put up a tent in the Market. Preachers Carmarthen, who had been called to their pulpits to show the duty of life to the wise man and the fool, denounced this evil thing of poles and ropes and canvas. Men and women were made acquainted with the perils of the theatre, perils for the scorchings of which there is no oil spiritual. Youth had to be weaned from temptation: Capels Tabernacle and Lammas Street and Water Street – Baptists and Independents and Methodists – paused in their quarrels about faith and doctrine, and summoned youth to nightly prayer meetings, at which there were no collections. 'Clever is Satan. For two pennies, or three pennies, or four pennies he will bang you headlong in the Pool of no Escape. The price of Heaven? What is the price of Heaven? You ride to Heaven on the back of prayer. And a prayer ride is as free as a ride on your own horse to market.' When Edwards London House passed a player in a street he drew his beard under his chin and spat. He sorrowed in Tabernacle for the young men he had seen staring at actresses whose hair was fiery and ravenous and at actors whose chins were as black as burnt heather. Said Preacher Lammas Street: 'People, keep from temptation. A certain pulpit giant wanted a coachman. "How near a precipice – a very deep precipice – can you drive?" giant asked. "To an inch," replied number one. "To two inches," replied number two. "I would not endanger – an English word is endanger – the life of a respected preacher, sir," said number three, "by taking him close to a precipice." People, there's a lesson for you.'

Amos resolved to hold himself apart from sin. On a Monday he testified his constancy to religion and the burden of his testimony was that it is senseless to pay money for the theatre when there is a prayer meeting for nothing. A few hours later that night the sound of voices disturbed his sleep. He rose from his bed and on the pavement below him he saw, standing under the street gas lamp, a black-chinned man and a flaming-haired massive woman, and the man folded the woman in his arms.

'Swear you'll not forsake me,' she pleaded.

'I swear,' the man vowed in a deep voice.

'Father and mother have I none. Of brothers and sisters I am denied. I have but my God. You will not cast me upon the cold, merciless, pitiless world? Promise me your intentions are honourable, or by this fair hand –'

Slim awoke.

'Play actors,' said Amos, 'not behaving respectable.'

'And now a kiss on those ruby lips,' said the actor. 'Ha-ha!'

The woman pushed him from her.

'Monster!' she cried. 'Devil from the deeps!'

He seized her by her shoulder and waist.

'This night you shall be my – mistress!'

They struggled and passed into the doorway of the shop.

Slim raised the window and he and Amos leaned out. But the couple were not in sight and they could only hear gurgling sounds and moans and gasps.

The man and woman came again into view.

'That ought to fetch the Taffies in,' said the actress.

'I rather think,' said her partner, 'you ought to chip in a few more Gods.'

With a ta-ta they separated, he going up the Square and she into the narrow Toll Gate Street.

Before going into his bed Amos prayed, it being a commandment that even if you leave your bed a dozen times in a night, you must pray on each return, for the Big Man is jealous that you perform His rites. It is also well known that death makes sudden visitations to the beds of the prayerless. Amos could not think of a new prayer, so he whispered one that he knew by heart. This is the prayer:

> Now that my journey's just begun,
>   My road so little trod,
> I'll come, before I further run,
>   And give myself to God.
>
> Then still, as seasons hasten on,
>   I will for Heaven prepare,
> That God may take me when I die,
>   To dwell for ever there.

Next Thursday was half-holiday. Slim and Amos and some assistants were sheltering in Coffee Pot's doorway. The kerb gutters were filled with water and women lifted their skirts in stepping over it. Slim's gooseberry eyes were opened with greed; and he had a remark to make on every woman: 'Mrs Lewis Watchmaker is wearing shilling-three stockings.' 'Thin legs for the wife of a fat preacher.' 'Diawl, nice calves has Mrs George Ironmonger.'

The actor and actress came along.

'Bad play actors,' said prentice London House.

'Now they shan't be long,' said Slim.

'A terrible prayer Mr Edwards told about them in Tabernacle. The spirit was in his inside. His whiskers tangled in his teeth like yarn and Nell Capel Keeper had to cut them with scissors.'

'Wild as actresses,' muttered Slim Jones.

'Much awfulness there is behind the scenes,' said boy Cloth Hall. 'That's how they tell.'

Slim and Amos followed the players. The actor was clothed like a gentleman: patent leather shoes, wide trousers, a frock coat, the collar of which was turned up. The woman, who had her arm in his, was holding up an umbrella, from which the rain dripped on his shoulder. They were followed to the village Pensarn, which is about a mile from the town and on the other side of Avon Towy; and there they entered into the Sheaf Inn.

'How you feel?' asked Slim.

'O-rait,' replied Amos.

'How you feel for a bloo of beer?'

'Slim bach, did not Miss Owen make me a Rechabite?'

'Diawl! Rechabites drink on the sly. Don't clap.'

'I don't clap,' said Amos, 'about my misdoings.'

'Drop dead and blind?'

'Drop dead and blind.'

'Chance we are asked, our feet were in a sticky muck and asked Widow Sheaf to dry them in the fire.'

The players were on a long settle under the chimney, a pint of beer before the man and of porter before the woman.

'How you are, Mrs Rees?' said Slim.

'Dear me, Mr Jones bach. And Mr Morgan, too. How was trade, say you?'

'Quite o-rait now just. We have a very special line in stair oilcloth.'

'What a one are you for special lines! How shall I say then?'

'Coldish is the day.'

Chub-faced Mrs Rees mulled some ale.

'No indeed, not for me,' cried Amos. 'Not a dracht. Not a little dracht.'

'Well I never!' exclaimed Miss Florence Larney. 'Fancy a Welsh boy refusing a treat!'

'Good afternoon, madam,' said Slim raising his hat.

She did not answer; rather she took Amos by the hands and drew him to the settle between her and her companion, and she raised the cup to his lips; and when there was none left, Amos said:

'Now-now, Mrs Rees!'

On the way to the town Slim was jubilant and boasted that Miss Larney had given him a wenchy wink. 'The drapery, mind you, I might chuck up for sure. O yes, I won prizes for reciting in eisteddfodau. A parcel of sparks is the actress. What ho! Tidy one for a stroll in the fields. Preachers say that an actress is a deep well of sin. Diawl! Her breasts are like a bladder of lard, and as tightly packed.'

'Diawl is Satan,' was Amos's reproof, 'and a curseword.'

They bought twopennyworth of potatoes at the stall of Will Chips and these they ate while peeping through the joins of the theatre canvas. Sickness overcame them and they yawned and vomited.

CHAPTER XII

THE price of sin is money. Amos was remorseful. The first cup from which he had sipped was not an offence because another had paid for it; but for the second cup he broke a crown, and therein lay a grave offence. How to build the crown again? You cannot possess that which is lost, and Amos's possessions would be short by fifteen pennies for ever and ever. At his bedside he ordered a miracle; and he had no ear for Slim's babbling. Dawn brought him no comfort and the day no peace. He walked dolefully backwards and forwards behind his counter. He pinched the lobes of his ears until they were scarlet and gone was his pride in the fair brush that was shooting up on his lip; he snipped his finger nails with his draper's scissors and the flying shreds reminded him of his pennies. He closed his eyes that God might perform a miracle in secret. But on searching his pockets he found that the miracle had not happened.

Yet the money was returned to him a hundredfold. While praying in Capel Lammas he felt something hard under his knee. He put down a hand and it was a half-a-crown piece and he placed it in his mouth and thereon to the amen his speech was thick with thanksgiving.

'There's a bulk in your cheek,' one said to him.

'Three lozenges in one for the cough,' he replied.

In the porch after the meeting a deacon cried out:

'A thief has thieved my half-a-crown!'

'Mistake! Mistake!' said another.

'Mistake by Satan's knots!' The loser unbuttoned his trousers and proved that he could put two fingers in the hole that

68

was through his pocket.

They searched for the missing coin and did not find it, whereupon Amos offered the man this consolation:

'What matters a hole in your pocket if there's no hole in your religion?'

He that loses shall gain; and Amos by losing fifteen pennies gained fifteen at prayer. Hitherto he had placed a penny in the collection plate every Sunday; hereon he would give a penny once every four Sundays. The only things that bring ineffable contentment are those for which there is nothing to pay; all others breed regrets.

Knowing that he was strong enough to look at sin without loosening his purse, he went with Slim to the Market. At the door of the booth the actor of the Sheaf Inn was upon a chair, on his head a silk hat and over his shoulders a flowered cretonne cloak which must have cost six-three a yard. He was addressing a company of about fifty people, and Amos saw that these thriftless sinners were wavering between falling into temptation and fleeing from temptation because all the time their hands were going in and out of their pockets. Said the actor in a high voice: 'What a play! What a drama! Not meat for boys and girls. A drama for fathers and mothers and engaged young gentlemen and young ladies. All the gentry and nobility have seen it and acclaimed it with unqualified praise. It is better than a sermon. Rather I'd see my tender daughter in her coffin than see her through tear-dimmed eyes in the coils of the villain. See the beautiful lady fighting for her honour! See Miss Florence Larney, the great London actress, as the poor persecuted heroine, thrown upon a cold, pitiless world, but strong with faith in the mercy and justice of good men and true. An unsurpassed performance. See her alone with the villain. Her clothing stripped from her body. First her hat, then her coat, then her blouse, then her beautiful gown. Does she retain her virtue? Come in! Come in! No one under the age of ten admitted. Twopence, threepence, and fourpence, ladies and gentlemen.'

Slim paid twopence. Amos crept under the canvas that night

and many nights. He did not know what made him go there. The Welsh are actors; they are make-believers. They act when they are alone because they are afraid to be alone with their melancholy thoughts. The best actors go into the pulpit, being men whose faces are canvases on which they can show the emotions and the passions and whose tongues are pipes which can laugh, weep, lament, and bellow. Amos liked to hear the firm eloquence of the righteous, the arrogant clamour of the evil, and the mean whine of the oppressed: he loved the pompous glitter of phrases more than their meaning.

One day Boss brought Miss Larney into the shop.

'Turkey twill, forward!' he cried.

In a moment Trots and the new apprentice were staring at her from the entrance to the hat department and Miss Owen was drumming her fingers on the foot of the banister. Amos was on a ladder and before he had time to come down, Slim was at the counter, smoothing his hair with spittle and drawing his paper cuffs below the edge of his sleeves.

He displayed a bundle of turkey twill on the counter.

'Best quality, madam,' he said. 'Feel it. Six-three a yard.'

'Have you nothing cheaper?' asked Miss Larney.

He brought another, saying:

'Four-three, madam. Don't recommend it though. The best is two times the better, madam. Absolutely fast colour.' He put a corner of the material in his mouth, chewed it, and stretched out his tongue. 'Absolutely fast, madam. Now a dozen yards. Six-and-six a dozen. Cost price, drop dead and blind.'

'I only want enough for two pairs of knickers. How much shall I want?'

'Miss Owen,' cried Slim, turning his head, 'how much for two pairs of knickers?'

'Two and a half I take, madam,' said Miss Owen.

'But I'm bigger than you,' said Miss Larney. 'I'll take six yards.'

'Now what about lace, madam, for frills?' He put boxes of laces on the counter. 'I recommend torchon. Valenseen looks

70

nice, but no hard wear in it. Now torchon washes like leather. Two-three a yard. Couple of yards are ample. And your next pleasure, madam?'

'That's all, thanks.'

'Where will we send the parcel, madam?'

'I'll take it with me, thanks.'

'No-no. I will send it at once. If in a hurry, I'll bring it myself.'

Slim ran to the door and bowing, said:

'Mind the step, madam.'

He put on his hat and went out with the parcel.

Amos descended the ladder.

Miss Owen did not move. Her mind was shaken by those fears which come to a mother upon seeing her child's soul in danger.

'I hope, Mr Morgan,' she said, 'you don't go to the thehatar with Slim.'

'Old thehatar! Miss Owen fach, why for should I go?'

Slim returned in half an hour.

'Bit of o-rait,' he announced.

'Say on then,' said Amos.

Slim looped a hand over his mouth.

'I'm going to her lodgings Thursday half-holiday,' he whispered.

But Amos was unconcerned and went on tidying his stock.

CHAPTER XIII

AFTER closing on Thursday, Slim dressed himself correctly in a fashionable black cutaway coat, white flannel trousers with puce squares, and brown boots which he had blackened. No: he was not going straightway to the den of vice. His fame was such that when he was abroad everybody said: 'Jones is a piece of a chap! Now where is he to?' He was too cute to have sermons preached about his iniquity. He would ramble to the Asylum grounds, throw a few stones at the mad folk, and ramble back through the by-streets to the place of mischief.

Amos gadded on the Pensarn road. He had no eye for the fishers in their coracles, for the hedges which were lively with new growth and murmuring with new life, for the low-lying fields which flaunted their fruitfulness. 'Dash it now! The old hedges want trashing. There's rusty is that machine hay-cutting. The wheels are three feet in the ground. Not proper to leave it out all winter.' He did not know one tree from another or one flower from another. Yet he could make likenesses of men: a nose like a carrot, teeth like a dead dog's, cheeks like red cabbages, a face like a turnip lantern. Peasants of towns are more concerned with men than with Nature. Their forebears lived by bargaining and bartering and they have inherited great skill in probing the motives that incite humanity; dazzling silence is often as plain as deceitful speech.

'Well I never!'

He lifted his hat.

'What is your pleasure, madam? And how you are?'

'You're in Manchester House, aren't you?' said Miss Larney.

With the peasant's distrust of open questions, he replied craftily:

'So they tell.'

'You're Welsh, of course?'

'So they tell.'

'What part of Wales do you come from?'

Again he was crafty.

'Some are South and some North.'

'It must be perfectly lovely to always live in the country,' said the actress, stretching out her arms in a gush of passion. 'Soon the foxgloves will be guarding the fairyland of the hedges like little musical comedy soldiers. Look at those frail little tendrils hugging that strong oak. Aren't they like lovers? Naughty! Naughty!'

Her head was thrown back and she declaimed as if to an audience of people; and Amos could not see the meaning of all her words.

'Yes, madam,' he said. 'Anything more, please?'

'O to be in tune with Nature! Everything growing. Growing is lovely, except growing old.'

When a profound thought strikes a Welshman, he halts in his walk to give it utterance. Amos halted.

'How much your age is?'

'Old enough to have a son as old as you.'

Amos gnawed his tongue and after a while he paused again.

'You are high for a lady.'

'I'm not higher than you.'

She placed her body against his body, bidding him to stand upright and very close to her.

'Why,' she cried laughingly, 'we're just about the same height. Leaves make trees look taller than they are. Skirts do the same with us. Now if I were a man I wouldn't be very tall.'

She drew her skirt around her legs.

'Do you think so?' she inquired, with a hungry laugh.

But she saw no riot in his eyes.

At the door of the Sheaf he faltered.

'No-no,' he said waveringly. 'Dash it no. Not now. Much obliged.'

73

But the woman wheedled him; and she called for a pint of porter and a bloo of mulled ale; and in the ale Amos found the courage that brings sorrow.

'Now, Mrs Rees!' he cried.

'We've had enough,' said Florence Larney. 'You shall show me the beauty spots on the way back.'

'Farwell, miss fach,' remarked the widow, in tones that were unquiet with memories. 'Sound will you sleep this night.'

Her stubby body was like that of a fat priest in short frocks.

'Farwell,' she repeated, wistfully and longingly.

Now after passing over lanes, field paths, and stiles, they came to a deep cattle trough and they leaned their backs against it. Before them the Towy glided shyly between her low green banks like a bride from the marriage altar, and the narrow murky quay-side houses cowered in the shadow of the towering jail.

'Tell me,' said Miss Larney, 'how the hool goes.'

She meant hwyl, the singing incantation by the means of which the Welsh preacher casts a spell upon his hearers and inflames their spiritual and carnal appetites.

Amos recited sermon pieces which he had read in Box-Bible. He was haughty and tender; he cajoled, whispered, shouted, and sang; he acted the violent ardour and the gentle warmth of the pulpit spirit.

The woman's gaze was far up the river, where the water was consuming the prodigal caresses of the dying sun. She slid to the ground and took him into her arms.

When they two arose the youth's face was as grey as that of the water and the woman's bosom as placid thereas.

CHAPTER XIV

SLIM Jones was a rip. He straddled beneath Coffee Pot, telling
lies that he had courted Florence Larney in bed. Apprentices
listened to him with wonder-hungry ears. Although they were
from cottage and farmhouse and as children had heard man's
commerce with woman talked about in plain words, they
knew nothing of man's desire which is born of the flesh and
is stilled by the flesh; and the knowledge, as Slim bared it with
coarse jest and clownish gesture, tingled their senses and
enlivened their imaginings. For many nights after the actors
had gone away in caravans, apprentices beset him with questions which had stirred them during the day; and enjoining
them not to clap, Slim added to the lies he had told and read
messages which he swore were from Miss Larney to him.

But wisdom is prudent, and concerning her misdeeds she
is silent, for the tongue, whether it utters a lie or a truth, forges
fetters which shall cripple our feet. Apprentices did not keep
their oaths. They blabbed to trot boys and Tom Trots to
Rachel Housekeeper and she to Miss Owen, and Miss Owen
requested her God to remove horrid passions from the heart
of the pensive one and to separate his ways from the ways of
Slim. To bring this about, she helped her God.

'Serving, Mr Morgan?'

'No, not now, Miss Owen.'

'Please help me mark off.'

Miss Owen's age was twenty-nine. She had been ten years
in Manchester House and Boss had regard for her and set her
over the affairs of the showroom, and therefore Amos was
upon his behaviour as to a superior power; and as he stepped

75

up the stairs Slim mumbled softly the base song which is called 'Our Mari's White Petticoat'.

Miss Owen was sorting into their several classes some women's clothing which that day had come from London. She examined each garment to see that it was whole and sound, and against the names of those which passed her test Amos marked a cross on the invoice.

'Well, now,' she said, spreading a cambric blouse on the counter, 'this is very chick.'

'How much wholesale?'

'Thirty-six shillings per dozen.'

'What is it to be?'

'Four and eleven-three each. There are three-twelfths.'

'Rait,' said Amos. 'Three-twelfths, thirty-six shillings.'

Miss Owen laid the garment over the blouse she was wearing.

'Reely,' she said, 'it is very chick. The lace is ultra splendid.'

Amos held the cambric against the light and mused over the lace, and he uttered his opinion, speaking as if he were uttering a judgment.

'Three yards cambric six-three two lace three-half hook-eyes cotton tape making fourpence. Cost price two-seven-farthing.'

'Reely!' Miss Owen exclaimed. 'Just the blooze for Mrs Jenkins Solicitor. Eben Lewis Pembroke is against white. He says black for living and white for coffin.'

'Eben is a speechy preacher for a student College.'

'God manufactured him a most holy gent.'

'There's tearful he was supplying in Sunday Lammas Street. Miss Griffiths Shop Burtche did "Wings of a Dove". Dash! She ought to win prizes of money.'

'She sings for love of Lord. Eben puts religious longing in her throat.'

'You are his wegen now then.'

Miss Owen blushed and her blush came of pride.

'The gentle word,' she said, 'is fianzay.'

They continued to examine and note. Six-twelfths calico

knickers, eighteen and nine. Rait. Six-twelfths union do, twelve and six. Rait. One doz. cambric chimeezes, fifteen and nine. Rait. One doz. chiffon boas, one damaged, eighteen and nine. Rait, one dam.

Miss Owen folded her thin arms on her flat chest.

'Man bach sly and skittish is Slim Jones,' she remarked in Welsh. 'And a big spender of money!'

'How do you talk then?'

'Two pennies every night to look at the thehater. And free he has been with the actress. Know you her, Mr Morgan?'

Amos breathed loudly and looked at her clearly and honestly.

'Indeed I don't,' he said with contempt. Then he wetted a finger and making the sign of the cross on his Adam's apple, he swore: 'Drop dead and blind.'

'Broken out he will be from Capel Lammas Street for misbehaving with the actress.'

Her maidenly conscience was distressed and she took Amos to her mother's house. She led him through Plumber's Lane, that lane the pavements of which were of broken tottering flagstones and the face of which was as rough-hewn as the floor of a stone quarry. Women in doorways, some with babies in their arms and some with swollen bodies, offered such remarks as 'New sponer, Miss Owen?', or 'Early to bed now,' or 'Where's Eben Pembroke?'

The house was next to the Red Cow which is at the entrance into King Street, the street which might have come from the mind of a medieval architect. The lower window was raised, showing a few haberdashery wares and sweets, and inside the window sat a lumpish old woman, who grieved for the bustle of the small holding from which her daughter had taken her five years before. Her grey hair was streaked with black like the coat of an ass, for the Welsh peasant's hair does not often turn quite white. Every boy in Carmarthen knew that she did not go to capel because of dropsy, and that on the Sabbath she would not refuse to sell a pennyworth of ju-jubes, or rock, or bulls' eyes.

Amos talked with Nanni about her custom and her profit,

which was a penny on every penny. But she was not inclined to talk. She sat on her chair, her eyes like raisins which had been squeezed into grey bulging flesh and her puffed fingers like bunches of bananas on her lap; she looked as if she had been moulded only yesterday and was waiting for life to be breathed into her.

Amos found Sara Owen in the parlour, and everything in that apartment was a pleasant symbol of her piety: a framed picture of Jesus reading a Welsh commentary of the Bible; a frame which contained two composite portraits of the Pillars of Methodists, a frame with the Pillars of Independents, and a frame with the Pillars of Baptists; two large sea shells, one at each end of the tinsel-draped mantel, which bore transfer pictures of Biblical scenes, and between these shells there were twenty or so photographs of students College; a small round table had on it a very big Bible and on the Bible was a silk hat; on a harmonium was a worn hymn book and a book of Band of Hope songs.

'Eben's preaching hat,' Miss Owen explained.

She struck a few keys of the harmonium. She had played to the singing of many students, but she encouraged none to touch her thigh with his leg or her breast with his elbow. She gave no heed to the ill that was gossiped about students College, in the belief that there can be no ill in those who are called by God from field and mine and sea to preach His word. Woe unto the woman who urges a preacher's flesh to overcome his religion; in the end religion shall triumph and she shall be thrown into Hell.

Sara Owen was watchful of her good name and kept herself free from evil talkings. On those July Sunday School trips to Aberystwyth she never wandered with a sponer, as others did, to the hiding places on Constitution Hill. She remained with the children on the beach, singing hymns to them in a slumberous voice. Adventurous young women and profane young men called her the Carmarthen Virgin; but before the next trip many a loving young woman had been shamed and many a daring student had run away.

Now Eben Lewis, this being the Eben whose bardic name Pembroke glorified the shire of his birth, told her that among all the women who worshipped in Nazareth and among all the women who washed their feet in the waters of Babylon, she was the most comely and pious. She was flattered, because he was without blemish. He lodged in her house and he gave her the sponer's ring which he said was the tape measure that marked the hours between promise and fulfilment. His age was thirty. He had a splendid sermon on his conversion: how on hearing the Voice, he uncrossed his legs, put clogs on his feet and clasped them, gathered his wax and the neddles and thimble and seized the neck of his goose. 'No more did I tailor men with buttons and twist. Off was I to tailor for the White Jesus bach.' A by-word was his piety. When he was rebuked that he lived close to a public house, he turned on his rebuker, answering: 'Blessed is he who can be in sin and not sin, for they shall sit in the Glass Palace.'

As Sara Owen was reverently smoothing the fur of his hat he entered into the room; he saw that which she was doing and said: 'Well done, Saran. A fresh hat I must have very soon, for she is not worthy.'

'The knees of his trousers are earthy,' said Miss Owen. 'Hap he fell.'

She used the third person because it is not meet to thee and thou a preacher. But Eben addressed her familiarly and called her Saran, that being her first name and the last letter of her second name. He took from his waistcoat pocket a thin copy of the New Testament.

'There's a friend in this,' he said, 'for each and all and all together.'

'And the toes of his boots,' added Miss Owen. 'Hap he fell?'

'Why iss, Saran,' said Eben. 'The earth is the earth of the Lord. Walking was I and talking to Him and I saw Miss Griffiths Shop Butcher and Eden jumped to my think and on my knees I knelt and there's a prayer I made.'

'His legs will get the cold.'

'The cold of the Lord!' He turned to Amos: 'Speak Welsh

you do?'

'Indeed, iss.'

Eben Pembroke complimented him, for Welsh is the language of the mothers of preachers and of the Mansion, but English is the language of the pool the bottom of which is without end.

His words brought from Miss Owen this timid excuse.

'I only do the English in the shop.'

They drank tea and ate bread sparsely covered with butter, and while they ate and drank, she told of Slim and the actress, speaking with the freedom of chastity.

'The actress is big with child and she has named Slim and Slim has confessed.'

'Ach y fy!' cried Amos in disgust.

Eben hung his head in sorrow at the fall of man. He scraped away the earth and twirled his long bardic hair around a finger.

'Is the actress telling the truth?' he enquired.

'Has she not named him?' said Miss Owen.

'Who saw the performings?'

'The Big Man,' said Amos fervently. 'Iss, the Big Man.'

'Eve tempted Adam,' said Eben in the manner of dispute. 'But learned preachers and scholars and teachers say he was not the father of Cain and Abel. That's how religion speaks. Eve was bad with the old serpent. Stroompets are they who do against the innocent.'

'But I heard Slim confessing,' Amos interrupted. 'Two times, three times.'

'Dear me,' cried Eben, resting the deep hollows of his temples in the balls of his thumbs. 'I will not buy a fresh hat silk as long as Slim is in Manchester House.' He took from the mantel a box which was covered with small shells and shook the money within it, saying dismally: 'Gold! O gold, what a bad sinner you are!'

'No companion at all,' observed Miss Owen, 'is Slim for you, Mr Morgan.'

Amos saw that the counsel was good and he shunned Slim.

The flood of scandal swept into Capel Lammas Street and

Slim, although he denied all the charges that he had made to his hurt, was driven out like a rabbit from its hole.

'You're too experienced for Manchester House,' said Boss to him. 'I've found you a berth in London – at Wilson's Oxford Street.'

Boss paid him the portion of salary that was due to him, and he also gave him two pounds; and Slim went.

CHAPTER XV

'HAT department Manchester House will soon stop. Who but Slim can keep such a stock of hats and caps, pants and shirts, collars and ties, cuffs and fronts, and scarves and mufflers?'

Thus spoke the prophets of other shops and they spoke foolishly: Amos was elevated to hats, and he had the ability to stand in Slim's place. He did more than Slim: he styled each mode of hat, calling one 'Royal,' another 'Duke,' another 'Prince,' and another 'Carmarthen Special,' but this last did not obtain favour and he changed its name into that of 'London Latest,' under which name it obtained more favour than any other. He was not out of his apprenticeship but Boss looked upon him as an experienced man, and trusted him, as he trusted Miss Owen, to order fresh stock from commercial travellers. He served through; and there was nothing, other than in the showroom, upon which he could not put his hand blindly. He had faith in his judgement and customers had faith in his word; and such was his pride in his high rank that he gave over consorting with boys shops under Coffee Pot. He spent most evenings with Miss Owen, in her house, or at a Band of Hope, or Club Rechabites; and she was glad of his company: maybe she was labouring to fashion his mind as a mother her child's. With that: Eben, his College days coming to an end, often sought inspiration for ode and sermon in the darkness and loneliness of country roads; often also he was in the house of Griffi Butcher, teaching Miss Griffiths to imbue her songs with love of Jesus.

He came to the shop to consider hats.

'Rait. Hat fach bowler?'

'Shut your noise,' was Eben's censure. 'Hat preacher.'

'Expect you a call? Supplying you are now every Sabbath.'

'The last Sabbath I preached with a view. A glossy hat I'll need if I try again.'

'Here is a hat,' said Amos, 'that shines like a mirror in the Mansion. You can shave before her and not cut your pimples. She is London Latest.'

But it was not easy to fit Pembroke because of the hollows in his temples, so Amos padded the under band with tissue paper, and he placed it on his head.

'Grand she is,' he said, walking around Eben. 'And weighty in religion.'

'How now then?' asked Eben.

Immediately the words were out of his mouth, a thought was born under the hat. He took out the pad which was on the right side and in the hollow he put his thin Testament in such a way that much of it fell on his cheek.

'There's to be a doings,' he said as one foretelling some great event.

Barely was Amos's feet on the threshold of the parlour that night, when Eben shouted this question:

'Are you boy Crist?'

Can a Welshman be any other? As every Welshman is a bard, so every Welshman is a Christian. What an asking!

'Saran has joined the band,' said Eben sonorously. 'She is a young lady Crist. Are you not, Sara Owen?'

She parted her short hard teeth and said:

'Yes. I'm a cloud that sweeps on sinners.'

'I will save each and every lady and gent in this big city of hellish evil,' said Eben. 'They will see the light eternal. I'm the cloud that swept the frogs on Pharaoh.'

The crusader began his fight against infidels outside the Red Cow; that is where Plumber's Lane gapes at Shop Welsh Whisky. He led in a hymn and above the voices rose the voice of Miss Griffiths, trilling like a wounded bird on its death flight. Then from a chair he addressed the few people who were gathered around him. 'What's in your hat, man?' The

Testament. A fire is the Testament to heat the brain box. A vision came in his sleep – the vision of a man who bellowed like a bull at the sight of a heifer. His sneezes were like fuses on fire. Now for the interpretation. The bull-man was the Diawl. The sneezes hell fire. 'The Diawl is on his way for to make sinners. People, who will be a boy Crist to drive him out of the city – iss, drive him along the Towy to the sea in Ferryside?'

Tomi Mami staggered out of the Red Cow and as he could not walk uprightly, he leaned under the red hand on the window, this being the hand that beckons men to perdition.

'Student,' he said, hiccoughing over and over, 'in the Crimea I slaughtered more men than you've seen of potatoes.'

Many laughed at the old drover.

'Why poke fun at Tomi Mami?' Eben chided them. 'The red hand has got his last pennies.'

'Hell's Diawl,' Tomi cried. 'For one pint I'll be boy Crist. What do we care if we got pints in the belly?'

Joni Bogus, reeling to and fro and greedily licking the moustache which hung like a curtain over his mouth, also hiccoughed:

'Bogus is the one boy for the bull. In the India a tiger ran to me for to eat me. What did Bogus do? I pushed my arm into his mouth and caught hold of his tail and turned him inside out.'

'Tell, Bogus,' one cried, 'about the lioness who tickled your feet when you were kissing the Indianess.'

But Amos was saying the last prayer. Perhaps he was uttering the sentiments he had heard expressed by the actors and praised by the people as he magnificently demanded that vengeance should fall upon thieves, drinkers, gamblers, jailors, workhouse masters, deceivers, and the despoilers of maids. When he was finished Miss Griffiths Butcher Shop was sobbing. Miss Owen offered her comfort and she too fell a-weeping.

Early in the morning Eben was in the shop.

'My think is changed,' he told Amos. 'Give me the eight-and-six and have the hat.'

'No preaching hat no pulpit call,' said Amos.

'Perishing is the mam fach in Boncath Pembroke.'

'Will you defile her funeral with a hat bowler?'

'Asking is she for her boy – her son bach. Stony-broke is the son and no coins for the old train.'

Amos cogitated; and he advised Eben to tell in Boncath that he had been robbed altogether in the train, and that he would pay on his return to Carmarthen, this capel owing him one pound for supplying, this capel seven-and-six, this capel ten-and-six, and this capel five shillings.

But the other would not be solaced, calling him the robber of widows.

Miss Owen had come into the department, grief in her brown spiritless eyes.

Eben turned and saw her and he departed with solemn tread as if he had not seen her.

The woman, saying nothing, went back to the showroom; and she came down again, a hat on her head and gloves on her hands; and she stammered:

'I am taking the sponer's ring to Miss Griffiths Shop Butcher. Eben only lent it to me. And with it on her finger the shame will not be so shameful.'

CHAPTER XVI

No one knew whither Eben was gone. Coracle men sent
hooks to the floor of the river and finding him not they said
that sinning preachers like leaking coracles should be burnt.
Town Crier proclaimed his loss and he was followed from
place to place by Griffi Butcher who offered a calf's head for
Eben's head on his chopping block. Preachers warned women
that a false charge is a deadly sin, punishment for which shall
be visited upon their bastards as it was visited upon the
unsprinkled stillborn male child of Miss Griffiths Shop
Butcher. Past understanding that the testimony of a chit of
nineteen years drove from the town – a town in which capels
should outnumber public houses – a tenor singer of the Christian Gospel. Eben Pembroke was not dealt with justly, he
being convicted by another's mouth. Humble are preachers
and in their humility they too often turn the other cheek. But
even preachers should have fair play.

As a bag of bones who has been cowed by her son's belt
was Miss Griffiths. There was nowhere, not capel or street or
shop, to hide her fleecy head and no salve to heal her wounded
heart. Her father's brother showed her pity and she went to
his milk shop in London.

If the fire through which she had passed had left its scar
upon her, Sara Owen's faith in the divinity of a preacher's
frock coat was not singed, and never once did she reproach
God. Her solace was the child Amos. Deacons Lammas Street
declared that he should become a preacher: they would have
a special collection made and a grand concert given that the
young saint be sent to a school to learn the religious laws of

the Independents. Sara tried to inspirit his mind to that purpose.

But no, thought Amos: one cannot be shopman and preacher; one cannot close one's eyes in prayer when there is money about. If Miss Owen had not closed hers hap the money in the box shells would not have gone with Eben. Consider Boss: what a sample to copy! No one knew whether he was Liberal or Tory; he attended every capel and church in turn; and what a scolding he gave Tom Trots for dropping a packet of laundry blue into the holy water font in Church Roman Catholics! Why was Boss a sample of a draper? Because persons of every feeling and belief came to buy at his shop.

In the holiday time Amos bought two pounds' worth haberdasheries, paying for every pound's worth only a shilling over and above the wholesale price, and with these in a box he set out on foot to Tyrhos, betwixt which and Carmarthen the distance is about thirty miles. He tendered his wares to small shopkeepers on the roads and such was the easiness of his manner and the glibness of his tongue that he did not have any left on the fourth day when he reached the moor, having sold even the box; and as he stumbled over the heather on the moor reckoning and re-reckoning his profit and gloating upon it, he saw Shan Tins and her children and her ass and cart in his father's quarry; this Shan was the sinewy half-gypsy who could out-swear any cattle drover, whose lightness was a byword, and whose thieving made the most slothful lock his doors at night. Amos told his father of her presence, and his father commented:

'Valuable is the quarry. Valuable is my moor land. And the old ass is eating the sweet heather.'

They both went up to the moor.

'Shan Tins,' said Ianto, speaking severely in the thin language, 'the rent is one shilling.'

'One shilling per day,' added Amos.

'Very cheap that is,' said Ianto. 'Your ass eats more.'

Shan whined a piteous tale, how that she was a forlorn woman and how that her children were fatherless.

'Children with many fathers,' Ianto expounded, 'have no father. Now off or rent.'

Shan wantoned her eyebrows and showed the gleam of her teeth.

'We will bring polisses, father,' said Amos.

Shan changed her naughtiness into a scowl and cursed with burning profanity.

Man and youth bawled against her and she bawled against them and her words came quicker and were more curseful than theirs and her voice was louder than the two voices together; and she made a gesture of throwing stones at them.

Ianto's grief at this robbery would not be quieted. Amos advised him to put a fuse of dynamite in the quarry, but dynamite is costly; Catti advised him to leave the harlot in peace lest he himself be contaminated.

'My think is of Ceri,' he replied. 'Not proper that she brings new evils into Ceri.'

It was not until Amos related his sellings on the roads and his profit of twenty-two shillings thereby that Ianto's interest called off his grief and formed a plan. Day by day he and Amos pretended to set rabbit traps on the moor, patiently waiting the hour that Shan would be in Ceri with her children, babbling for food at every house and entreating the people to buy her pitchers and buckets.

Their diligence was rewarded and they lured the well-conditioned ass to them and they took him to Tyrhos, Ianto riding on his back and Amos prodding his hindquarters, for they were in a great hurry. Shan went here and there as one demented and accused every man of stealing her ass. She pleaded and bullied that the doors of outhouses be thrown open to her, but all spoke as Ianto had spoken: 'Do we keep lockless doors when Shan Tins is in Ceri?'

Ianto and his son behaved as if they were of one mind, hence the son was not surprised on an evening to see his father sitting among Shan and her family.

'Has the ass showed himself?' Ianto inquired in a friendly way.

'No,' replied Shan.

'When he is starving he will come home,' said Ianto. 'The starving prodigal always comes home.'

'How can he find us? We have so many homes that we are homeless. I'm longing after my ass.'

Shan snivelled, and each of her ten children screamed or yelled.

'The bowels are shaking for you,' said Ianto. 'Live here you could –'

'Your heart is not stone then,' said Shan, drying her eyes.

'I am firing a large dynamite in the quarry the tomorrow after tomorrow. Amos the son is sick and he is stopping home for ever and he must work. No use is your cart, Shan Tins. No use without the ass at all. I'll break up the old cart and here is one florin.'

Shan spat on the coin and snivelled afresh.

'Eleven years was the old ass with me,' she said. 'He was a suckler when I picked him in a field. That day my first child was born. He could smell a policeman before a policeman could smell us. He slept with us at nights. The fathers of my children strayed, but he strayed not. He got his food in gardens and hayfields and cornfields and was never caught. He came of a sacred family. He had the touch on his shoulders that Jesus left on the ass who took Him into Jerusalem. And we cared for him for Jesu's sake.'

'Now-now,' said Ianto. 'I take the cart.'

She scowled again and cast a daring eye.

'He will not like his cart broken.'

Ianto was about to blurt out, but Amos quickly prevented him, asking:

'Was your ass the best make?'

'The great God never made a better!' she cried. Then definitely: 'No, I will not go. My ass strayed from here and here he'll stray back.'

'Father,' said Amos off-handedly, 'if an ass you need there are three sucklers in a field as you go into Carmarthen. The best make they are. The field has a bit of pond in it and at the road cornel of the next field is a Capel Methodist – Methodist Capel.'

Shan addressed her children thus:

'Gather the things. We are going very early.'

Ianto seized one shaft of the cart and Amos the other, and Shan and her children followed them to the edge of the moor, noisily lamenting the image that they saw between the shafts.

'The food of an ass is as nothing,' observed Ianto.

'Bargain quite respectable,' said Amos. 'Harness too.'

'Pity the woman gypsy opened my purse so wide, boy bach. In my think is a travelling little shop.'

CHAPTER XVII

Amos was in Commerce House, Barry Docks, he having left Carmarthen three years before; at which leaving he was counselled by Lammas Street to read the Bible and by Boss to read 'The Drapers' Record'. He aspired London, but London is far from Wales and there are pitfalls on the way, and he who runs too hard pants and falls. Knowledge lent him prudence: Thomas and Davies were discharged in the seasonal clear-out at Ben's Swansea and Slim Jones within two months from Wilson's Oxford Street. In Carmarthen you are number one; in London number ninety-nine. A preacher whose words he had read in Box-Bible said that to arrive at the meaning of the entire Word one must linger at each word in the Bible. Therefore to come by the sleekness of the London draper one must be lopped in this shop, hewed in that shop, and smoothed in that other shop. It would lower him if having reached London he would have to come back through lack of skill and art. The big London drapers are like God: they call many but choose few.

He had experienced the trade at Merthyr and Aberdare, and while he was at Aberdare Commerce House advertised for a 'smart young gent for quick trade able to dress windows salary twenty pounds and spiffs live in apply own writing.' He offered himself and on the notepaper appointing him to the post there was a picture of a shop with carriages in front of it and fashionable ladies at its door. A Welshman confides his purpose in no one, in father or mother, in brother or sister, and he confided in no one. Down as the heart of a maid whose lover has broken his promise was his heart when he beheld a lock-up shop with its side-door leading to the dwelling rooms, and with its two small windows of garish feminine wear and nothing priced over one-and-eleven-three.

But after a few weeks his mind was at ease and he found contentment in a street of frowsy women crippled by man's haphazard love, and of children whose faces were in the likenesses of the Chinamen and Japanese and Lascars and Arabians who came into the docks. This was experience. No man can foresee in what sphere God will set him to gather money. Therefore no man can know too much. The shilling of the harlot rings as true as that of a preacher's wife. All money is clean; and money was squandered in Commerce Street, as it always is by the mindless folk who inhabit ramshackle streets. All the day he and Mrs Rees were busy at selling those perfumes and unguents and gaudy, flimsy articles of dress with which woman throughout Europe is able to bewitch the sailor in port.

The husband was Picton Rees, who was as often tippling in the Sailors' Rest as he was in the shop. In sobriety he was an offence. If a girl and a sailor were at the counter, he would put his head between them, his hands behind his back flapping his coat tails, and ask with a foolish leer: 'How's the business doing, miss?' Howsoever many sweethearts a sailor has and in howsoever many ports, he believes that each is faithful to him until he returns to her and will remain faithful even after his death. So many a good sale was lost, for when a man suspects the fidelity of his woman the first thing he denies her is money. He slithered up and down the little shop on the heavy feet of the forty-year-old draper, fondling his smoky wisps of hair and thinking out obscenities. On Sundays he ministered unto God Capel Horton Road with the zeal that he ministered unto himself on week days in the Sailors' Rest. If sobriety made him obscene drink inspired him with the unctuous oratory of the trickling nose... He had lisped prayers at his mother's knees and went to capel three times on Sunday. Look at him now: the most prosperous draper in Barry Docks. Cash trade; ready money all round; no bad debts. What religion has done for him will do for all. His place is a gold mine and Alice a nugget. Since he married her ten years ago, she has twiced, thriced the trade. There's a head is on her. There's a noddle. She's small, but all there. Size don't count. Experience and age does. Why Alice is forty-three though she does not appear. A wife better than rubies. What a saleslady. Dam, she could sell the young ladies in Sam's Cardiff before breakfast....

Yes: Mrs Rees was a great saleswoman. With her thin fingers – the greyish black of faded ink was the hue of the half-moons of her nails – she turned common wares into the uncommon and the tawdry into the elegant. With her tip-tilted nose she would sniff at a bottle of perfume and behave as if she were going to faint with delight. The sailor who shopped alone she cheated with a loose smile and tinkling words into the belief that he could lie with her. Her eyes, which were as if they had been stretched and screwed at the sides, glowed with understanding. A flicker from a sailor's girl would at once bring the reply: 'Of course, dear. Come alone, Mr Naughty Mans. Take great care of her. She's honey,' and with mincing steps she would take them to the street and ushering them through the side-doorway, sing to her servant woman: 'Lee-lee! Best room.' A whisper from another would cause her to unlock a case and bring forth a box of pills or a bottle of medicine.

Her mother was Welsh, but she was unlike the Welsh: her thighs were narrow, and her black hair, rich and hard, was brushed back over her head, falling thereon like thick yarns of silk, and wound into a heavy skein over the nape of her neck; and she spoke no Welsh and her English was odd.

Amos slept in a room on the third floor, which room was between that of Picton and of the large boned, broad-shouldered Lily; and almost every night his peace was broken by Picton's body thumping against the banisters as it was being dragged up by Lily and tumbling down as it was being thrown into its room, or by Lily shouting to the lets on the second floor: 'Shut your row! Where do you think you are?' But he was not distressed by what he saw or heard. Other people's affairs were not his. His only concern was his own fortune; everything else he shut out from his life. His spiffs were seldom less than five shillings a week, the food was good, and Mrs Rees dealt kindly by him and placed her trust in him. He opened the shop in the mornings and watched over Lily while she dusted and swept the floor; he made a count of the money at closing time, and padlocked the doors, and delivered the money into Mrs Rees's hands.

Mrs Rees had a room with a bed in it immediately over the shop, and thither one evening he brought the money. She was lying on a couch. He saw that there were flowers and a bottle of whisky on a table and that the bed, the curtain being withdrawn, was covered with a sheet of purple silk and on the rail thereof were shawls of several colours. She was clad in a scarlet dressing-gown, which was also of silk, and which was streaked with the strands of her loosened har, and her legs were bare to the knees and of the colour of summer clouds wanly tinted with yellow.

Holding his head aloft, Amos cried business-like:

'Cash, please.'

'Totals?'

'Thirty-three-three-and-six.'

'Put it away.'

Amos drew from under the bed an iron box and placed the money within it.

'Anything else, please, madam?'

'A shawl.'

'Any particular colour you fancy, madam?'

'The black.'

She commanded him to lay it over her from her feet to her armpits, and he having done so, she said:

'You puts my hair long out on top. Was that the bell?'

'I don't know for I didn't hear. It is very early for Mr Rees.'

She drew her lips together.

'My hair don't show off on black, does it?'

She turned down the shawl and bared her breast.

'If you arrange it like a veil for my skin I'll be much grateful.'

Amos smelt her perfumed body.

94

'Anything else I can attend to, madam?' he asked.

'No, thanks. Good day. Tell Leelee to catch the bell.'

She came down in the morning, the perfume the like of which was not sold in Commerce House, still about her presence, and at noon Amos at her behest went to see if the ship *Gwyneth* was in port, and he returned saying that she was... 'And Captain Roderick?' Well, Amos had not inquired. Perhaps he was gone down into the sea. Perhaps he was with a wife. Sailors are like that. And captains are rich, and spend money...

'Painted girls gather on them,' she said bitterly, 'like flies on the deads in mortuaries.'

By day she was betwixt fancy and fear, but after each closing, even on half-holiday, she sprayed her gown and her shawls with Bouquet d'Arabia and smoothed her body with perfumed unguents, and decked it in scarlet and veiled her skin and rested on her couch like a chaste, longing wife waiting for her husband; but by the by a girl coarsely rejoiced to her the going away of her lascar in Captain Roderick's ship.

That same day a woman and her man needed a room for an hour or so.

'This is not the house you want,' she replied, angrily.

She was further angered by a girl who came to her for medicine. She looked at her with the unblinking stare of a good woman.

'Was I like you I'd drown me.'

She had no smile for customers. Her fingers lost their cunningness, her eyes their mischief, and her voice its tinkling music. Her kindliness was murdered. She kept Picton without money and so he was held in the shop, and with his lewdness and her uncharity, custom took flight and Amos was out of heart at seeing his spiffs falling under a shilling a week.

'Trade is damaged, sir,' he complained to Picton.

'She's always like that,' said Picton, 'the times he don't come. I've never known her spiteful ways to last so long. But pity about the lets and pills. I always banked on them if the shop failed. There's a fortune in a house like that. Of course

I can't do it here because I'm too well known. But London –'

It happened that Florence Larney and her players came to the town.

'Grand stuff in the Sailors' last night,' said Picton, making arrows on the linoleum with the edge of his boot. 'An actress. But a lady. Acted to the King and holl the Royal family.'

'Indeed,' said Amos. 'Dear me.'

Picton and Miss Larney became friendly. Then articles were missing from the stock: a belt, a blouse, and a lace collarette. Mrs Rees began to make a count of the money herself; and Amos found the depth of her mind and perceived the thing that she thought. He was troubled and he breathed in urgent sincerity to God Independents that that which was lost was found. God harkened unto his plea, and as he was walking, his eyes upon the ground and his heart sore in affliction, he heard a voice saying: 'Well I never!' and he beheld Miss Larney and on her body were the belt, the blouse, and the lace collarette. He pointed to them one by one and asked:

'Where from are these?'

'Aren't they lovely!' she exclaimed. 'I love lovely things. They are presents from Picky. Aren't they, darling?'

Amos smiled in his happiness.

The actress was so talkative and he was so lightsome that neither saw Picton's lip curling against his nostrils.

Amos would have hastened away to impart his good news, but he could not free himself from the woman's chattering. She patted his face, his hands, his shoulders, and his waist, but she could not add any warmth to his joy.... That afternoon in the fields. Lovely! Wasn't it the first time? She knew it was. A woman can always tell. They must meet again. Are the fields very far away?...

Amos hurried to Commerce House and he told Mrs Rees and she kept him in her room until she charged her husband with stealing her goods for an actress.

Picton, drunk and righteous and unctuous, drew in his stomach and stretched his finger at Amos.

'Get from my shop,' he shouted. 'The wife won't have you

here. I shan't trust you with her. She's an honest lady. You'll die by your neck and when after you're dead remember what I Picton Rees told about you. What did you do with the actress in a field? What did you want in the field for? Ho-ho! Hay? Ho-ho!'

At that announcement the wife took her husband's part and they both reviled Amos with much heat.

The deeds of a drunken man and the wounds of an abandoned mistress are beyond God's repair.

CHAPTER XVIII

Amos was given a week's notice to leave, but the words were spoken in vain.

'You can stop on if you like, Morgan,' said Mrs Rees.

'Mr Rees, madam? There's he.'

'He!' she cried disdainfully. 'A sober assistant is more handier than a drunken husband. I'm sorry, Morgan.'

'Don't mention it, madam,' said Amos.

'What you've done have nothing to do with me. Everybody do it. We all got to wake up. Sooner we wake the nicer. It is the big joy. For it we make money and sing songs and keep sober. Poor silly boozers, how they crush the sweet flower!'

Her tongue was active and its text was love. She was like a woman who after wonder-gathering in far places finds the most precious wonder on her hearth. As a hungry woman's eyes glistening at a feast were her eyes; as a gentle nun's voice beseeching alms in the name of a saint was her voice; as a covetous maid scooping her hands in eagerness were her hands.

Amos's spirits were high and the little meaning that he found in her words also caused his eyes to glisten beneath their cold lashes. He had been given more than pardon; he had won grace. In the shop he could do no wrong and at closing times he was trusted with the reckoning of the money. Once Mrs Rees gave him supper in her room and after they had eaten she had him draw the couch before the fire. Telling him not to look around, she skipped behind the bed-curtain. He heard the tinkle of her voice rilling a tune and he smelt her perfume and as he sniffed the cream of his cheeks rosed and he creased his forehead in wide understanding. She returned to him in her yellow gown with her hair like flowing jet, and she fell upon him, sighing, sobbing, tearing apart his garments, and crying:

'I didn't know! I didn't know! Love me! O love me!'

Amos knew her.

Soon he was at the window, oppressed by melancholy.

'All this snow, madam,' he said dismally, 'is no good at all to trade.'

Declining spiffs worried him.... Dash, only ten-half last week. Picton was an old hen, but he didn't kill the trade. Mrs Rees killed the trade. Girls take their sailors to shops where they are obliged. What you think? The think is Sam's Cardiff...

Though Miss Larney appeared on a white horse as Lady Godiva, not her plump arms, or the billowy folds of her body, or her fleshy legs, or her bold winks seduced many people to the theatre, and it was so that the manager became afraid of the face of his players and ran away. Hence Miss Larney remained in the town, and so greatly did she and Picton like each other's company that where one was there also was the other. The harlots, apprehensive that she would add herself to their traffic which in winter dwindled tragically, grimaced at her and called her by filthy names; respectable wives kept jealous watch on their lovers and husbands; chaste women licked their lips and tattled and ennobled their virtue; drinkers in the Sailors', remarking that Picton drank less, sneered at his temperance and said that of woman and beer the more glorious is beer. But Picton stood up for Miss Larney. Modesty: she was adorned in modesty, as untarnished as a baby, and as faithful as a saint; and he said further that the hour she declared her pure love for him was more magnified than all the hours in his life.

About a week after Miss Larney had left the town, Picton said in the presence of Mrs Rees and Amos that he was going to examine the flaws in Commerce House.... Fresh stock was wanted. No more buying from the samples of little whipper-snapper travellers from little whipper-snapper warehouses in

Bristol and Cardiff. The fountain head is the place to buy. There is a fountain for all things. A fountain for religion and a fountain for stock. And where is the fountain for fancy drapery? London. Why, London!...

Thither he set forth. On that afternoon Mrs Rees gave Amos twopence and told him to go and wash himself in the public baths, and when he got there an attendant instructed him in the business, that being his first entire cleansing since he was born. Now one night in bed he disparaged the perfume which was sold in the shop and congratulated Mrs Rees on the perfume which she sprinkled on her bed, her gown, and her nightdress; and at a slumbery moment he dreamed a dream that a great number of people were in the shop. They were standing on the floor, the counter, and the shelves, and hanging from the ceiling; many were lying on the ground, gasping in pleasant ecstasy; and they were all tied in couples, each couple being a sailor and a girl. He interpreted the dream to be an order to put that perfume in the stock, for it was clear that men and women hungered for it by the vast number he saw in the vision and that none could stand up against it by the couples who were in ecstasy on the ground.

'Your perfume will mend affairs,' he vouched.

Mrs Rees, who was vain of the perfume and wished to have it remain a secret, at last agreed; and she also said that again she would start the lets. But she relented too late. The harlots, embittered by the poverty with which winter visits the ports and docks, had hardened their hearts against her, and they meted out to her the measure that is always meted out to the samaritan: they blackened her, saying that her beds were verminous and that she robbed the poor sailor of his hard-gotten money.

Picton returned on the seventh day and he heard that which was cried about his wife and his conscience was in a turmoil. Thus he moaned:

'Dam! After all the years I built the business. I ought to be stricter. But I can't do everything.'

'Perhaps the new stock will bring them in,' said his wife hopefully.

'I didn't buy after all,' he announced. 'I had a feeling all was not right. I blame nobody but myself. Women don't manage.'

Mrs Rees's temper was roused. In a voice that was full of rage, she said:

'You'd bankrupted but for my cash.'

Without appearing excited or reproachful, he replied:

'That was the first big mistake. Cash from a house like you kept was dirty cash. Trade's gone down steadily. I had no idea there was carryings-on here. No idea whatever. If I had, in a fire it would be. A big, large fire. You always told me they was sailors and wives on a bit of rest before sailing.'

He resolved to sell the business, and entreaties and tears did not prevail upon him to change his mind; and for the stock and the fixtures he obtained one hundred and fifty pounds.

His last words to Amos were:

'Be just and fear not and go the middle of the straight path. Clean money makes a clean conscience.'

He then addressed his wife as if grief was overwhelming and shattering his heart:

'Forty-three and cribbing for a berth and been on my own. But an experienced man like I ought to be snapped up in London. I'll send you the money. Goodbye, the true, true love!'

CHAPTER XIX

ON the morning that Amos was going to crib Cardiff for a berth, he and Mrs Rees stood in the doorway of Commerce House. The backs of the windows were adorned with sheets of silk, one in the colour of purple and one of scarlet, and on the floor of each window were bottles of Bouquet d'Arabia, and on the glass of each was a strip of paper with words elegantly written in yellow ink, these being the words: 'Scent that tickles sailors senses.'

Picton had been away a month and no message had been received from him.

'Mr Rees,' said Amos, 'will be unexpected to see the shop when he comes home. When you think he will?'

'I hope he shan't come back,' Mrs Rees replied. 'There's no place for him. The rooms are always let.'

'But he is the husband, madam. He shall come back rait enough.'

'He's sure to. The world is round and that's why bad pennies always turn up.'

The rain which had been beating people into the Sailors' Rest was thinning.

'Well, madam, so long,' said Amos.

'Goodbye, Morgan. Be sure you drop in if you are in Barry.'

'Very pleased, madam. The ref o-rait?'

'Of course. I puts down I know you better than the husband,' she said airily.

'You shan't joke, madam. Put about Amos Morgan, I am honest and industrious and civil and cool and calm and collected.'

They clasped each other's hands and there was no regret at the parting.

Amos moved his large feet, which were beginning to turn outward. His umbrella, enclosed in an alpaca case, he held by its middle, that being the gentlemanly fashion, and his six feet of leanness was folded in a fawn mackintosh. On his way to the railway station and thereon to Cardiff perhaps he thought on a year-old letter from Miss Owen telling him of the death of her mother and of her inclination to leave Carmarthen. Perhaps he thought of his father's letters bemoaning losses: Shan Tins had robbed him of two shillings, for the old ass brayed himself unto death within a week of her departure; the pigger swore that he had sold him two pigs who were in swine fever and came with a policeman for the return of his money, and so pigs and money were lost; had he known that the goats were sick he would have forestalled death and killed them and sold their flesh; coal was very costly for the smithy and peat will not blow into a flame; Deio Blind Eye had started a smithy in Ceri; Catti was big with too much eating. Losings and losings and losings.

Amos had answered only a few of Sara Owen's letters, and he wrote seldom to his father and he had not been to his father's house since he left Carmarthen, he having whiled away his holidays in studying other shops. . . . A penny stamp costs one penny and men railways are mean. You do not put one hundred pounds and a little more in post office by spending. . . .

He thought on Sam Samson, whose grey massive building was like a castle set in a dun street. He had heard tellings of Sam: his farm over against Dinas Powys, his Cawdor Hotel in the centre of the town, his scorn of mayor and councillors, his tempestuous rage against which none could battle; he had heard of his cute buyers of departments, of his shopwalkers whom nothing escaped, of his toffish counter-jumpers who were keener than terriers, of his eighty-nine rules, the breaking of one of which was punished by a fine. Yet young men and women fought to serve Sam, for Wales has never seen a greater man of affairs and there was no other place in the provinces where they could be trained up so completely for London.

But when he looked at Sam's counters spreading out farther than he could see, it was of himself that he thought and for the success of his purpose was his silent prayer to God Independents.

A man below the common size with a stomach like a bladder of wind, and with legs and feet like a fat baby's, came to him.

'Please can I see the engager?' asked Amos.

'Cribbing?'

'Yes, please.'

'This way.'

Roberts, the buyer of the Manchester Department, was plagued with corns and he hopped before Amos singing thus: 'Abide with me fast falls – dam-dam-dam – the even – o dam – tide the darkness deepens – dam the corns.'

He left Amos at the counter which was over a well, this being at the middle of the store and the place from which Sam surveyed the drapery departments before him and the departments of furnishings behind him. That which Amos saw and heard made him again crave to be one of this kingdom: assistants fawning money out of ladies: frock-coated shopwalkers splaying their feet and saying: 'Walk this way, madam;' clerks writing at high desks on the other side of a glass door; porters in the well folding purchases for dispatch; young ladies in black gowns beyond the balustrade of the lofty showrooms; voices crying, 'Sign, please,' 'Forward,' 'Ladies' gloves first on left, madam,' 'Gents' hosiery third on right, madam,' 'Tulle in lace department, madam, fourth on left,' 'Rubber sheeting in ladies' waterproofs upstairs, madam,' 'Millinery upstairs in showroom, madam.'

On a sudden the shopwalkers quickened their movements and became more servile to customers and more exact to assistants, and assistants increased their readiness and deepened their smiles. A short, broad man had come to the well. His frock coat and square-crown hat were grey; his face was as grey as the stone he had digged as a youth in Carmarthenshire quarries, his eyes were as fiery as those of the ferrets which delivered rabbits into his boyish hands, and his wide nostrils had the power of the man who has conquered by terror and lives by terrorism.

'Hey, mister!'

His words sounded like the cracks of whips on a frosty morning.

'You, Jordan!'

Amos had heard of Jordan, who was despised by everyone who had gone through Sam's. His second name was Jones, but he favoured the sacredness of Jordan; his nickname was Pig, because he came from Pembrokeshire and Pembrokeshire Pigs is a scoffing term which every Welshman knows. He was also so called because as steward of Sam's table he provided bad food and skimped it, as overseer of the men's bedrooms he inflicted a fine of a shilling on each of the six or seven men in whose room the caged gas jet burned after eleven o'clock at night, as leader of 'Praise God from whom all blessings flow' before every Sunday dinner of roast mutton and potatoes and as shopwalker in the silks he punished with fines everybody who said 'pork' or 'pig' in a voice loud enough for him to hear. It was said that he was worth three hundred pounds a year to Sam in fines. But in a high-class trade he was a sorry draper, finding a lofty joy in cheap stuffs, and it was for that reason that Sam made him the steward of his table.

Jordan's knees knocked against each other and he stooped his neck before Sam.

'Yes, sir,' he said. 'Yes, sir.'

'Look at me, mister.'

The flash of Sam's eye turned even daring men into middle-wits.

'Where the hell you saw sheep washed in dripping?'

'Please, sir –'

'You're gullish, mister.'

'I made a mistake.'

'Mistake be dam! I don't give sixty pounds a year and food and lodging for mistakes, mister. The next one out you go. I told you get a ton of dipping. Dipping, mister. Fetch the dripping from my farm and don't get butter till it's all eaten.'

Sam turned to Amos.

'Well, mister?'

'I want a vacancy, sir.'

'There aren't any, mister. I've got all the idiots I need.'

'Then,' Amos responded, 'you shan't want me.'

'Hey, mister?'

'I have expected here one hour and half, sir.'

'Don't tell lies.'

'There is the gentleman who carried me here now just, sir.'

'Hey, you Roberts!'

Roberts puffed up.

'Yes, sir.'

'If you don't cut your corns tonight, mister, you best cut your neck. How long has this young man been here?'

'Eleven o'clock, sir.'

'I said how long?'

'T-t-two hours,' Roberts stuttered.

'Damn you, can't you see my customers walking out without being served?'

Roberts hopped away.

'You're a liar, mister. Where you from?'

'Cardiganshire.'

'Every Cardi are liars. You told me one hour and a half.'

'The lie was in the right, sir.'

'And you're for a vacancy, hey? What department?'

'The experience is all round.'

'And when I've taught you, you'll go to London?'

'No, indeed. Drop dead and blind I shan't.'

Sam went into his counting-house and returned with a blank sheet of paper which he had torn from a letter, and on it he wrote Amos's name, the name of his father, and the names of the shops in which he had worked.

'Refs all right, mister?'

'Indeed yes, sir. I have never taken pins or string or anything.'

Sam was pleased, for he hated his vices in others.

'If you steal here, mister,' he said, 'I'll clap you in prison for your life. You can start on Monday. Thirty and spiffs. Minute's notice on either side. Be here at nine and see Jordan.'

CHAPTER XX

'STRIPPED am I altogether,' Ianto wailed. 'Deio Blind Eye steals my work.'

'Well, now! What think you of that? There's a brass forehead.'

Thus Amos, who was at Tyrhos, the railway fare being less than the cost of a lodging in Cardiff.

'No misery is in me for you,' Catti cried out. 'Sluggish you are. All the time you peep at pieces in Box-Bible. For what how do I know? The old box is your bed wench. Is she made of gold you fondle her so.'

'Bits religious,' said Ianto, 'are in the box.'

'Bits of easy speech. Blind Eye stays at his anvil. What a worker! To the sea-shore I'll jaunt and throw the old box in the sea.'

There came over Ianto the fear of the man who sees a corpse candle going from his door toward the burial ground. He reproached Catti:

'Destroy the Beybile I won't let you. Don't talk sin on the brink of your grave.'

He also recalled the atheist who shredded the Bible and whose teeth consequently became live coals and fell from his gums and set his beard on fire.

But Catti would not be reproved.

'Good, Ianto bach, are teeth of fire. Hap if you put them instead of clods and peat on your poor coal the coal would burn. When jobbins come you cannot heat the iron. Closer to you is the money than the trowsers you don't have on.'

There was about Catti the boldness of a mare tethered in

barren pasture when she kicks up her heels and breaks her string.

'Blow you the bellows now,' said Ianto, 'and see the flames.'

He drove a piece of iron into the coal and he bent forward and tried to catch the few sparks which flew upwards.

'Foolbert!' Catti jeered as she went out. 'You're a pretty man. You're mad without the fever and like persons in the madhouses.'

Ianto lifted his apron, scratched his naked legs, and tightened the cord over his waist with the jerk of a man going to make a pronouncement. This was the pronouncement:

'The sparks of one year would make the fires of one half year.'

'Who is stripling Blind Eye?' asked Amos.

'Ho, a stripling. Ho, a greedy stripling. Is not one smith enough for Ceri? Why does a damaged collier come here for to take the jobbins? Greedy are persons Ceri. They hold what they have and steal what you have. I turned the water from the road ditch into my fields and in the night they took it back. I complained to polissman. What did poliss say? "No man owns water." Poliss is a rag. Do I say I want your oats and hay and mangolds? Then for what they covet my water?'

'Sensible. Quite sensible,' said Amos.

'All sinners they are. The chiefest is Katrin. She gabbled. "Big money has Ianto Tyrhos." That was her gabble.'

'How much now?' asked Amos.

'All will not fill a baban's palm, Amos bach. The taxer heard –'

'Bad are the saying about tax-gatherers in the Beybile.'

'Taxer said they were under the roobob. There's laugh my stomach gave.'

'Bitchish is Katrin,' commented Amos.

'How can I rant about the wife of father who is in his grave? No, I can't rant. But her telling was no telling for her telling led astray.'

'My inside's on stir for you, father bach. Hap taxer will put you in shail.'

'Go you off! Nothing in taxer's head.'

'Men bach are strangled every day in shail Cardiff.'

'Clever will be taxer if he finds the money.'

'Easier it is,' said Amos, 'to defraud God than tax-gatherers.'

Ianto was alarmed. He had collected his money halfpenny by halfpenny, penny by penny, threepenny-bit by threepenny-bit and the yellow sovereigns into which these brown and white pieces had grown were dearer to him than land or cattle or smithy; he loved them with a lover's jealousy. As had been his intent to make money so was his joy to look at that which he had made. His plight made him sorry for himself. He enlarged his labour. Must the trace of his toil be effaced as is the trace of last year's furrow by this year's? He who had nourished his land into fruitfulness and had struck his anvil into a song is at nightfall begrudged a kiss.

Amos approached Catti with blandness in his countenance and addressed her as his second mam fach and promised to send her from Cardiff a fashionable gown.

'Whisper now,' he cajoled, 'the hiding of father's money.'

'Could I tell,' Catti replied, 'my cows, pigs, fowls, would perish from the eatings.'

Ianto came upon them smiling happily.

'Ho-ho!' he cried. 'In the bank goes the money.'

'Do I have nothing after you perish?' asked Catti.

Ianto brought forth a sack which was nearly full of white stones.

'On the day of my funeral I shall rise and go to man bank and say to him: "Give you now Ianto Morgan my yellow soverens".'

But Amos was perturbed.

'Gone will be your soverens, father,' he said dolefully.

'O-rait they will be under locks.'

'What of the keys? Stealers are boys bank. Father bach, keep your money I will.'

'Well no, indeed.'

'Will you let taxer rob you and cast you in a hole in shail?'

'Bank is the place for the soverens. O iss.'

Amos rose up before his father.

'Father bach,' he said, 'hurt the limbs of your limbs you have. Can you find a better place than in the pocket of your son?'

Ianto's purpose did not shake, and he said this and that.

Amos bit his nails and shook his head as a man impressed by another's reasoning.

'Sense I see now o-rait, father bach,' he allowed. 'If man bank claps to taxer?'

Ianto gaped his lips questioningly.

'A small think is in my head,' said Amos. 'But no odds. No good is the think.'

'Say you the think.'

'Tie the money in a box and write you your name on the box and in bank Cardiff I put it for you.'

'Far is Cardiff.'

Amos placed a sovereign in his father's hand.

'Not rait,' he said, 'for money to brew your brains into a boil. The soveren will pay the old train. And, father bach, take you also this piece of six pennies for to eat in Cardiff.'

Ianto took the sovereign and the sixpence as earnest of his son's earnestness; and he went to a secret place, and came back with three hundred pounds, which was half his fortune, and in entrusting it in Amos's keeping, he said to him in the thin language:

'Honesty is the best policy.'

CHAPTER XXI

AMOS lodged his father's money with his money in a bank, and in sovereigns the amount was four hundred and fifty; and so that peace should fall upon his father he wrote to him that the bank man was not of the Welsh but of the English people. The business of banking he discharged on Saturday, and many times that day and the next day he returned to the bank fearful that the spiked iron bars had been torn from the windows and his money stolen by robbers.... A temptation also to bank man are so many soverens all together....

He was inside Sam's door before the appointed hour. Roberts, damning and hymning, was making notes of lines which were running low in the sections of his department. His coat was off and his shirt sleeves were rolled up, and Amos could not without thinking tell his back from his front, he being the same both sides. Coatless young men were decorating yellow brass rods which beamed over their heads and young ladies were bedecking the many-armed brass standards which were on counter and floor; and under Amos's eye the rods became like garlands at a rich man's wedding and the standards like flowers at a rich man's funeral. At nine o'clock the shopwalkers appeared, and they all wore frock coats and wavy moustaches, and not one was under six feet in height. They splayed their feet in comely order to their several departments, gravely murmuring: 'Lavatory,' whereupon the ladies, their scissors swinging from their waists, and the young men, their coats hanging from their arms, stepped to the basement to tidy themselves.

'Well, mister?'

Jordan was speaking.

'I am the fresh assistant,' said Amos.

'Where's your sir, mister?'

He intoned his words in the manner of Pembroke folk, and his thin voice was a poor copy of Sam's.

'I cannot know,' answered Amos.

'Left her at home, hey, mister?'

'Please –'

Jordan thumped his fist upon his palm, and Amos remembered the sound of clotting butter thumping against the sides of a churn.

'Don't back answer, mister, or you shall have a fine. Now you are fair warned. You shall sir here, mister, and sir you will have.

'Sir,' Amos said timidly.

'What's your name?'

'Amos Morgan.'

'There's no Morgan here so you keep it.'

Jordan knocked his knees against each other on four flights of stairs and on the fifth floor he took Amos into a room which had a low slanting roof and on the wall of which were a mirror and a framed card headed 'Fines'. There was little space in it, because of the washstand, with a jug and basin and a towel, and a double bed with a clothes trunk at its side.

'You lay in this bed,' said Jordan. 'Where's your box, mister?'

'By there just in the station.'

'Get English teached you, mister. You're in Cardiff now.'

'Yes, sir.'

'My man shall fetch your box. That'll cost you sixpence, deducted from screw.'

Jordan sat on the bed and drew up his socks and turned down his trousers which were folded high above his boots.

'Squadding seven to seven-forty-five, breakfast seven-forty-five to eight, counter eight sharp. Best be previous than not; late arrives are fined. Watch your swaps; if you let go three customers a day without selling them you shall be sacked.

113

And if you pinch, mister, I'll have you to jail as long as I live.'

Amos was put in the flannelettes, which counter of the Manchester Department was opposite Sam's staring throne; and when his first evening was come his spirit was down with the thought that nothing could hew him into London shape; and he had no mind for his supper of bread and cheese and dripping and coffee, but went to his room to study Fines. He read that no one shall enter his bedroom in business hours, take a swap line without signing a shopwalker, go to the lavatory without signing a shopwalker, cheek a customer or buyer or shopwalker, lose a leaf from a check book, sleep out without a permit from Mr Samson, enter the premises after eleven o'clock at night. The breaking of these rules and over seventy others was punished by fines of from threepence to five shillings and were taken away from spiffs, it being unlawful to take them from salaries. Amos vowed to keep these laws. He also read that makers of bills that were short in their adding were fined and had to pay the money by which they were short, that buyers and shopwalkers were empowered to fine for any misdemeanour not mentioned on the card, and that three shillings a month were taken from every salary for the services of a doctor, a library, and a boot cleaner.

Amos was in bed, imprinting the laws on the tablets of his memory, when his bedfellow came into the room.

'Good-nait, sir,' said Amos. 'How we are?'

'How are we – not!' said the other drunkenly.

Burns leaned his arms on the bedrail; his goitred neck hung like a plum-duff and his nostrils were clogged with snuff.

'Pig said there's a lodger,' he said. 'Lodger! We're all lodgers come down from Heaven for a holiday in Hell. You're the – there was Thomson, Westaway, Oakshift, Byron, Scott – you're the sixth in five months. They were all in the flannelettes and got sacked. What you expect if you're always under Sam's ponk?'

Burns took off his outer garments, put out the light, and fell into bed in his drawers and undervest.

'Bet your name is Jones or Evans,' he said.

114

'No, sir. Amos Morgan.'

'You may be luckier. The other chaps were all Joneses. I'm Jones. But they call me Burns because I drink a glass of beer. If it wasn't for the Joneses and Evanses and Williamses and Thomases and Davieses the rag trade would close up in Cardiff for no shop assistants.'

'Dear me!' said Amos.

'Bloody fine lot we are! The English spit on us here and we take it. We Welsh are ideal shop assistants because we are meek and mild hypocrites and born liars. As real top-notch drapers we don't count. Where's our Billy Whiteley and Peter Robinson and Tommy Wallis? There's not a Welsh draper anywhere who can see further than his one small cash desk.'

'There is Sam now, sir.'

'He's different. His father was a Scot land surveyor who left a bundle of sin with a Carmarthen farm girl. We're throwouts – remnants. Lookme! Experience in London, Manchester, Bristol, Liverpool, Glasgow. Yes, Glasgow, where whisky comes from. In Glasgow I swallowed enough neck oil to drown old Sam and his shop and Pig. What's the rag trade done for me? Lookme! Sixty-three and in Sam's Carpet Department. But by God, there's no flies on me.'

His tongue stilled, his throat gurgled, and he slept.

Amos mumbled the rules as one rehearsing a prayer and through the chinks in his sleep they sprang up in fantastic shapes.

CHAPTER XXII

It was Bethlehem's arms that received brother Amos as a trust from Capel Horton Road in Barry Docks and the Reverend O.B. Edwards, D.D., pronounced benediction upon him. O B E was a mighty preacher and a strong pulpit warrior against the evils of the streets, and Sam and many of the Welsh who kept shops sat at his feet.

Burns scoffed. He said that O B E's eloquential sweat slimed his hairy pink cheeks into the likeness of a newly littered pig's stomach. Amos protested: 'O B E can't assist his face.' Burns answered: 'He'd have another face if he drank less oil and more vinegar. It's vinegar these capel chaps want – these chaps who hum with sanctity on Sundays and don't care a dam where their money comes from in the week. Look at Tim Rowland. Amening in Bethlehem on Sundays and collecting Crouch Square rents on Mondays.' Amos again protested: 'But O B E is in the pulpit, not you.' Burns said: 'Don't I know the preachers? Lookme! Wasn't I a year in college in England learning to be one? Wasn't I turned out on account of the insurance refusing to take my life?'

... Well-well! A preacher at the beginning and an atheist at the ending. Burns ridiculed religion. He was cheeky about the three Miss Trevors who did the Tuesday Bible Class in Sam's dining-room. Too bad that. The Miss Trevors were rich and lived in a very grand mansion in St Fagan's....

One night Amos was pondering over O B E's words: 'Happy is he who is called to God while his harness is still bright with his labour.'

'Fat oil,' observed Burns. 'Dead shop assistants are rarer

116

than coracles that are no good. The fishermen burn the coracles, but we haven't the pluck to burn ourselves.'

'Dash!' Amos cried gladly. 'Living for ever!'

'When a shop assistant dies he's been out of berth so long
that he's forgotten he ever was in one. You see the names of
bosses on headstones, but never an assistant.'

'But smart men can always find jobbins.'

'You can't be smart if your feet have gone. And with the
feet the brains go. That's why poor assistants can't think of
short cuts to the Holy Land.'

Amos was depressed and tried to make joyful conversation.

'What kind of counter-jumpers at London?'

'They don't jump counters in London. They daren't show
the holes in their trousers under their coat-tails.'

... With all considered, Burns was the smartest assistant in
Sam's. He never measured floors and stairs with a ruler. He
measured with his eyes and his estimates were always correct.
He cheeked his buyer and shopwalker and gave back answers
even to Sam and he was never fined. Sam said to him: 'Give
your nose a blow, mister.' Burns replied: 'I got no time to.'
Sam replied: 'Then do it in my time, mister.' Burns replied:
'I prefer it snuffy.' Does London want cringers? Jim Page,
who was in the handkerchiefs' stall, had been at London. He
bent and hit his nose on the counter every time Sam passed
and his nose was quite flat....

Now in the hour that Amos was sifting his thoughts, Sam
told Page that if he did not stop his monkey tricks he would
have to pack his box. Page then signed to go to the water
closet, and he stuffed the pan with paper and pulled the chain
until it was full of water and he put his head in the water and
was drowned. Sam's rage was hot and he commanded the
shopwalkers to publish to his people that self-killing must be
done after the hours of business and away from his establishment.

... Does London want sneak-snakes? They had no department for Pembroke Pig. As squadding boss of the assistants
who swept and dusted the floors and counters, he drew an old

line under Arriveds as the clock began to strike to have a longer fine list. He was fond of going into clothes-boxes to search for stolen articles...

Yet the days sped too quickly for Amos. Once Sam's wife Mrs Samson came to his counter, and he feigned that he did not know who she was, and having served her very politely he asked: 'Will we send the parcel, madam? Much obliged. Name and address, kindly please, madam?' Sam praised his civility. 'Morgan will go far, mister,' he said to Dam Roberts, 'specially as he didn't know who the customer was,' and when Amos was told this he was as exalted as an agnostic who has caught a glimpse of God.

Dash, Sam was great! Sam to a buyer: 'I don't pay you three-fifty a year, mister, to lose me my money. Get at the back of your bad stock or you'll get my boot in your back.' Hence there was not much bad stock. How then the bargain sales 'stocks must be cleared?' Ho-ho! For two nights before the sales everybody stopped in to prepare the bargains. Manchester men made remnants: blouse lengths of prints and voiles, shirt lengths of flannels and flannelettes, apron lengths of cotton checks, ladies' knickers' lengths of white calico and nainsook; brown calicoes and sheetings and tickings were folded in lengths of twelve yards, and table napkins, diaper towels, turkey towels, bolster cases, pillow cases, and so on, were bundled in dozens. Reduced tags were pinned on the lengths and the bundles, and on the short lengths there were halfpenny spiffs and penny spiffs on the dozen lengths and bundles....

Although he was not entitled to serve through the Manchester unless a customer had made her first purchase at his section, Amos did so. He would bend over his counter, waylaying people and asking: 'Will I direct you, madam?' The half-a-yard matchers he sent to the right places, but to the good lines he offered a chair and brought to them that which they required. He nabbed pretty Mrs Jacob, who kept a short-time house in Crouch Square and who at every summer sale bought dozens of yards of sheeting and ticking and bundles of bolster and pillow cases; he nabbed county ladies who came for remnants of apron checks and prints and voiles and nainsook and flannels for Christmas presents; he nabbed charity manageresses who bought brown calico and remnants of flannelettes for shirts and knickers and nightgowns. Of him assistants said: 'If the Virgin Mary came for swaddling clothes he'd make a spiff on her!'...It was o-rait to gabble like that. Is not the preacher esteemed by his collections and the draper by his takings?

Amos was learning. He acted in a mirror in common with the best preachers, practising ingratiating smiles and gestures and saying: 'Good-morning, madam,' 'Take a chair, madam.' 'What's your greatest pleasure, madam?' 'What can I have for you, madam?' 'Here's a special bargain remnant, madam.'

Every day he was progressing. He was familiar with the ways of woman: knowing her boast of intuitive vision, he affected honesty and candour before her; knowing the scorn which she loves to cast upon those who serve her, he showed meekness unto her. He flattered and lied and wheedled and he knew when to overpraise and underpraise; he made spiffs to the sum of five shillings a week. He was not as foolish as Emlyn of the silks, who had to pack his box at a moment's notice. Emlyn thinking a lady to be of the English said to her in Welsh: 'Tell me now how is your belly bach?' The lady shouted in horror and told Sam that the young man had been obscene to her. The Welsh in Cardiff take pains to hide their origin.

So confident was he in his excellences that he back-answered a woman who came to match a remnant she had bought at a bargain sale.

'Here are we, madam,' he said, 'fourpence-three-farthings a yard.'

'But,' she protested, 'I paid a shilling and eleven-pence for the remnant of four and a half yards.'

'Do you say so?'

'Why, yes. And you told me it was under cost price.'

'The quality of remnant is best, madam. O quite rait, the quality is best.'

'But the patterns are the same. Your bargain sales are not honest.'

119

Amos said:

'I apologize close to your face, madam. You are a liar.'

'Funny,' said the woman.

'Don't talk,' said Amos. 'May the Big Draper up in the sky keep me straight in lies. It isn't funny to be a liar.'

'Funny,' said the woman, 'that you can never trust a Welshman.'

'You're not a honest lady.'

The woman misunderstood Amos's meaning and complained to Sam, telling him of the affair from first to last; and Sam answered:

'A young man who can't lose his temper, madam, isn't worth twopennorth of cold gin. Good da, madam.'

After that all lines bearing a pattern had to be cut up entirely into remnants: Sam being keen for the good name of his business.

Amos was proud of being one of Sam's men. He did not go to the open air meetings in The Hayes where assistants stood on boxes and reviled their employers, he did not cavil that he could not stand upright in his bedroom, that he had to clean his boots, that there were only about fifty books in the library box which Pig kept locked, that the doctor dispensed the same prescription for every ill, that the week-day dinner hour was only fifteen minutes and the dinner always mutton and potatoes, and that every year on two half holidays he marched with Pig's 'compulsory volunteers' to gather in Sam's hay.

He was obedient. He joyfully obeyed every command be the doing of it ever so irksome. Tredegar, in the ladies' hosiery, used to be cloakroom attendant on the occasions of balls and dances at the Cawdor Hotel. But his stubbornness in refusing to squad on the mornings after was a vexation unto Pig, who also had to provide 'compulsory volunteers' for the hotel; and Pig moreover suspected that he held the money tips which people gave him instead of taking them to the counting house. Amos accepted that office and that he should not be late at squadding he did not go to bed on those nights he was employed.

In the winter months his spiffs and tips amounted to over seven shillings a week.

Albeit his obedience and meekness Pig disfavoured him, badgering him at squadding and imitating his accent before customers, but Amos would not lose his temper or answer back, and thus thereby transgress some written or unwritten law and be fined.

He was one of the two hundred or so young men and women who had been drawn into Sam's from the shires of Carmarthen and Cardigan and Pembroke; they were the children of small holders who had skimped and borrowed to call a few acres of land their own, and despite their sufferings and cheatings they could not pay the interest on their borrowings, for there was no profit in their labour; and they who had demanded that God's land should be for the toiler and not for squire or rector found their holds passing to lawyers and shopkeepers and politicians, these being the lenders whose hearts were stiffer than those of squires and rectors. They vowed that their children should not tread the barren hills and the sterile valleys, and that they should prosecute a calling at which their shirts were drenched by neither rain nor sweat.

Most of the elders had worked at Sam's since their youth and every morning they were qualmish with the fear that the day would bring them a moment's notice. How could they offer their bodies in the market place, bodies from which the spirit of courage had flown? The only market they knew was Sam's. The only god they knew was Sam.

The women curtsied and madamed and waddled about the showrooms like puppets whose clocks are running down, and the men smirked and whiffed and strutted like aged husbands wheeling the carriages of their young wives' babies begotten of lovers, but their curtsies and smirks inflamed the haughty contempt of lady shoppers.

Burns carpets said:

'In all life's nooks there is no creature more cruel and callous than the lady who goes shopping.'

But if Amos humbled himself his imagination was in a far

place, and in that place there was a store which was bigger than Sam's and a man who was more despotic than Sam, and the store was his and he was the man.

On some evenings he mingled with his fellows at Sam's doors; a gathering of pale weeds, said Burns, like a compound of consumptives. The store was on the decent side of the street called St Anne, the side which was graced by a chapel and a church; the other side was known as the harlots' parade, for its dawdling women in gay clothes, many of them servant women who had been abandoned and shop women who had packed their boxes at a moment's notice. On Bank Holidays men came from the coalfields to St Anne Street, and they drank, cursed, swore, sang hymns and fought one against the other. On such nights the street women and their men often had to file, two behind two, at the doors of the short-time houses in Crouch Square and Myrtle Avenue.

The talk of Sam's blades who lounged and gazed began with spiffs and fines and shopwalkers, but it always turned to women, one telling that for two-and-nine at a riverside shop he had his hair cut, a boot clamped, and a cut from the joint; another that a crying baby on a bed was told by its mother: 'Hush, darling. It's tomorrow's milk'; another that he had paid a girl with two silvered halfpennies and a farthing; another that a certain woman's agility was proved by five broken bedsprings in her bedroom.

The women of St Anne Street set a high price upon their bodies and they trafficked in that street until their sores were such that no paint could hide; then some went among the black and brown and yellow men in Bute Road, and some to other parts of the town. There was no quarter in Cardiff which had not its harlots, its row of dismal short-time houses, and its herbalists and quacks for those ailments which men beget of love. Preachers and reformers called for the cleansing of the streets; none called for the cleansing of the houses.

There are moods when the flesh is stronger than wisdom. In such moods Amos, his body like a tall stalk and his cheeks like roses painted on a china vessel, went hunting in the cheaper

122

parts of the town. Perhaps it was his reverence for the chapels in St Anne Street that caused him to go to other places, but there is a chapel in nearly every street in Cardiff. Thither in such moods he journeyed, heedless that his conscience would reproach him presently with: 'There now, now! The two shillings is in another's pocket.'

Other than on his desire, there was little to spend: ninepence a week for laundry, a penny a month in Bethlehem, twopence a month at the public baths, twopence every six weeks for his hair cut; a suit of clothes every two years at two-ten, two shirts a year at two-eleven-three, two pairs of socks a year at six-three, two collars a year at four-three, one pair of boots a year at nine-and-six.

On Tuesday evenings he attended the Miss Trevors' Bible Class. The sisters, who were triplet and orphans, had dainty bodies and soft clear skins; their eyes gleamed with adoration of the Lord, and each comported herself as if she had crushed all worldly tumults; and one was so like the other in height and girth and feature that it was not easy to tell which was which. They were famed for their goodness and charity and their wealth and beauty ravished men's eyes, and many men desired them in marriage; but their love for one another was too deep for them to part from one another. Miss Gertrude said the opening prayer, Miss Winifred read a portion of the Bible and explained that which she had read, and Miss Blodwen sang three sacred songs. They brought into the class their chauffeur: God's message is for the high and the low; and it was the chauffeur who placed a hassock for Miss Gertrude's knees and found the pages in the Bible for Miss Winifred and the songs for Miss Blodwen.

When the chauffeur did not come any more, Amos performed his duties with enjoyment; the ladies stirred him and he had never seen any as grand.

'Now what is truth?' asked Miss Winifred one evening.

Miss Hunter corsets defined it as God fulfilling His promise, elderly Miss Stagg millinery as serving one's employer loyally, and Holland umbrellas as shaming the Devil.

'But,' said Amos, 'God is the truth and the truth is God.'

'God means,' said Gertrude, 'that we cannot be untrue to Him if we are true to ourselves. Each of us must carry her own cross, feeling we do so for His dear sake.'

'That's a little selfish, don't you think?' observed Miss Winifred, shaking her auburn hair. 'One's cross should be one's joy and therefore shared.'

'A cross,' said Miss Blodwen, 'is a great possession. Both of you are always anxious to help me bear mine.'

'If the cross is the result of a sin,' said Miss Winifred, 'the sin must be washed away before one can unburden one's self.'

'Yes,' said Miss Blodwen, 'when it is a sin.'

'If I do not know the nature of a sin,' said Miss Winifred, 'my sin is no sin.'

In that sort they talked until Miss Gertrude asked God's blessing upon the class.

Then she announced that she and her sisters would not attend the classes for perhaps a year.

'Pray for me, dear friends,' she said. 'Pray for each of us. Pray for our well being as you would for your own.'

As Amos was holding the door open to them, the sisters looked upon him as with one eye.

'Poor boy!' exclaimed Miss Gertrude. 'You should take a holiday.'

'I am quite o-rait, much obliged,' said Amos.

'Your poor mother will break her heart if she sees you,' said Miss Blodwen. 'Where is she living?'

'Miles and miles from here indeed,' replied Amos.

'My dears,' said Miss Winifred, 'we must mother him.'

The sisters moved a short distance away; upon returning, Miss Winifred spoke:

'You must come to St Fagan's every half holiday and Sunday. And you can spend your summer holiday with us too. We'll soon make you well and – and strong.'

Miss Gertrude added:

'And fat.'

With a tremulous laugh, Miss Blodwen said:

'Fit you mean, Gertrude dear.'

During Amos's first visit to St Fagan's Miss Gertrude asked him to send to them so many yards of fine nainsook and so many pounds of cotton wool.

'No, dear,' exclaimed Miss Winifred. 'You should get silk. It's more comfortable.'

'But nainsook is ever so much cheaper,' said Miss Gertrude. 'And nobody will know.'

'I too insist on silk,' declared Miss Blodwen. 'The best china silk, Mr Morgan, and charge it to my account.'

During the second visit the sisters were quilting the silk and cotton wool into bands, and the width of each band Amos judged to be that of his two hands stretched to the utmost. Miss Winifred held up one of the bands, saying:

'I knew silk would look nice.'

Miss Gertrude and Miss Blodwen agreed.

Now the sisters' bodies began to swell. Yet the girth of one never rose above that of the other; and when Amos was out with them he saw men nudging and winking, and women casting brazen glances at them. But the sisters passed on with a smile as if they had not noticed anything.

By the by they went away and when they were come back after three months, Amos found them at a cradle in which there was a baby.

'Do look at my baby!' the three cried.

They spoke as with one voice, and Amos could not tell which of the three said that the child was hers.

CHAPTER XXIII

MISS BLODWEN: 'Isn't he our bootifoo – our bootifoo baby.'

Miss Winifred: 'Our bap's toes are so scrumptious I could eat them! Yes, every little toe!'

Miss Gertrude: 'Baby's eyes are just like twinkling stars!'

In that sort the three Miss Trevors almost continually. The cradle was lined with silk and the coverings and the canopy were of silk. Wherever the sisters there also was the child. When he was asleep they tiptoed about and spoke in whispers, when he was fretful it was in her turn that each was privileged to take him in her arms and soothe him, and when he was taken abroad it was in her turn that each had the pleasure of carrying him. There was tattling on every side of them, for the child declared what was done.

The poor and the aged, prophesying the end of the mansion's bounties, said: 'If one of us had done this, there would be a song'; the better-to-do people, glorying in the fall of the elect, said: 'Those girls don't know what shame is.' The sisters were negligent of opinion and the countenance of each was that of the woman whose desire has been gratified to the uttermost.

Amos was no longer their ward. He ate and slept in the cottage of a childless widow, which cottage was on the Trevor estate, and if he went to the mansion he was kept apart from the child. Once upon meeting them he cringed toward the child, but Miss Blodwen drew away from him and hugged the child closer to her bosom. 'Our baby is so frightened of strangers,' she explained; and Miss Gertrude added: 'Too much admiration will make the little one vain.'

Miss Winifred said:

'Baps is going for a long, long walk. Isn't he, doodums?'

Amos's spleen was like that of a man who has a collection plate thrust under his nose after a refreshing sermon; it aroused horrid thoughts within him and he belittled the sisters on the cottage woman's hearth.

'I puts two and two together,' said the widow.

Amos interrupted:

'One and one is two and one a gentleman.'

Her hee-heeings made her cough and beat her breast.

'Of coorse! Of coorse!' she guggled. 'But what one of the three?'

He twisted his forelock and closed an eye.

'On my oath I shan't tell,' she swore. 'See? I lives in their house.'

Amos stretched his legs and clicked his tongue, thereby tormenting her curiosity and covering his ignorance.

'I puts two and two together,' the widow repeated.

'One on two together and a made-to-order bastard. Ho-ho!'

'The motor man goes. Poof he goes. Mrs Daniel Post Office says he goes to Australia. What for?'

'Bastard,' Amos replied.

'If he don't come back we will not know from what one. Tell me now.'

Amos asked another question:

'What one is he like? Find that and you find the mother.'

'The three got the same face. Perhaps their underneaths are not alike. Have you seen their underneaths? Perhaps the three are one mother. The three comes from the same pod the same time. A commercial tells Mrs Britannia Stores that three triplets have like aches. They have the flu together and Mrs Dentist says they have the same toothache. I remember Mrs Dentist says that motor man had his tooth out the same time. Yes, that makes motor man the father. But why three family ways for one baby?'

The aged and poor were annoyed that the sisters were not discomfited, yet they behaved pleasantly in their hearing and

127

all was deceit; the better-off who called at the mansion to ask subtle questions were told by a lying servant that the Miss Trevors were not at home. Being pressed hardly on all sides, Amos named each sister as the mother. He too was deceitful, inasmuch as he meant to report every tittle and so get him a name. But on his departure he saw neither Miss Winifred nor Miss Blodwen. Miss Gertrude he saw and she tried to demean him by saying that every little child is a gift of God the Father.

At Sam's he testified with pride how he had refused to succumb to the temptations of the three holy sisters, and how he had fled from their mansion and was pursued, and how he was given shelter at the house of a Baptist preacher. 'The bitches,' he said, 'are no better than the whores of St Anne Street.'

He thought of Sara Owen. She had been at Bulkley Lloyd's in Queen Street since the spring of the year, and in his vanity at being the guest of the Miss Trevors he had dealt with her loftily and disdainfully, passing her by with a 'Good-nait. How you are?' One evening after Bethlehem, Miss Owen was at the door when he came out and she gave him her hand and looked at him with the love of a mother greeting her wayward son.

'You are as high as my father was,' she said. 'I couldn't keep my eyes from you in capel for thinking of him. Well, how are you? Buyer, I am certain.'

'Yet at Bulkley?' asked Amos.

'I'm in the mantles now.'

'Bulkley is high-class trade.'

'Most select. You heard about Boss? Well –'

'They sleep out at Bulkley?'

'Yes. I'm in a room.'

'How much for the room, I ask you?'

'Five shillings per week. I got the harmonium. Come and hear it singing.'

'Pianos are the latest style,' was Amos's comment. 'And organs. My grand friends in St Fagan got two pianos and two organs.'

'Mr Morgan bach, you will have money.'

'Yes perhaps. No perhaps. What the spiffs like?'

'Commission on sales we have.'

'O-rait. How much?'

'It pays for the lodging.'

'How is the screw?'

'Thirty-five per annum is the salary.'

'And no more to pay out.'

'Well, yes, I am saving. How much have you in Post Office?'

'Goodness me,' replied Amos, 'not one penny.'

'You're making jokes.'

'There's father and the second mother.'

They were by St Anne's Church as the clock struck eight.

With a 'Dash!' and 'I hurry to supper, so long!' Amos left her.

He cleared his mind to think on fines. They said at the open-air meeting in The Hayes that Sam's walkers produced eleven hundred pounds a year in fines, not counting Pig's three hundred pounds. They said that the money for boot cleaning and library and doctor went to Sam, the doctor having resigned because his salary did not pay for his bottle corks. They said that Sam gave spiffs and took away spiffs. Amos's imagination spanned the road to London and London experience. There was waste at Sam's: gas should be turned out at ten o'clock, brown paper should be smoothed out and used again, and potatoes with meat are a relish and it is a proverb that he who eats a relish with relish dies in poverty. Brown soap makes a white lather and brown pennies make white silver, and on every penny there is a puzzle picture and for those who have eyes to see the picture is a shop.

Burns swayed at the bedrail.

'The way of life is death,' he said. 'I believe in enjoying myself. Death always makes somebody happy – usually the coffin-maker. Why shouldn't I enjoy myself in life like he will in my death?'

'I don't know how to advise,' said Amos.

'There's nothing in the Bible against enjoying yourself.'

'But there's a lot against wasting cash.'

'What's the use of keeping cash?'

'Cash can begin a shop.'

'And when you begin, the thing you didn't expect happens and there you are.'

Death is the gloomy companion of the aged man, but for youth life is everlasting. Death is a scavenger who removes refuse that the virile shall walk in his place. Amos contemplated his father's rare letters. The penmanship of each was different, as if all had been written by different men and not any by his father. He could not solve the problem, knowing that his father held his secrets as close as God holds His. They told of perplexities. Ianto had gone to gather life stones as far as New Quay, and the lighthouse was an old man in a white shirt spying on him and the houses were the shirts of the old man hanging on ropes drawn across the sky. The birds have their nests and the moles their tunnels, but he had nowhere to put his money. The crows watched his diggings from the trees and came down upon the places after he was gone, and they told the owls, who hooted his secrets in the night. There were scratchings on Box-Bible and Catti said that they were made by a rat. The rat must be killed. 'Send poison for to poison the rat at once.' Amos coveted his father's money, and he wrote to him as darkly as he had written to him, thus circumventing post-men's curiosity. Amos's words: 'A certain man bought three hundred soverens' worth of tatoes and stored them in a dry storehouse with thick walls and the profit in four years was about thirty soverens. O B E preaches a grand sermon on thirty-seven ten Luke.'

'Go, and do thou likewise': that was the text. Was his way in accordance to the word? Was he a mitcher like a truant schoolboy? Or a grappler whose store, howsoever abundant, never suffices? Over four years had passed with their summer and winter bargain sales and fresh spring goods and new autumn fashions; and in these years he had sown with a heavy hand, but his four-year harvest was only a pound and a few shillings over a hundred pounds. 'Awake, awake, put on strength'... Now Miss Owen is a oner for saving. She seldom buys clothes and never rides on trams. Maybe she has a tidy sum.... A thrifty woman squanders her body and the thriftless woman her soul.

He questioned Miss Owen straightly, but he got no answer; he questioned her covertly: she had nearly a hundred pounds. On half-holidays he went to her room, remaining there until they said, 'Let us go now, for it is supper time.' She played her harmonium and sang hymns, and in her motherly care for him she mended and laundered his garments; but she would not let him still upon her the anguish that stormed his breast. Once she asked him if he frequented bad houses. He thought out a device to overcome her and feigning shame he replied that he did; and as Miss Owen was not moved he thought out another device, answering saucily: 'That's how coins go.' Miss Owen, her eyes filled with horror, told him that money paid for ill-composed love is wicked. But he grinned brazenly as if he was doing nothing amiss. Then one evening she determined to woo him from his extravagance. She put out the light and went on her bed and she whispered to him: 'Take me.'

So Amos added three shillings a month to his savings.

But he was ill at ease. He must be a doer. Cardiff was for the backward and the timid. He was slim and straight and when in wax his moustache seemed thick and stylish. Miss Owen was a little bent; her stockings were of cotton and much darned and her petticoats of flannelette. He looked into the *Nonconformist World* in the Free Library, that weekly paper of sermons and prayers, of exhortations and expositions, of poems and good counsel, and of the charitable deeds of Liberal politicians and preachers, being famed for the 'Wanted Drapery Assistants' advertisements of shopkeepers in the London suburbs. He wrote three letters, each of which beginning with 'In reply to your advert' and ending with 'Anticipating a favourable reply to your most obedient servant.'

Thus he planned the heaven over which he was going to lord.

About eleven o'clock Pig came in to see about the gas.

'Sam's wife Mrs Samson,' said Pig, 'has passed into the light beyond.'

Burns, mimicking any preacher at any thanksgiving service, declaimed in Welsh:

'Dear people, not two brown pennies would I give to be in Mrs Sam's place now just.'

'You're worser than a socialistic,' cried Pig with exaggerated awe. 'I shall tell about you.'

Every day to the eve of the funeral Sam stood at the dispatch well, roaring commands in a dreadful and terrible voice, and on that morning he stamped through his departments, his face as grey as his coat and as forbidding as a rock which has withstood age and dynamite. He paused at the flannelettes and that which he saw made his face seem as if a snarl had been chiselled on it.

'Here, mister! Who pulled the blind down in the Manchester window?'

'Jordan, sir,' replied Amos joyfully.

Pig was on the floor and Sam crept to him and when he was behind him he seized his ears and drew back his head until the man hee-heed from pain.

'Pull that blind up, mister! What you think my windows are for? And if you don't look out, mister, you'll soon find yourself in your own dam coffin.'

CHAPTER XXIV

ONE day Sam was at his throne and below him on the counter of the well were stocktaking sheets. He called his buyers and shopwalkers before him one by one, and all of them he addressed as follows:

'Some stocks are short, mister. The staff are thieving. Catch them or I catch you and throw you in the street. I'll fill the jail with them.'

The buyers and shopwalkers rocked their heads and made hissing noises, it being a shame for their persons to have to do with thieves.

Sam also said:

'I've been up all night, mister – understand, all night, mister – with these stock sheets. And this is the way I'm treated!'

The good servant is more vigilant of his master's property than his own. So were Sam's headmen. With nods and 'of courses' and 'tisint honest' and 'thief scot to be found' they assured Sam that they would trap the offenders and bring them before him. They weaved snares of temptation: throwing shop-soiled gloves and handkerchiefs and bits of ribbon on the floor as worthless and surprising assistants with 'Turn out your pockets.' The snares failing, they set men and women to pry on one another and none knew who was his friend and who his enemy. But howsoever ready all were to betray the guilty, their diligence came to naught. After a week, Sam having said no more about the business, the buyers and walkers put the matter aside and said that only by means of a miracle one could pilfer under their watchful eyes. Moreover Sam's nature had been tamed. The god who hurled his words as if

they were stone pellets and whose judgements were without
pity was become a son of man with the manner of a nagging
scold.

Albeit Pig did not slack. He remained watchful to the end
that he might win renown above all others. He fingered and
turned the coats of men while they were squadding or dressing
the rods; he did not find even a threaded needle or a button.
His mischievous tricks were a laughing-stock. Four men, of
whom one was Burns, conspired against him and resolved to
make him small. One of them told him secretly that Burns
stole the tin-tacks which were for nailing down carpets; in a
similar manner the second and the third. Wherefore Burns
appeared before Sam and with a show of contriteness he confessed to his thefts. Sam cried as from pain and made his losses
out to be thousands of pounds a year; and he demanded the
value of the tin-tacks and their return.

Burns answered: 'As I lay carpets I carry a mouthful of tacks
and I always swallow half them.'

At this time Amos was behind his counter and he laughed
and Pig heard him and fined him half-a-crown for laughing
during business hours. He also warned him:

'You best pull up your socks or you shall see.'

But sore though the fine made him, Amos was unafraid,
for that night he received a letter from J. Hampton-John the
Bon Marché in Kentish Town appointing him to a post at a
'salary of thirty-five pounds per an spiffs live in moment's
notice either side.'

Early on the next morning, even before he had unfolded
the ends of his trousers, Pig was at the well with Sam, and
Sam called Amos to him, saying:

'You're to be searched. You miserable thief to take my
goods.'

Pig then withdrew a sock from a pocket in Amos's coat.

'Look at me, mister,' said Sam. 'You pinched this.'

'No, I did not. Drop dead –'

'Where's the other? On your foot, hey?'

Amos rolled up his trousers and showed that which he was

wearing. He unbent himself and delivered his mind with firmness.

'I am not the pincher, Mr Samson, sir.'

'I shall go to his box, sir,' said Pig, 'for the other sock.'

'Very well, mister, go.'

At this Amos cried out:

'The thief is Pig and Pig is the thief. The other sock is on his leg.'

'My sock,' Pig protested, 'is the other of a pair of two.'

'She is fresh from stock,' said Amos.

'It looks new because it's been in the wash,' said Pig.

'Why is the price tag yet on her?' asked Amos quietly.

Having rebuked God for clothing a scoundrel with the face of a fool, Sam gave Pig a moment's notice.

Pig went and then Amos spoke to Sam:

'An affair that can't catch pinching shopwalkers is no good at all now indeed for experience. I leave of my own accord.'

CHAPTER XXV

'GOD watches u.'

The phrase was on a bit of cardboard and Drake 48 was interpreting it to Amos as he rewrote it letter by letter; and the tracing of the letters made him peevish: he was short-sighted and with forefinger and thumb he held aside the thin point of his long nose from the way of his pencil.

'See? "g" one penny. "g/-" one shilling. "£g" one pound. "g-" penny-farthing. "g=" penny-hapenny. "g≡" penny-three. "o" is two and "d" is three, and so on.'

He restored his nose to its place and blew open his nostrils and spelt:

'G-o-d-w-a-t-c-h-e-s-u.'

Amos thanked him with a much obliged.

'God watches you, maister. I hope He does. Now get on with it.'

Drake turned to the floor which he walked and Amos to learning by heart the letters which stood for pounds, shillings and pence, and by which goods were priced at the Bon Marché, and to the silks and velvets and velveteens which were on the shelves behind him.

A heavy man, whose face might have been free from veins, so brightly did it shine with the colour of the yolk of a new-laid egg, and whose thick blonde eyebrows and benign countenance was like that of some good shepherd, came out of an office which was hidden by a curtain. At about twelve paces from Amos he stopped and catching his thumbs in the armpits of his white waistcoat, he delivered himself softly and with mirthful exaggeration:

'Inteet to goodness me! There's a fine Taffy! Whateffer! Look you! Taffy wass a Welshman! Taffy wass a thief! What about the widoo fach fair you wass seen in the train?'

The assistants laughed and giggled over boxes of ribbons and gloves and laces and bundles of calicoes and cretonnes and muslins as servants do at the hearing of their masters' grotesque jests.

In that way Amos made the acquaintance of Drake, he being called 48 because everybody had to sign 48 to him for permission to go to the water closet; also in that way he was made acquainted with the characters in which articles were priced at the Bon Marché and with its owner John Hampton-John.

The crown of the hill which he had reached did not reveal the lively shops of his imaginings: shops of long avenues and wide staircases, frock-coated shopwalkers with the sombreness of schoolmasters, assistants with more art than honesty, fashionable ladies in motor cars. The Bon Marché was a higgledy-piggledy place. About two-thirds of its floor was a maze of counters and shelves containing a disorderly, confused stock of general drapery and beyond this was a showroom of women's outer and under garments. These sections were separated by a wooden partition, against which was Hampton's office. Other than the four street windows, each of which bore the notice 'H-J for Honest Value', the shop had neither skylight nor window, hence much of it was lit all day by electricity. Most of the assistants were clothed like farm servants on Sundays, and they carried themselves with the dull cautiousness of the peasant who stands on the borderline of town and country. The customers were the wives of artisans, and as these women are greatly dependent upon the mere will and pleasure of their husbands, they have little to spend, but they spend wisely, showing infinite care over purchases and alertness in detecting the good from the bad. For neighbours the Bon Marché had beer houses and pawnbrokers, and business which traded in fried fish and chips, cooked ham and beef and trotters, second-hand clothes, china and glass wares, and junk and rags and books; and at a short distance a Congregational chapel, a Roman Catholic Church, the Working-men's College, and a statue of Richard Cobden.

Hampton-John was prosperous. He had a place among the Apostolic Troop in the Big Seat of the Welsh Tabernacle which is in Holborn and of the ten his precepts of sacred truths were the most ready, the most profound, and the most cheerful. On the monthly occasions that Tabernacle added new members to her limbs he was handy with advice to the youth and age who that night were made partakers of the bread and wine of Tabernacle. These are a few of his sayings: 'Never forget you are as good as the other man.' 'Jack is as good as his master.' 'No good young man and young lady have ever been sacked from the Bon Marchey.' 'Laugh at obstacles and they'll go off.' 'If at first you don't succeed, try, try again.' 'The Devil never wins in the long way.' 'Put a pinch of salt on the Devil's tail and he'll take the nearest hole into Hell.' 'Honesty is its own reward.' 'Work never kills.' 'Give to the poor and lend to the Lord.' 'Luck in business is flapdoodle.' 'There's no place in the Metropolis for skidaddlers.' 'Put your trust in Him and He'll watch over you day and night.' These sayings he delivered in English, for he was tolerant of the English people. 'There are good and bad everywhere. Now you wouldn't consider me Welsh, could you?' He was of the Cymrodorion, of the Sons of Wales, and of that group of educationalists who make puzzles for the National Eisteddfod, and at gatherings of these bodies he also spoke in English, but he never pretended that he was English.

The well-to-do Welshman ennobles himself with an English name and a hyphen, it being his way to take the name of an earthly mansion while he awaits his Heavenly Mansion. John Hampton-John was John Jones when thirty years before he opened his first shop. He had then one assistant, and she was Miss Sanders, a crisp haired, agile heeled Fen woman, the wiles of whose sharp mind and the use of whose virile body were at his call. At the time that she discovered her state she did not murmur against him, but went for a while to the house of a woman who lived in the neighbourhood, and thereafter to a secret place; and when she came back her hip was crippled and she was no longer desirable in any man's sight. Hampton moreover had fallen in love with a woman in his shop and although she guessed that the woman was with child, she confided her sorrow to none other than her pillow. Hampton showed his displeasure, snapping at her and seeing faults in all her work, but she answered him to his teeth that she would not depart from him. He was afraid and consented to his condition. Whereupon he made her his housekeeper and married the woman; and although Miss Sanders was in the shop only during his absences, she never ceased to employ herself in his interest. She kept his account books, caught thieves, paid the assistants their salaries, and overlooked his stock sheets; she fashioned remnants of awkward lengths into bows or collarettes or flowers, or into whatsoever ornament was the order of the day, and she increased the value of Christmas cards and toys by sprinkling over them jack frost which she made from broken glass. She transformed the worthless into money. She attended Mrs Hampton-John in her illness and held her to her bed during the strugglings and bellowing which ended in death; and she washed her body and enshrouded it. She did not give over the symbol of her trade: her scissors always hung at her lame side, striking the floor as she moved about the corridors or the kitchen or her little sitting-room. At night she sat at her window, her body bunched like a bluebottle tied in a spider's web, working for Hampton by mind or hand.

She dealt coldly by the forty or so assistants who crowded the bedrooms over the Bon Marché, and the food she distributed to them was poor and meagre. Those who complained of scanty bedclothes, she answered: 'You can lay closer together, can't you?' Those who grumbled at her food, she answered: 'Take it or leave it.' She hated the frailties and strength of youth with the malice of a decayed woman. But her concern was great for Hampton: she made his bed in the large room which was set apart for him, she prepared the food that was placed before him in the room adjoining, and none but Hampton was allowed into the bathroom.

Amos slept with three others above the furnishing shop which was across the road. The room contained two beds: the first was at the side of the door and the second against the wall, and to go into the second he had to step over the first. His bedfellow was Gould, who suffered from a malady, and as the water closet was in the yard below the room often stank in the mornings. But life in bed is short and ambitious youth is not fussy. You closed your eyes and lo it was day and you had little time to put on your clothes and run to the Bon Marché for a wash before squadding. Moreover Gould was generous with the cakes and stewed rabbits and such dainties which he used to receive from his Somerset home and which he stored under the bed.

Between squadding and breakfast there was a religious service. This was held in the basement stockroom and conducted by Drake 48. Drake was a sermon taster and his imitations of Dr Parker and Dr Clifford and Mark Guy Pearse made pretty prayers, but those that came from his head were faulty.

Amos wanted to hear of the steps by which Hampton had risen, and he weakened Miss Sanders by his appearance of false humility and praise; and he sat beside her in her room and heard of work-days measuring twelve and fifteen hours, of walks backwards and forwards to City warehouses, of breaking crates for fuel, of tearful pleadings for extended credit, and of a basement stockroom lit by paraffin oil.

'The Big One dispatches these orders to try us,' said Amos.

'Perhaps,' said Miss Sanders. 'The misfortune was fortunate. He else might have broke. And you can't tell.'

'Tell what?' asked Amos.

'I mean God thought Jack – Mr Hampton-John – couldn' be done without.'

'Only quite the very best can't be done without,' said Amos.

She told him how the first little shop was burnt by fire and how by the help of the One mighty to save Hampton conquered his mishap, the Bon Marché now standing not only on the ruins of the first shop, but also on the ground of three other houses.

There were constant comings and goings among Hampton's assistants. The staff changed almost as often as the seasons. When a man had saved enough to keep him in the Royal Hotel or in some other cheap lodging house for a week and to buy a frock-coat suit, a silk hat, and an umbrella, he would turn away from the Bon Marché and go to crib the West End; and likewise a woman. The advertisement was every week in the *Nonconformist World*. After Miss Sanders and Drake, Miss Temple had been in Hampton's service longer than anyone else, her term being three years. This was the huge buttocked woman from whose ears small bells dangled at the ends of long chains. On occasions she was paid money for singing music-hall songs at smoking concerts. Then her name was Miss Temple Bells, but in Bon Marché her nickname was 'Indispensable', as on some afternoons she helped Hampton in the office to select new lines of underwear from samples which had been sent on approval. But Amos disregarded the ding-dong chatterings about Miss Temple, as he disregarded Hampton's mockery of his Welsh accent and his jibes when he did not know the way to switch off the electric light. As he had ordered his life in the confidence of success, so he lived it.

On half holidays he did not seek the entertainment of the music hall or the theatre or the cinema. He walked in the streets, measuring the frontages of such shops as bore Welsh names, judging the quality of their trade by the things in the windows, and fancying stories about the small beginnings of their owners. When he was abroad he had paper folded over his cuffs and he wore an indiarubber dickey below his collar to keep his shirt front from soiling. He did not go and eat in the ham and beef shop, the proprietor of which boasted of his trade with Hampton's people. He held to his money. A man with no money is a man with nothing. He fought against his need, but when his need overwhelmed him he found some draggled wretch in Primrose Hill and took her to Mrs Richardson's house in Primrose Crescent; and then he chided himself hotly as if he had sinned against his nature.... Now if Miss Owen had a berth in London. He would be saving a bit more. There would be nothing to pay.... He still thought of her as Miss Owen. Howsoever intimate a Welshman is with a woman before wedlock he addresses her familiarly only after wedlock.

He worshipped in the Tabernacle on Sundays, gazing from the gallery on those who sat in the first pews and in the Big Seat, and counting them as witnesses of God's promise to endow with riches those who keep the Sabbath.

One morning as he was setting out, Miss Bartlett overtook him.

'Where are you going?' she asked him.

He told her.

'I'm going to Hooke-Hunter,' she said. 'Why don't you come? He's fine.'

He was led, as many of the Welsh were led on Sunday mornings, to hear the famous Wesleyan preacher whose gospel that money is the reward of godliness and that there is no Hell, enlightened by countryside sayings and parables, was satisfying; many there were who loved Hooke-Hunter's God.

'I always go when he's preaching,' said Gwen. 'Drake says it helps to learn English too.'

Over his dinner of cold pork and boiled potatoes, that being every Sunday's dinner, he resolved to improve his English and he told 48 where he had been and with whom.

'She's a very nice young lady,' said 48. 'She didn't ought to be here. She ought to be somewhere stylish.'

'O well,' said Amos.

'She ought to be the Indispensable,' remarked one of the men.

'The Temple bells are ringing a long time,' another remarked.

Drake held up his knife and fork.

'Say that again,' he cried, 'and I'll fine you. Why, I've known Gwen Bartlett since she was a baby. She's Cornish like I.'

Again Amos Morgan was with Gwen Bartlett at Hooke-Hunter's. He was turning over the leaves of their hymn-book, when she seized his fingers and whispered:

142

'What lovely moons you got!'

The trembling of her lips as her shrill voice rose in praise, the heaving of a lace ornament on her small bosom during the pauses between the verses, and the pressure of her body against his scraggy thigh bone thrilled his blood. On their way to the Bon Marché she paused at shop windows, exclaiming how she would like to have this and that and the other thing. Amos was learning that in love the eye must be satisfied as well as the palate.

One day Mrs Richardson, a fat woman with small hands and eyes like eyelet holes, came into the shop, and Amos was afraid that she was come to report his midemeanours. She sat at his counter and Hampton seeing her came up to her.

'I've a fine line of madras curtains,' he said. 'Madrases all the rage now. Fetch some, Morgan.'

When Amos brought them, Mrs Richardson was saying:

'I don't see why not. I'll have a chin-wag with her.'

She examined the materials, which Amos held up as if they were curtains; and she asked:

'This the best you got, young man?'

'Absolutely,' Hampton replied. 'It would cost you double up West.'

'Then I suppose it must do. I'll have it on all my windows. Put it down to me.'

'Drake will measure how much you want. Now the sewing? I'll send Miss Temple. She's a very clever young lady with her needle.'

'How long can she stop? It can't be done in a day. You understand that. If it was it wouldn't be successful.'

'Keep her as long as you like,' said Hampton. 'I got to go off for a few days.'

Miss Temple came back from Primrose Crescent in four days, and the insolence was gone from her buttocks and the peal from her bells; after she had been at her business three days, Miss Sanders charged her with stealing some underwear garments.

Miss Temple lowered her face which was as white as the

143

false pearls over her neck.

'He gave them me,' she said timidly.

'Gave them!' Miss Sanders cried. 'As if any gentleman would! You're discharged without salary.'

'He gave them me,' she repeated.

Then as if she were born again, her face grew scarlet and she turned her head and pealed her bells.

'The old fool,' she shouted. 'He told me to put them on for him to see what it was like to sleep with the quality.'

'Your sort,' Miss Sanders retorted, 'always end on Primrose Hill.'

'I'm lucky I don't end in Primrose Crescent.'

'Clear out or I'll call the police.'

Miss Temple sat on a chair and threw one leg over the other.

'I want a pair of knickers,' she said. 'The best silk knickers. Send them to Miss Marie Lloyd in the Bedford Music Hall. Who's that withered spud-face hobbling about? O you're Miss Sanders, are you? My God! These ear chains, dear? They're my lavatory chains. I pull them when I look at you.'

'What you waiting for?' cried Miss Sanders.

'For the police, dear, or my money for a month.'

Temple Bells was paid a month's salary which was forty shillings and she was paid for the days that she spent at Mrs Richardson's; and the money she counted over and over and over, in the while galling Miss Sanders with unanswerable taunts. Then she swayed her thighs to the door, saying:

'I'll send for my box. And don't you muck my things or you'll hear about it you – you bag of dirty tricks!'

Shortly before the closing hour Hampton returned and he seriously rebuked Miss Sanders on being told that Miss Temple had been dismissed.

'I won't have it,' he said. 'I can't turn my back before this sort of thing happens.'

'Not only did she steal,' said Miss Sanders, 'but she went on holidays without a permit.'

'Ah! No! I shan't stand for that.'

The next morning he was on the basement stairs unbeknown

144

and heard 48 doubting God's wisdom, saying that the serpent plays like a kitten and bites like a tiger and that fair words and shining faces are not Christianity, and asking God to help him to bear the dark secrets of his leaden heart.

'Who're you?' cried Hampton, jumping to the floor, his forehead as bright as a yellow-varnished pew in Tabernacle.

'If I was God –' 48 began to say as if he were possessed. Then he kneaded his nose as if he were freeing himself, and mumbled meekly: 'Do you speak of me, sir?'

'Secrets! What secrets? What secrets you tell? Your very own secrets, ai?'

Man reveals himself in the presence of his superior: 48 admitted that he had gabbled dreamily and in an ungrateful manner.

'Don't be frothy,' said Hampton. 'I shan't have my young folk taught atheism in a religious meeting. This will be the last of them. You'll open the premises fifteen minutes earlier than the rule. That'll teach you. You've put God out of the Bon Marchey. That's what you've done and accomplished. And on Saturday too our busiest day. You only consider yourself. Damit! Pardon the language, God. I only keep you because I'm sorry for you. I've been too good to you.'

He who is not in the good will of his master is not in the good will of his master's dependents; hence many of the assistants foretasted the joy of seeing a man being brought down and in their assurance they displayed their contempt for 48 and dallied in coming to his 'Forward, please.'

'Drake will be pushed and he should,' said Amos to himself.

He thought of his berth, for no man had been as long as he at Hampton's; his period was eighteen months. But he had no frock-coat with which to decorate that office, and he consulted 48 and 48 advised him to buy a second-hand coat from Moses in Kentish Town Road.

A few were apprehensive of the going of Drake.

'We may fare worser,' said one. 'He never fines us. His fines wouldn't pay for Hampton's white waistcoats. And if we want to go for 48 he lets us. Not like old Hampton's "What! Again miss?"'

But behold! At the end of that Saturday Hampton was speaking comfortably to 48, and 48 went aside the counters saying: 'Religious services as per usual. By special request.'

The days were added. On each Sunday Miss Bartlett wore something new and pretty: a chiffon scarf, white suède gloves that reached to her elbows, a tulle bow fashioned by Miss Sanders: and of each she said to Amos:

'Aren't they nice! Mr John gave them me.'

Her face glowed with the vanity of a virgin on the brink of sin.

'Really indeed!'

'I don't think the Bon Marchey at all bad now. I hated it at first.'

He found himself alone with her in the stockroom. She was gazing at some of the top shelves and her head was held back. He put his arms around her and tried to throw her on the floor, for the fire was burning madly within him, but she stayed his intent.

He thought of her in his bed; he made a picture of his wish, tearing off the clothes that covered it and leaving only those which were lacy and flimsy.

Hampton sent to Gwen and she became the Indispensable and as it is with women who sell themselves for gain and favour, so it was with her: she blazened her weaknesses, carrying herself with the aloofness of chastity, consorting with none of her fellows, haw-hawing in the elegant English fashion, and laundering and drying her pretty underclothing at Miss Sanders's fire.

'If H.J. sees me with you,' she said to Amos, 'he'd kill me!'

Hampton took her to the Zoological Gardens, to Madam Tussaud's, and to a Welsh concert; and even at the sinking of her cheeks he dealt kindly by her.

'He'll marry her,' said one.

'The wages of sin is the Bon Marchey,' said another.

'Bet you a bob she's knocked up,' said a third.

A report to her shame was spread and on 48 hearing it he stood still like a drunken man trying to gather himself together;

146

and he kneaded his nose and when he was come to, his nose pointed to the office, and he gave utterance to these words: 'God watches you.'

Miss Sanders began to appear in the shop and she was constantly deploring Hampton's illness.

'You're completely run down,' she said to him one day.

'But I'm all right,' he protested.

'No, you're not. You're out of sorts. Never mind about yourself. You've got to consider the Bon Marchey and us. If anything happened to you –'

So Hampton went on a holiday.

Miss Sanders was compassionate; and eager that Gwen should be spared the gossip of the assistants, she put her in the stockroom to make a count of the stock; and she put Amos with her, but he, perceiving the woman's design, said to Gwen: 'Get you round my back, Sataness'; and he forthwith returned to his counter. The evenings were foggy and Miss Sanders would not let Gwen go out and endanger her health and so they two sat together in the sitting-room. She named one man after another who might have undermined Gwen's virtue, but the answer was a No to each name. They played the game of confessions, each writing on a slip of paper her favourite preacher, or colour, or actor, or book, or man, and for the last Gwen wrote 'Mr J Hampton-John.' Miss Sanders looked awry on the writing and with jealous eyes. She killed a kitten and yet no sickness came over the girl. Thereafter she employed her in crunching broken glass into jack frost for the Christmas trade, and once at bedtime she gave her a cup of milk. In the morning Gwen was ill. 'You must expect this, you know,' Miss Sanders said to her. That night she also gave her milk and likewise the next night and the next. On the fifth morning Gwen could not rise from her bed, and Miss Sanders said: 'I quite understand, dear. You'll get the room to yourself.' For some time she walked to and fro before the door, her scissors tapping the floor like a blind man's stick; and when Gwen began to bellow very greatly she entered into the room and stifled the cries with a towel. She collected tribute money

147

to honour the dead from the assistants, collecting in all five pounds, and after the coroner had praised her acts and deeds and announced that Gwen had killed herself with ground glass, she sobbed and mumbled

'The Bon Marchey will bury the body.'

Hampton came home and went to bed and in the morning he looked as if the hours between had been so many years of sickness, his hands trembling as if they were caught in the eyes of a hangman.

'I'll have her sent home,' he announced. 'And pay the difference out of my own pocket.'

They took Gwen's body to Paddington Station on a foggy night. Drake 48 was on the platform. Amos with him; only God knows why.

'The night is as black,' said 48, 'as the night before God made light.'

He spoke in a voice that was faded and worn:

'Is death the end? It didn't ought to be after all her worries. You sent her here on appro and your messenger fetches her before she has time to see if she likes it. Really and truly it didn't ought to happen. Your mysteries are past me. If you are the God people say you are, stretch your hand to her, for she was a very good girl.'

He knelt and drew his nose over the floor.

'What you lost, 48?' asked Amos.

'I wonder if the words went up or has the fog beaten them back.'

CHAPTER XXVI

DRAKE and Amos walked into the black fog.

'I shall go cribbing,' said Amos,

'Two years' Bon Marchey ref did ought to get you a berth.'

'Kentish Town is not go ahead. West End is the place. Large stores there. Not little cornel shops.'

In a self same manner 48 had heard youth speak. There is no purpose in disputing youth whose bent is on conquest but whose mind can comprehend neither the present nor the future.

'Little cornel shops!' Amos repeated. 'Why people come to them I don't know.'

'They come to Bon Marchey for the advertisement in *Nonconformist World*, thinking it's religion before business. It's only before breakfast.'

A fit of coughing seized Amos and he put out a hand to feel for a wall against which he could lean.

'Rest on me,' said 48. 'We're in the middle of the road.'

Amos recovered and turned up the collar of his jacket.

'It can't do,' he said, 'mixing religion and business.'

They shuffled on warily like bears through a trap strewn thicket.

Drake as if asking himself said:

'Is Gwen clear of this fog yet?'

'People must behave in London, 48.'

'She didn't steal.' In the doomful fog 48's voice sounded like a man speaking in a deep pit. 'Stealing is the deadly sin. It takes a thief more than the years of his life to earn his salvation.'

'I shan't have a thief in my shop,' Amos vowed.

'Thieves are honester after prison and don't get much salaries.'

'O well then, that's talking.'

They were at a wall in which there was no opening. Turning from it, 48 remarked:

'There are no black fogs in Cornwall. Soon Gwen will be in a white mist. I'd marry her but she wouldn't.'

'Personal applications are best for cribbing, eh, 48?'

'Yes.'

'I'll tell Hampton I got toothache and go West End on spec.'

'He doesn't believe the Welsh.'

'For why not for?' Amos asked angrily. 'Don't we all want to get on?'

'The fog is heavying,' said 48. 'My words won't go up now.'

'Don't make me laugh,' said Amos.

They went on, losing their way and finding it, and knocking against each other, for neither could see the other's face.

'Catch hold of me,' said 48. 'We're at the Regent's Park Canal. Many thieves have found their last berths here.'

They reached the furnishing shop.

'It's four o'clock,' 48 announced. 'It's a vrosty morning.'

'Good for the Christmas trade,' said Amos, opening the door.

'My words are vrozen stiff by now. Good-night. I'll take a stroll. If I go to bed I may not wake.'

When 48 appeared at the religious service the nap on his silk hat was like the fur of a drowned calf, his frock coat was like a garment on a scarecrow, and his nose was like a smouldering poker.

Hampton made one of his surprise visits and laughed roaringly. Then he changed his mood and sought to ease his torture by delivering it upon another. He snorted:

'Of course you would muck up the first day of my Christmas bazaar! Of course you look like Father Christmas, don't you? More like a chimney sweep I shall say. I can light the pipe on your snout. When was your last bath, ai?'

The congregation sneered and sidled from the unclean thing; and 48 sniffed and grinned feebly as if he were expected to enjoy the banter.

'Had your last bath in a big house, ai? With attendants in grr-aand uniforms, ai?'

Amos would ask 48 for the whereabouts of the baths for which there was nothing to pay.

Snow fell airily. Hampton, in a muffler, an overcoat, a silk hat, and goloshes, inspected his windows with their cotton-wool flooring glistening with jack frost; he inspected his bazaar and ordered a more lavish use of jack frost.

At noon the poet-preacher of Tabernacle came into the shop, and there was none to greet him, 48 being resigned and down-cast and forgetful of his duties. Amos stepped down from his counter and bowed to him and offered him a chair, and he addressed him in Welsh:

'Fair day to you, religious preacher.'

The Rev. Sadrach Windsor-Daniel unbuttoned his coats and lifting the skirts thereof, he put his wide softness on the chair.

'Fetch your master,' he commanded in English.

He then disordered his white hair and his hair and beard became a halo around his red moon-like face.

He shook Hampton's hand solemnly.

'I'd have come earlier,' he observed, again in English, 'but the flu had me low.'

'You shouldn't be out,' said Hampton. 'Of all the Tabernac-lites we can afford to lose you not at all.'

'Flu deaths are few this year,' he remarked crabbedly. 'A man of sixty-five is not old enough to die.'

'Sure not! Sure not! It's real religion to come out on such a cold, raw day to comfort the lowly.'

'You should wear on a cheerful face.'

'An inquest takes the coyness from a man.'

'Now-now, Hampton-John. And you are always so witty.'

'I always do my best to my young ladies. I can't do more, can I?'

'She was English?'

'Yes.'

'You know what they are. Vanity, frivolity, and pleasure. Let them be merry today for tomorrow they die.'

'Merrying at a great price – the unforgivable price.'

'So-so.'

'Come and eat a dinner.'

Windsor rose and picked up a tinsel dressed doll which sparkled with jack frost.

'The frost,' he said, 'is like the hoary frost.'

'Made on the premises,' said Hampton.

In going Windsor paused to think, as preachers do when people are within their voice; and the following issued from his lips:

'The vain flower that bedecks her petals with frost will never smile again.'

'Good! Very good!' Hampton exclaimed. 'In your best form.'

'Wait. The Lord spreads the lily on her pedestal, and He adorns the thorn with the rose, and He weaves the fern to her rib. Ah, me! The Lord giveth and the Lord taketh away; blessed be the name of the Lord.'

Which visit made Amos examine himself and he found that he was good: thinking only of his business, taking not another's burden for his own, going upon no unprofitable errand, prosecuting no idle entertainment, above all believing in the God who never fails His children in Tabernacle.

He did not again profane the Sabbath: morning and evening saw him in Tabernacle; afternoons saw him at the Sunday School, sifting and stirring the Bible with the cream of his people, these being the dairymen whose trade denied them the morning flowers of Windsor-Daniel and who were assiduously conversant with the mingling of the seen and the unseen. Thereby he was strengthened: from Tabernacle comes peace to your house, custom to your shop, and money to your pocket; from Tabernacle comes immunity from the faults of your senses. He did not smoke or drink strong drink; he shunned the wasteful company who in the evenings went from Tabernacle to the Crown and Anchor; he did not tarry with the fly girls at the steps of Tabernacle.

His father rejoiced to him in a letter that he had tested each of the twelve hundred stones and that they all struck fire. He was going to put the stones in the coffin which he was making for himself and his dead body was to be put in their midst and it would be so that the men carrying the coffin would tumble and toss it because they hated him, thus striking the stones into a flame and the flame would kindle his life anew. He was keeping the matter a secret: of all people in Ceri he only was worthy of immortal life. Amos answered rejoicingly. His father wrote that he dribbled for the sight all at once of his sovereigns. He answered that the sovereigns were as secure from thieves as the gold in the sky. His father wrote that Catti had returned to parson's cottage and parson's church and that Deio Blind Eye was courting her in bed. He answered that their sin shall find them out. His father wrote that Catti had robbed him of all she had brought for it is the law that a woman's possessions become her husband's on marriage. He answered him to summon the policeman. His father wrote that he could not summon a policeman without sovereigns. He answered: 'Father bach you know you are a very bad liar what is the matter with your old talk your loving son Amos Morgan.'

Ianto wrote to him again and again and the writing was always different, threatening and wheedling for his money, but he did not answer him.

His mind was lively on the West End; and the days were like elastic, every day stretching and stretching and he resolved to go cribbing before the elastic was stretched to the autumn. Moreover Hampton was nagging him that he gasped in the presence of customers.... Well now. How can you help gasping when you are spent with running up and down the stockroom?... On three occasions he haggled with Moses over a frock-coat and on the fourth he bought it for a pound; and he put it on himself and swaggered.

'I got a toothache,' he said to Hampton.

Hampton seized each side of his coat, which fell below his knees, and folded it around him so that it was like two coats, in the while sneering:

'Inteet to goodness me! You wass a Welsh preacher who wass not in the pulpit! What wass the hymn now? Why wass you talk when there iss no talk to be? Look you, Amos Morgan.'

'I got a toothache. Very painy it is.'

Hampton jerked up his teeth, the plate thereof having dislodged itself.

'You want an hour off. O yes! You will have an hour off. Two hours. Two days. See? How will the Bon Marchey do without you? Three days off. A million days to crib in. See? Two million days. See, ai? You're sacked.'

Being greatly perplexed about the coat, Amos determined to consult 48 and 48 was sorry for him and went with him to Moses.

'Mr Moses,' said 48, 'you're an honest man.'

Moses turned on him a wondering ear.

But in 48's eyes there was the trust of a sheep dog's.

'What's the catch?' asked Moses.

'This coat will make two coats and fetch two pounds.'

'Then it is a bargain for a pound.'

'Mr Hampton-John sees it and says urgently if Mr Moses has the twin I'll buy it for Sundays.'

Moses bent his elbows, showing the palm of his hands.

'For another pound,' said 48, 'you can do the young man a frock-coat suit.'

The three men rummaged through a hillock of overcoats and frock coats, and it was not until many had been tried that one was found narrow enough and long enough for Amos's body; and while Moses was searching for a waistcoat and a pair of trousers Amos kept by the hillock with the coat over his arm as if he were afraid of losing it; and when the three garments had been found and paid for, Amos said:

'I'll carry them without packing and save you the paper.'

'You'll get on, my young friend,' said Moses.

'Much obliged,' said Amos.

CHAPTER XXVII

THE words of Hooke-Hunter: 'You will never find Miss Happiness by running after her, because she is always with you. God give you eyes to see her.'

Amos was wiser: the proper name of Miss Happiness is Miss Money. Perhaps he knew without reason that her hiding place is among the secret recesses beyond the horizon, that the quest of her has no end; and perhaps that is why, like his people, he was never entirely happy. The hymns of death, with which one prepares oneself for the House of God, were always in his mind, and the savour of them was as bitter as a wild apple; and he in whose thoughts death is ever present is much afraid of death. At the moment Amos was exalted unto heaven he was brought down to his grave.

> O carry me, my four friends dear!
> From house to grave I must be borne;
> So lay me deep down in the earth
> Until the Resurrection morn.

He was in Soho, wandering between decayed houses from whose tall doorways men and women had gone forth in quest of Miss Happiness. An umbrella, which had been lent to him by 48, hung from the breast pocket of the overcoat which he had stolen from Moses and in his hands were his cribbing clothes bundled up in paper and a silk hat in a box. He was melancholy: yesterday he was earning money and there was nothing to pay for food and lodging; tonight two pounds for Moses, eight-and-six for a silk hat, and a shilling would go to have his trunk brought to the Royal Hotel; maybe for many tomorrows, maybe for many weeks, there would be no money coming to him and much money going away from him.

He turned into Corsica Street, the narrow road which goes from Wardour Street into Dean Street, and in which was the Royal Hotel. The hotel was one of three houses which belonged to a German baker and it was between his bakery and Mother Griff's dairy shop. It had two entrances: one into a restaurant which was frequented by carmen and porters and their kind, the other opened on a staircase which led into the rooms above. The three houses were renowned in the sight of shop assistants: the hotel for cheap lodgings, the bakery for slabs of moist currant cake, the dairy for Mother Griff's four-penny sago and stewed fruit. The most favoured was the milkshop, which was owned by Evan Griffiths. Young men stood at the high board that ran against the wall the length of the shop, feasting on penny slabs of cake and sago and fruit and chattering about the affairs of the day. So used many shop assistants to appease their hunger each week-day night. Maggie waited upon them and they had named her Cowslip for the colour in her cheeks and the ripeness of her body. She was civil and slighted no one; she was mirthful and chaste, laughing at jokes and despising coarse words. Amos peered through the window. Griff, gaunt and haggard, was bending over a huge pan and about a dozen young men were at the board. Presently Maggie came from a back room with some dishes in her hand and she held them before Griff and while he was ladling stewed fruit into them, she lifted her face and Amos saw that she was Miss Griffiths Shop Butcher. He had heard tell that neither Griff nor his niece went to chapel and that Griff was a stormy heckler of the Christian Endeavour men in Hyde Park on Sundays.

'Hap,' he said to himself, 'she will sell cheaper if I don't tell.'

He moved away and entered the restaurant of the hotel. As he could not see anyone he called out.

'Shop!'

'We're closed since seven.'

He followed the voice and came behind a man who was on

his hands and knees scrubbing the floor; and the man's bald pate was black and blue and pink and red.

'What you want?'

'Lodgings, please.'

The man shouted:

'Forward, Florrie! Lodgings!'

He rose to his feet and he was Picton, and he gazed closely at Amos.

'Dam man!' he cried. 'You've grown down to nothing.'

'How shall I say Mrs Rees is?' asked Amos.

'That woman! She could kill any men and she's killed you. I know nought of the slit.'

'O like that it is. A commercial at Cardiff said she did a big trade in scents, keeping three young ladies assistants. Piling a fortune.'

Picton continued his work. Then he spoke testily:

'You are very Welshy to run a lady down behind their backs. Who hasn't got their faults? If I go for holidays I shan't be ashamed to look in Mrs Rees.'

The stairs had creaked and a woman stood by them, and she said:

'I hope to God you do and stop with her.'

Picton rubbed his discoloured pate.

'Is the carnation very sore, lovey?' Florrie crooned sneeringly.

Her hat was like an upturned nest, her fringe of golden hair was bright with dye, and her bosom trembled like whey in a straining net.

She drew half-a-crown from a waist pocket under her apron and gave it to Picton, remarking:

'Here's your allowance. That'll keep you till stop-tap.'

Then she took notice of Amos and exclaimed:

'Well I never!'

Amos followed Miss Larney to her room.

'Well I never! Fancy meeting you after all these years. What you doing?'

'Cribbing,' Amos replied. 'But I am pleased to serve you.'

157

She laughed merrily.

'No, my boy, all that's over when a woman's in the winter of her discontent.'

'You know I mean I'm pleased to see you,' said Amos. 'What about sale prices for lodgings?'

'A shilling a night I get. Of course food's extra.'

'Quite a big sum,' he said, adding craftily: 'A swellish place you have, madam.'

She was astonished; but the Welsh always astonished her. A Scot cribber would first see his room and having seen it say that the walls were smeared, that the ceiling was hung with cobwebs, that the window rattled, and that the house smelt of stale onions and vegetables and fish-oil, and then offer her sixpence a night.

She could not turn away money. It was a poor man's eating house and the prices were low, and she had to pay a wage to Miss Johnson and two women helpers and to keep Picton in clothes and food and beer, yet with her other employment she was able to gain a little profit. Picton was idle. He slept in the garret because the clock of St Anne's Church warned him on Sundays when it was time to arise and prepare himself for the Welsh Baptist Chapel which is in Castle Street, but on week days he did not get up until the mid-day meal. She went away with him because she was sensible that her body had overlived its grace and her smile its lure; and she thought that he had riches, but he did not have enough money to pay for their lodgings at the end of their nineteenth week together; she thought that he had been driven to the public houses by the wantonness of his wife, but her own chastity did not prevail to keep him away from them; she thought that when she paid fifty pounds for the Royal Hotel and all that was in it, he would be diligent in the business, but he wanted to make it a short-time house. All that he did was to scrub the floor and the tables at the end of the day, and that labour he performed with a grunt in his face.

'You ought to be an actor,' she remarked on a sudden. 'You have such speaking eyes.'

'How much for the lodgings?' asked Amos.

He told her how his mother being dead, his very aged father was in his keep.

'Well–well, he is the only father I got and I must do the duty.'

'All right,' she said, 'ninepence for you.'

The while they were thus employed she was squeezing her bulging feet into brocaded shoes, and wrapping her body in a chintz mantle which was ornamented with red and black and yellow dragons and moons and which fell in loose folds to her feet, covering her food-stained blouse and frock. She put paint and powder on her face and blackened her eyebrows, and she put bangles on her wrists and rings on her fingers.

Then she called Miss Johnson and told her to show Amos his room and to give him some bread and milk.

'Half a mo,' Amos cried, thinking that this was a trick to rob him. 'How much will that cost? You can't steal from me you know.'

But she was half-way down the stairs.

Miss Johnson's age was about fifty-five. Her speech was thick as if the words were still-born in her throat and she walked with her feet apart as do women who have trodden for many years on carpeted and wooden floors. In common with dependants she praised her benefactress in the hope that her words should be repeated to her benefactress.

'If it wasn't for madam, I'd have starved long ago.'

'Refs a o-rait?' Amos asked.

'Why, yes,' she answered. 'And from the smartest shops in the West End. And I always left on my own accord. Shop life is for the young and slippy. Customers think you must be young to know the latest fashions.'

Amos ate his bread and milk; he was considerate, not speaking that which was in his mind: 'For why did not the old woman then save money?'

She sat upright, as if she were afraid of bending her neck, her sagging cheeks were crimpled like seaweed in the sun.

Young men, one by one, each in a frock coat and silk hat and with an umbrella, passed through the room, and of each she asked: 'Well?' Sometimes the answer was a No and sometimes 'Tommy Wallis on Monday' or 'Billy Whiteley' or 'Peter Robinson.'

She took Amos to his bedroom.

'You'll get the bed for yourself tonight,' she said. 'But tomorrow you may have a lodger.' She lit the gas on the landing. 'We do that as Mr Rees is often late. If you don't sleep warm let me know. I'm in the next bedroom. And I'll give you some of mine. Good-night, Mr Jones,' she said forgetfully, as she went into her room.

Amos dallied in the street. The public house opposite was noisy. A 'Closed' card was on the baker's door, but the shop was lit. There was a cradle on the floor and the German and his wife, both dusted with flower, were continually coming up from the basement and framing their lips into a kiss over the cradle.... Dash, why did they not go on with their baking, and put the little old baby in bed?... At Mother Griff's door Maggie was with a man. In the public house someone was singing 'Rescue the perishing,' and as he was saying to himself 'Picton is now quite drunk,' he heard Maggie's companion saying: 'That's old Carnation. He'll get monkey brand tonight'

They saw Amos.

'Diawl!' the man exclaimed. 'Amos Morgan Manchester House.'

'How are you, Slim?'

'You know him, Cowslip? You remember Miss Griffiths, man. Shop Butcher?'

Amos bit his drying lips.

'Yes, indeed,' he said. 'But I'm pleased to meet you, Miss Griffiths.'

They took him into the shop and the girl called her uncle to see a boy bach from Carmarthen, and then detained him until she made ready for him a dish of sago and stewed fruit. Slim was grown stout and his red moustache was abundant, but baldness was eating into the hair on his temples. He discussed, with concern, the divers medicines which Griff was taking for his complaint. Cowslip sat beside Amos and spoke about Carmarthen: the people, the shopkeepers, the streets, the monuments, the river Towy, the cemetery.

'Stop you,' remarked Amos, 'where did you go to capel?'

'Pity your Manchester House boss died,' she said. 'He was a good man.'

Amos recalled Miss Owen trying to say something to him.

'How much money did he leave?' he asked.

'Stopping at the Royal?' Slim inquired.

'Well –'

'How's Miss Johnson there?' asked Griff. 'I don't see her about much. When I was in the trade she was with me in Marshall's. And a very smart young lady she was. But what a goer. She had some swells about her and no error.'

Amos walked with Slim, for Slim had to be in his bed at Hall's Oxford Street by eleven o'clock; and Slim prayed him not to reveal his whereabout to Miss Larney because he was going to marry Maggie.

'She has a bastard from a student,' said Amos.

'But she'll get the milk trade,' said Slim, 'when old Griff dies. And he won't see more than six-twelves of clean shirts. I'll buck things up very quick. I'm sick of the rag trade. Diawl! All day it's you bloody Welshman.'

They were walking so quickly that at the end of Wardour Street Amos was panting a little; and he returned. In bed he saw a shop which bore the words: 'Amos Kentish-Morgan,' and a linoleum floor the pattern on which spelt 'Amos Kentish-Morgan.' His sleep was disturbed by the banging of a door and the noise of irregular footsteps and by the singing of 'Rescue the perishing.' After a while there was stillness and then he heard Picton declaiming: 'I rescued you from the stage and worst. From a living death I rescued you. You seduced me from my gold mine of a shop and my religious wife. And look at you. What have you done for me?'

Amos turned and there was someone in his bed and the hair was that of a woman. He gathered as many of his garments as he could and sought another room.

On the landing Miss Larney was in her nightdress and Picton's head was gripped between her thighs and she was beating the pate thereof with the heel of a slipper, at each beat crying:

'You ugly baboon!'

CHAPTER XXVIII

'GOOD morning, brother.'

Peacock of Peacock's Knightsbridge lowered his guileful eyes and continued his writing. This was the Peacock who was known among the City merchants as Prophet Peacock for his likeness to the Bible prophets and for his saying as a young man from Nottingham: 'God Almighty made Knightsbridge a drapery shop'; and this was the room where the cribbers were catechised and the law-makers of the Baptist Union occasionally met to confer. Its shape was square and its six lofty windows were flung open. The yellow varnished desk at which he sat was raised about three feet from the ground so that the man behind it was as a ruler unto the Baptists who sat on yellow chairs at a square yellow table. There was one picture on the wall: a long, narrow photograph of Peacock, Mr Lloyd George, and the Rev. Dr Clifford standing in front of a motor car, each with a foot on the running-board.

Peacock read that which he had written, performing wondrously with his grey beard; he twirled it into an S, rolled it into a ball, and made of it a face veil.

'Good morning, brother,' he repeated. Then he blew his nose and sniffed at a bottle of salts.

'Go nearer the door, please. Now what can we do for you?'

'I call *re* the advertysement in the *Daily Telegraph*,' Amos replied.

'My dear good brother, we are suited.'

As if his throat were greased with syrup was the sound of his voice and the fatness of his manner as if he were bestowing a gift; and for that Amos gathered his courage to speak up.

'The advertysement is for every department. And I had all-through experience.'

'We're suited.'

Peacock unlocked a cupboard, this being the cupboard in which such medicines as brandy and whisky were kept in the event of a Baptist fainting in conference, and brought out a small Bible, which he gave to Amos.

'Prepare for the shadow,' he said. 'The shadow is always over the most stalwart of us. God bless you, brother. No vacancies today. Next, please.'

Amos passed out and another cribber passed in. There were yet twenty to thirty in the line and as he went by with the Bible in his hand he heard several remark: 'He's got the bird.' He reached a corridor over which hung a board and this was the writing on the board: 'Staff only read mark and inwardly digest'; and on the walls of the corridor frames bearing 'Be sure your sin will find you out. Numbers XXXII 23,' alternated with those bearing 'Don't expectorate that dirty habit brings DEATH to hundreds of THOUSANDS per year.'

The advertisement said 'Apply 10 sharp'; Amos was the first at Peacock's door and had waited thereat two hours and had gazed in silence on Peacock for fifteen minutes and the morning was far gone. At the mouth of the Goods Yard, which is in Cuthbert Street, he waited in the hope of consolation in the misery of others. The seasoners, men and women, the broad soles of whose feet had trodden many miles of West End shops, hurried away with their Bibles in shame and dispirit. They knew that it was their duty to seek work and that it was the duty of engagers to deny them work; and they knew that the only berths which were open to them were as sale hands and Christmas bazaar hands. The women were frumpishly dressed, it being well known that pertness was shameful in the sight of Peacock inasmuch as it weakened the strength of his male overseers; the men were worn and frayed, Pea-cock's sayings being also well known: 'The future of religion like the future of industry is in the keep of the young man.' The younger men – they too had had London experience – paused

164

and discussed Peacock, appraising him and disparaging him. He had built Peacock's. He had fought the London County Council and his ground landlord over the design of his premises, and he was the designer; he had issued a pamphlet saying that the Council and landlord were denying him fresh air – God's fresh air which belongs to no man and to all men. 'And he sleeps them six in a room and one chap caught fifty bugs in a night and pinned them on the wall and old Peacock sacked him without a ref for pinching the pins.' He claimed that man should be at liberty between business hours and gave his staff the choice of sleeping in or sleeping out. 'I should say so! And he allows half a dollar a week for lodgings. All right for nice girls and pretty boys.' He conducted his business on a gross profit of twenty-five per cent and insisted that his buyers kept that rule. 'And he pays buyers hundred and fifty and assistant fifty all round. No spiffs and no com.'

'He's a slim old swine.'

'He can smell the chaps he wants before you open the door. If he doesn't want you he calls you brother and gives you a bloody Bible.'

'He takes dam good care to drop the brother and Bible if he takes you on.'

'For what? Shall I tell you? He's afraid you'll read the Lord's Prayer.'

'He's not so bad if you know him.'

'Shut up for Christ's sake. Nobody are bad when you know them. The trouble is to get to know them.'

'He's a cheat – with all his palaver about religion.'

'Absobloominutely! He cheats the almanac of a day. He says February ought to have twenty-nine days and when it hasn't makes you work overtime an extra day.'

So the cribbers spoke. They separated and moved off in groups, the men looking like companies of disheartened undertakers in a land in which there is no death.

The cribbing line did not get smaller; as some fell out, others fell in: seasoners with the timorous jaws of ancient horses, and maids and youths panting for the race.

165

Precious mornings spent themselves and Amos was not chosen. Most of the engagers were trim Jews and Scots whose ages were under fifty, and who had the clear eyes of the man who buys stock for his breeding stable. They questioned rapidly and judged quickly, and seldom gave anyone a moment in which to spruce up his accomplishments. One regarded Amos and then said: 'Ours is a very quick trade and you couldn't stand it. Good day'; another used to him a phrase the meaning of which he did not know: 'We don't carry passengers in this show.'... Why did cribbers from Hampton's and Sam's Cardiff get the berths? He did not know. He could do anything: dress windows, shop-walk, keep stock. Why were there no Welsh engagers? Burns carpets had said that they were of no use except behind the counter.... Every morning he was early at his quest, heedless of the 'Hullo, cockey!' and 'Aren't you got up?' gibes of the errand girls who were matching for dressmakers. One day he saw a girl copying on paper a Paris model gown which was in the window of Merry's Regent Street. He entered the shop and a man stood before him with a silk hat on his head and he reported to him that which was being done, and the man went and snatched the drawing and he returned swinging the door in Amos's face. Amos was disconsolate: he had expected to open out a talk with him and for the man to say: 'You're smart. Start on Monday.'

In the fourth week he was left at the Hotel with about ten seasoners. The Tabernacle God had failed him and man had forsaken him. But the timidity of the seasoners in front of the engager was departed when night came, as with rallied spirits they gathered in the restaurant of the Hotel and reviewed work and life. Maybe the cause was the nearness of sleep and forgetfulness.

'Rotten bad luck today.'

'Today? Last berth I had was Whiteley's Christmas bazaar.'

'It's four months to the summer sales.'

'Perhaps death will intervene before then.'

'I wish to God the soles of boots were eternal souls.'

'What's wrong with brown paper?'

'I don't wear socks, so they don't get wet.'

'Old Fowler used to say cold feet made you a sooner.'

'I don't get you.'

'Nor do I neither.'

'Sooner after customers.'

'He died before I came to London.'

'You missed a hell of a man.'

'He's dead anyway. God rest his merry bones.'

'So you'll die. We'll all die if we live long enough.'

'Wonder if there's girls where Fowler has gone to. It's real hell for him if there isn't.'

'What happens after death?'

'Why don't you read Darwing?'

'You start in the same department, of course.'

'Hell!'

'Moderate your language, please.'

'Quite right. If you've got no religion you're not on the safe side.'

'Do dead men dream?'

'I hope to God they do.'

'The best dinners I've ever had in the whole course of my life was dreaming.'

'Dam bad luck –'

'I heard Dr Palmer preach a sermon on a chap – an atheist chap – that stripped his feather bed and ate the fleas.'

'Old Palmer ought to be an actor. He's great.'

'If he could tell me how to blow my nose by acting I'd be much obliged. Half my shirt is gone in handkerchiefs.'

'Bloody awful luck. Gate Folkestone advertised for a smart window dresser, apply 10 St Paul's Churchyard. I was as near as dammit to it when old Gate asked if I belonged to the Y.M.C.A. Of course I said I didn't. Then old Gate said his shop got no lavatories and the staff got to use the ones in the Y.M.C.A. premises.'

'Why don't you join up?'

'Nobody can go wrong if they believe in the Lord.'

'Briggs' young ladies sleep over the way and got to go through a speciality shop to bed.'

'Hell! Living in ought to be abolished.'

'Hear, hear.'

'Yes! And if we'd lived out we'd have married.'

'With our screws? Don't be a fool.'

'Yes, we should. We'd marry just to sleep with a woman for nothing. And we'd get kids.'

'And they'd get kids.'

'Naturally. For they shouldn't be rich enough to buy things in speciality shops.'

'The young ladies at Haywards' have a latchkey if they go in at twenty-five pounds a year.'

'Shop girls got no brains. Clothes and how to get them is all they think!'

'And some old man's key.'

'I was in Jackson's with that Miss Tumilty that went to prison. She got a key and shot a Jew chap in Hatton Garden dead. What a fine piece of goods she was. Never seen such thighs and bubs. Ought to be a pantomime boy.'

'Look at Miss Temple. Always got the bullet. I was in Briggs' with her.'

Amos said that he knew Miss Temple.

'Well, you don't know her any more. She's singing to theatre queues. Doing all right, I bet. Got brains that girl.'

'There's plenty of brains in the rags if it was found out.'

'Brains be blowed! Think we're in this bug-ridden, goddam hotel for our brains? I don't think. The only brains in this trade was H.G. Wells.'

'I know. Swears and Wells.'

'Brains! You don't want brains behind the counter. If you're a footballer you'll get a berth anywhere and special dinners of rump steaks.'

Thus.

But Amos's mind was burdened with the money he was spending: gone was the price of twenty-three breakfasts at fourpence each, and gone were twenty-three slabs of moist cake and twenty-three nights' lodgings. One cribber smoked a cheap, heavy navy plug tobacco because it made him vomit and vomiting turned his stomach against food.

'If the stomach becomes used to it,' Amos thought, 'she will need the pipe and the food. That will be expense indeed.'

At Westbourne Grove he met a Sam's man, who told him of Sam's death in a fire. The fire broke out on the top floor. Sam said that he would find the man who had done the mischief and sack him on the spot, and he called for a ladder, but the Fire Brigade had no ladder high enough. So Sam climbed the highest that there was and seized a window sill and got through the window.

'How much did he leave?' Amos asked.

'The new manager,' the other went on, 'sacked all the old hands. Even old Burns had to go.'

'Tell to me what he left,' said Amos.

'Well, I don't know. But wasn't it too bad? They couldn't help Sam being up the pole.'

One morning Amos was in the line outside Fowler's extra sleeping house in Heather Lane. Fowler's manager, who was nicknamed Mastiff, gazed at the cribbers from the opposite pavement. He was a thick man and his brown mutton-chop whiskers met his ears in grey curls like paper frills. He stepped across and walking along the line tapped the arm of every man who was not in a frock coat and silk hat, and every man and woman who appeared to be over the age of forty, and said: 'No vacancies today.'

Six men were admitted into the room at the same time. Each was given a form and told to write on the empty spaces, and after he had done this he had to do likewise on another form; and the questions on the two forms were the same but set out in different words, the question 'Reasons for leaving last employment' becoming 'Did you leave your last employment on your own accord?' Mastiff examined Amos's papers and said to him:

'If your refs are all right, you can start Monday in the laces. Salary thirty-five and spiffs.'

Amos laid aside his cribbing clothes and went into the restaurant and called for a dinner, it being his first dinner since he had left Hampton's, of toad-in-the-hole and potatoes and the cost of it was sixpence-halfpenny.

CHAPTER XXIX

IN Fowler's dining-room there were three tables for the men and two for the women, and to each table there was a carver and a waiter and for all the tables there were three beermen; and before each person there was a pint measure which the beermen filled with beer, and the persons who abstained from drinking gave their measure to those who did not. Amos drank beer: it was costlier than water and there was nothing to pay for it. The assistants went to their meals in parties each of about two hundred and there were three parties; and they were always scrambling for chairs that were near the carvers.

When Fowler was alive, Misery the steward had to see that every assistant was appointed a certain chair, the newcomers beginning at the bottom and moving upward as other places became free. But Misery was in love with Siren – Siren was the cook whose eyes goggled when she was in drink – and since she sat in a cauldron of boiling green vegetables he had refused to leave the kitchen while cooking was in progress. The carvers, who were chosen from the dispatch room, were given their food and ninepence a day in addition to their weekly wage of twenty-five shillings; and they sold the good places for little trinkets which could be easily stolen from stock and which they took to their wives or daughters or sweethearts.

Food was plentiful: sausages or cold ham or bacon rashers were breakfast relishes, there were meat and two vegetables and rice pudding for dinner, tea and bread and butter in the afternoon, and bread and cheese and beer or coffee for supper. But in Fowler's day there was also cheese at dinner, and cake

171

at teatime, and meat at supper. Some blamed Mastiff. Some blamed the other four directors, saying that they pulled Mastiff apart from the pleasant ways Fowler had set them and kept him on the harsh ways that Fowler had also set them. Meekanmile, who bought the linens and was weighty at board meetings, declared of Mastiff: 'He's too rough altogether. He's all right in Carlisle I got no doubt. But in London, no. Still, don't say I say so.' Jerry, the head of the correspondence office, said: 'There are now too many mouths to feed. Mr Fowler had only one – his own.' Meekanmile had Miss Fowler in his pocket. Whenever Miss Fowler came to the shop he bowed her to the departments, caressing his goat-like beard and bloating her with praise. He advised her in her buyings, and her mind was as easily tipped as the dishes of a scale.

Fowler claimed that Fowler's was built on beef and beer, beer for blood and beef for flesh. 'Three things will remain for ever,' he said, 'the Thames, the British Empire, and Fowler's.' Three wives had cast him away from them and he died at a great age, death finding him in bed with his parlourmaid and in a room which was papered with pictures of naked women. He left Fowler's to his lawful offspring, a daughter by his third wife; he left three thousand pounds to each of his nine natural children and sums of money to their mothers, whether he had known them in their wedlock or in their spinsterhood. But there was one son who sold his inheritance to the World of God Society for five shillings a week and a parcel of tracts a week. He was Dismal Jim who was condemned (so he said) to bring the souls of a hundred thousand sinners to the feet of Jesus that his father's guilt might be washed away. Every night he was at Quaker's Yard, Fowler's private entrance, with his tracts, and every day he slunk by the shop windows between Holborn Circus and Oxford Circus, approaching passers-by from behind, pushing tracts into their hands, stretching his head over their shoulders and saying: 'Come to Jesus.' His pale carcase looked as if it had been buried and come to life again. Every day, in heat and cold, in rain and snow, in thunder and lightning, he prosecuted his work of absolution.

Fowler had been dead two years and the ashes of his frame, which was like a wide-bellied bottle standing on its neck, were being forgotten.

A relic of Fowler's harshness was the Private Letter announcement, copies of which hung in places that the customers who looked could read. This was it: 'Customers are requested to report any incivilities on assistants' parts to Mr. Fowler himself. Mark your letters "PRIVATE". Postage refunded by return.' Fowler never revealed the nature of such reports, discharging the offender: 'Private letter about you. Here's your docket.' Now Mastiff did not see a private letter for nearly a year after Fowler's death; then a woman demanded an apology that her letter had been returned to her with 'Gone Up' written on the envelope. Mastiff sent for Jerry, who had been in no other employment and who had not ceased to mourn Fowler.

'What do you mean by this?' Mastiff asked.

Jerry raised his face, which looked like a dog-fish caught on a hook.

'Yes, sir,' he replied. 'It's quite all right, sir.'

'What impertinence!' cried the woman, adding with a scornful smile: 'Everybody knew what sort of loose man poor Mr Fowler was. "Gone up" indeed.'

'I wanted,' said Jerry, 'I wanted to put them right.'

The account was told to Amos by Mansel and Bucky as they three were preparing to go to bed.

Mansel, a young man with the fair skin of a child saint, was spreading carbolic soap on the soles of his socks, which were moist with the heat of his feet.

'Private letters not fair,' he observed. 'They're not right. Women are awful dam liars. Aren't they, Bucky?'

Bucky was leaning at the open window, his broad fingers in his thick black curls.

'Nice bit of skirt,' he remarked of a woman in the street below.

Amos having joined him, said:

'Tart.'

'Hell! There's old Come to Jesus shoving a tract on her. Wish he'd serve the customers with some.'

'A dozen to the directors,' said Mansel.

'And a gross to old Meekanmile – the slithery, slimy swine.' Bucky imitated Meekanmile's torn voice: ' "I'm always trying to improve things. But I'm really nobody here." The old skunk. He'd cut Mastiff's head off tomorrow if he could.'

'Mastiff is bloody, but a chap does know where they are with him.'

Though Amos's mind was thoughtful, his tongue was shy of English speech, for often his accent caused mockery and his words laughter.

'Ignorant to customers,' he said, 'is not o-rait, you know.'

'Shut your chops!' Bucky cried.

'Ignorant be dam!' said Mansel, drawing his fingers between his toes. 'I could learn them a thing or three. If you say "good morning" to them they're insulted, and if you don't they're insulted. What the hell do they want?'

'Dam fine thing for Jerry he's a legacy,' said Mansel. 'Else he'd been shot out.'

'Yes,' said Bucky, sleepily. 'Shot out like an old glove.'

There were about fifty legacies for whom Fowler had willed life employment in the business named Fowler's. They were a burden to Mastiff and the people who were over them. At every reproof the women whimpered: 'Mr Fowler wouldn't speak to me like that. Poor Mr Fowler! But he was a gentleman'; the men answered: 'Go to hell with you! I was in the trade before you was born.' The chief culprits were the three Beefeaters: Navels who walked the linens and was so named because his nose was like a collection of babies' navels, Captain Fitz who walked the fancy and was so named because on Saturday half holidays he wore a yachting cap and a blue reefer jacket which had yellow brass buttons on it, Cutitshort who walked the gent's and was so named because he had to shorten the stay of assistants who dallied in the lavatories in the mornings. Some said that they were brothers, such was their friendship for one another.

'No bloomin fear! If they were brothers they'd be at each other's throats like hell fury.'

When slightly drunk they hinted that they were the sons of noblemen. One day a small girl sitting at Amos's counter with her mother cried out:

'O look, mummy. There's Admiral Fitzgerald! He was at Southend with his battleship.'

Fitz heard her and went out to the Old Bell for a drink.

They were unmarried and lived in; they were lean and crooked; and their moustaches, howsoever puce and shiny on the morning after screw day, were muddy grey before the month was out. The nights following each pay-day they spent in the bar of the Old Bell, ordering drinks, drinking drinks, and throwing coins on the counter with the remark: 'Plenty more where that comes from.' But they remained in the common room the last six or seven evenings in the month. There they set a bad example, awakening in young men unwholesome thoughts. Navels had a bass voice and in singing smutty songs the pimples on his nose shone like rubies. Captain Fitz spoke of the battleships he had owned and the titled ladies he knew. Cutitshort read from a notebook as if he were crying out items from a catalogue: 'Miss Noble has lace on them. Miss French has real lace on hers and I wonder who paid for it. Miss Jameson's got bloomers so very sorry not much to report. Miss Boyd's got no petticoats which is not quite respectable.'

'What's Norman got on?'

'Ah!' said Cutitshort. 'That – that is a secret.'

One morning after pay-day Fitz tottered across to Lamplight the chemist for a pick-me-up, having signed pass out to no one. When he returned Mastiff was in the department and Mastiff said:

'The next time I hope you'll be run over and killed.'

Fitz was embittered. He followed Mastiff here and there, saying over and over:

'You look down on me, don't you? Just because I'm a bit seedy. I ought to be in my bed with my little head on the pillow. But I can't afford to lay up. Who'd look after my titled connection when I'm not here? Yes, who? You? I don't think.'

Meekanmile took him aside and said:

'It isn't for me to say anything. But at your age it isn't right to be spoken to like that. Still, it's your business. If you like to be made discontented and look silly, it's your affair.'

Fitz would not be comforted, saying that the honour of his family was smirched. During the afternoon he and Navels and Cutitshort were continually in and out of the Old Bell, and towards closing time a red haired woman with the cheerful face of a whore entered the fancy departments, and she banged her parasol on the counter, shouting noisily: 'I am the lady of title and I want the Admiral.' Meekanmile came to her and showed her where Mastiff's office was and she went there and cursed Mastiff with many curses.

Amos was at Fowler's but not of Fowler's. He joined in none of the assistants' levities. He could walk up Quakers' Yard on screw nights without fear of being waylaid by the women who were come for the rewards of love on trust from the skirt-sniffers. From the turmoil of the dodgings of the debtors and the chasings of the women he was free. 'Dam fools,' was Bucky's description of the skirt-sniffers. On Saturday and Sunday evenings Bucky stood under the arch of Gray's Lane in Holborn, surveying the girls and women who processed east and west. When he fancied an animal he grinned his teeth and lifted his eyebrows, and often the woman would slacken her steps, turn her head, and follow him into the lane.

In business Bucky had what is known as a connection; many ladies would be served by him and none other. Middle aged women sometimes waited half-an-hour for him, and as his fingers drew a kid or suède glove over theirs, they fell into a reclining position in their chairs and closed their eyes lightly.

'Disgusting exhibition!' Norman used to exclaim.

Norman was the lace buyer. He carried a lady's walking-length umbrella and put paint and powder on his face. The high heels of his patent leather shoes made him appear taller than he was and his frock coat, bulging over his chest and

176

drawn tightly over his narrow waist, fell over his broad thighs like a woman's skirt. He was mindless of the 'God's truth!' of the men assistants and the 'Ughs!' of the lady assistants. He was a mighty judge of lace. He knew both the real and the imitation, but his delight was in the real. Young men who designed garments for fashionable women came from Kensington and Mayfair and Piccadilly to buy and to fondle Norman's precious examples of the 'patient toil' of nun and peasant and gentle lady. He was the only buyer who lived in. His bedroom companion was Tawny, the fat pimple-faced youth who was in the cash desk against the lace window, and who had come from the Drapers' Benevolent School. The two sometimes quarrelled, Norman nagging and the boy sulking. The day that Norman charged him with unfaithfulness Tawny put ink in a pepper box and sprinkled it over some lace in the window. But Norman spoke up for him to Mastiff. Norman taught Amos, who had handled only coarse-thread imitation laces. He taught him how to pick up the delicate real laces and how to display their designs to an advantage on velvet pads; he taught him the difference between handmade and machine-made, between drawn work and needle point and between Swiss and Brussels, and so forth. Once, seeing Amos pulling real point d'Alçenon to make it measure more than it should, he clapped his thumb-balls on his eyes and shrieked as if in agony: 'You're hurting it! You're strangling it! My dear, lace is made for kissing.' He never used the pads. 'What is it for, madam?' According to the answer, he would lay it on his chest, or his thigh, or his leg. Buck viewed this business with contempt, twisting his lips as if he were sick at the stomach; and when he had to pass Norman he used to squeeze his nostrils and cry: 'What a stink! I'm off to the bog for a breath of fresh air.'

Meekanmile brought Miss Fowler to the counter. Norman was engaged with Capel Clark, the buttery skinned town traveller who carried the lines of a Nottingham house, and so Amos placed before her a few designs. She was like a sheaf of corn and the colour of her face and dress was the colour of straw, but her great hat was yellow and looked like a posy of dandelions caught on the top of the sheaf. Norman left Capel Clark and took Amos's place and what time he was looking for other laces, Clark addressed Miss Fowler:

'Excuse me, madam. You are the daughter of the late deceased Mr Fowler. He was the noblest man I ever knew in the whole course of my existence. I honour his very name.' As he spoke the last sentence he took off his hat and held it as if he were passing a funeral.

'Real valensay, Mr Norman,' said Meekanmile.

'He was a real man,' said Capel Clark. 'A real man.'

Miss Fowler repeated unmeaningly:

'A real man.'

Norman inquired how the lace was to be employed and then, as was his custom, showed it off.

Clark closed his eyes.

'This,' remarked Norman of one, 'is an exquisite copy of eighteenth-century valenciennes.'

'It is perfectly sweet,' said Miss Fowler. 'How many yards do you think I want?'

'Really, madam,' interrupted Meekanmile, 'I don't fancy you'll fancy that in the long run. Now what do you think of this? Very smart, you know.'

'Imitation,' said Norman. 'A very ordinary pattern.'

'Still,' said Meekanmile, 'it'll wear, you know, and wash.'

'Very well then, I'll take your advice and have that.'

While Norman was unbinding the lace, Clark opened his eyes and they looked like buttercups surprised by the sun.

'Excuse me,' he said, taking a piece which Norman had not shown. 'Don't you think this is very dainty?'

'That!' Norman smiled, politely hiding his annoyance at having his judgement criticised by a traveller in cheap lines. 'Mr Clark doesn't understand real lace.'

Clark put on a smirking grace.

'Dainty for the dainty,' he said.

'Yes, it is nice, isn't it?' said Miss Fowler, after a moment or so. 'I'll have that after all. Thanks ever so much.'

Clark noticed Meekanmile's displeasure and said smoothly:

'If your father had searched the whole of the wide, wide world he couldn't have left the firm – your firm – in better hands.'

He followed her to the door and to her car, Meekanmile folding and unfolding his hands as they went.

That was the day of the night that Dismal Jim, with burning urgency, called sinners to the feet of Jesus, for God was to visit Fowler's with terror and death.

'Funky?' asked Bucky.

'Amen and amen,' said Mansel with mock fervency.

'What about it, cocky? What's the size of your order of sins?'

'Well, I don't know,' replied Amos. 'I'm not a digressor.'

But he transgressed unwittingly. In the morning Mastiff sent to him.

'Lady complains you coughed in her face,' said Mastiff gruffly. 'Put a handkerchief before your lips. And don't do it again.'

While Mastiff was speaking Amos was praying to God to guard him against a docket, and with man's ingratitude he did not thank God. He was sore: already he was soiling a handkerchief a week because of the blood that came from his mouth.

'Marvel you didn't get a docket,' said one.

Said another:

'Cheer up! Mastiff's keeping it till after the sale.'

So life proceeded. Amos trimmed the hedges of every example and good counsel, sifting the good from the bad and storing that which was good. He contended with no one. He did not enter into the quarrellings of the Welsh of whom there were many at Fowler's, and who reviled one another with the term 'bloody Welshman'. The words of the Rev. Hooke-Hunter: 'Gather your strength on earth and it shall be your armour against the buffetings of the water of the Jordan.' That was a parable, Amos thought, the Jordan meaning the river that separates master from man. In a year or so the son of Ianto would pitch his shop the other side Jordan, and remain there for ever with the blest of the drapery kingdom.

179

CHAPTER XXX

A WOOD-PIGEON in a park gave Amos a message. It was this: 'Take two cows, Taffy. Take two cows, Taffy. Take two –'; and Amos interpreted it to mean that he should begin with two shops. The places advertised in *The Drapers' Record* were going concerns and there was so much to pay for stock and good-will and fixtures. Why were they selling them? A horse is not sold in the fulness of his strength or a cow in her milk or a sheep before she is shorn. He must make haste, but not be hasty; and he must not be outwitted by rascally talks. He would implant himself in empty shops, and put over them the name of Amos Kent-Morgan, and he would cause trade to grow where it had not grown before.

He was rich, possessing together with his father's money eight hundred pounds. As a workless draper hides his condition with a bold shirt-front he hid his riches with poor garments. At Mother Griff's: 'I really don't imagine I can grant fruit-sago'; and often Slim would say: 'Put it down for me, Cowslip fach.'

Thrift and wisdom were joined in him; thrift enabling him to gather money and wisdom to keep money. He was contented with his situation. Others grumbled: 'I'd like to be an actor,' 'I'd like to be a jockey,' 'I'd like to be a writing chap,' 'I'd like to be anything but a bloomin' draper.' At Fowler's they clubbed for daily and weekly papers and snatched the papers away from one another that they could read about sport, the theatre, books, divorces, murders, and such light things which are not of the trade. Few opened *The Draper's Record* and none interrupted Amos in the studying of it with 'After you, Taffy.'

Sara Owen sent him many letters which he did not answer. But one was of great importance. In it she told how she had trimmed and relined a plain felt hat which cost her four-and-eleven and sold it for ten-and-nine. As a good field which yields an after-crop of hay is a good shop.... Miss Owen was very smart....

As he was thinking he beheld two wasters. He was in Drury Lane, and Miss Larney and Miss Temple were contesting with each other before a long line of people at the pit and gallery doors of the theatre. Miss Larney was in her chintz mantle and Miss Temple was in a frock that flashed with sequins of many shades. 'I was here first,' said Miss Larney. 'Did you put your grandchildren in bed, dearie?' responded Miss Temple. 'With your kind permission I will give you an impersonation of Ellen Terry as Portia,' said Miss Larney. ' "The quality of mercy is not strained –".' Here Miss Temple said: 'Moo! Moo!" Then Miss Temple began to sing, and Miss Larney interrupted her: 'We boil old fowls in our home.' The people laughed very much, and one shouted: 'Why don't you toss up who's first?' They did accordingly and having accused each other of cheating, Miss Temple went away and Miss Larney recited speeches, some of which he had heard her giving in the booth at Carmarthen, and when she was at an end she made a collection of money and went. Miss Temple then returned and announcing herself as the girl with a bell in her throat, she sang, so she said, like Melba and Patti and Marie Lloyd and she also made a money collection.

Amos passed on toward Mother Griff's, dwelling on the unseemly quarrel. They were bad women. They were wasters and wasters soon come to street begging. He thought out English words with which to describe what he had seen.

'Their heads,' he told the company at Mother Griff's, 'were waving and fatally comforted with illusion.'

The men horse-laughed and jeered, but Slim reminded them of the strip of black board which was nailed over the window:

'We got to respect the dead.'

When by and by Amos was preparing to leave, Slim gave him a razor.

'Old Griff,' he said, 'has left off shaving.'

'Does she cut?' asked Amos.

'We're marrying four weeks today.'

'Dear me, what you want to do that for?'

'Must have someone in the shop. And when the assistant is the wife it's very handy. Twig me? I'm giving a treat and you shall come. Making a night of it. Get a sleep out pass and stop here.'

Profitable thoughts are born out of time, and Amos rued that he had not asked for Griff's shaving brush and soap and sharpener. O yes: he would go to the treat, but as to sleeping out? Sleeping out passes had to be signed by Mastiff, and the assistants had to advertise their reasons on the pass and the name and address of the person in whose house they intended to stay, and if he thought that they were telling a lie, he went to a directory. 'And if he catches you,' said Bucky, 'it's goodbye Dolly Grey to you.' The flighty young ladies – the young ladies who went to Frascati's with German and Jew agents – used to say that their father or a brother or an uncle was in London. Then a girl threw vitriol on a man and to the next Mastiff said: 'If I were you, miss, I'd get him to marry you. No. You must sleep in.' But they outrode Mastiff, for they were able to make gifts of money to Siren and she spoke up to Misery in their behalf, it being his duty to mark in the assistants at night and lock the doors; at the beginning he demurred, and Siren said: 'Right-o, my lad! If you object to them young ladies having their bit of fun I object to you doing your little bit.' Meekanmile was on the side of the assistants. 'I believe in liberty after hours. But I'm not the manager. Now if I was –'

Slim held the feast of his wedding and offered pork pies, buns, plum cake, and tea and coffee, and of the twenty guests he took six to the gallery of the Holborn Empire and Amos was among the six; and while they were waiting with others at the doors, Miss Larney and Miss Temple came and quarrelled and recited and sang and gathered money as they had done in Drury Lane.

There were more people in the building than Amos had seen at any preaching meeting and they were more orderly. He saw Siren in the first row of the gallery and on the floor, close to the band, the three Beefeaters, who were smoking cigars and cutting their finger-nails. In a space between the going of one player and the coming of another Siren shouted: 'What-o, Beefies!' They did not take notice of her, and at the next interval she threw an apple which fell on Fitz's head, whereupon the three stood up and shook their fists at her and misshaped their faces. She threw a second apple and a third and a fourth but they struck other people, and though these people aimed things back at her they also hit others than Siren. Presently many on the floor and in the gallery were engaged in pelting apples, oranges, bananas and pears backward and forward.

Said Amos to Slim: 'Like an eisteddfod, Slim bach.'

Slim answered: 'O dam, no. It isn't as bad as that.'

The people who were for peace cried: 'Chuck them out!' Siren and the Beefeaters were thrust into the street and they met and went into the Old Bell; and they came out very drunk and at the entrance to Quakers' Yard, Fitz stood on a box and demanded a bigger Navy, and as he orated Siren stood in front of him and allowed his hands to rest on her head that he should not fall, and her he called Britannia. There were gathered about them hundreds of assistants, making a mock of them; and in and out among them Dismal Jim glided, urging them to be saved from the wrath to come.

On the third day, being the second day of the July sale – terror fell upon Fowler's. Three assistants – a girl and two men – were stricken by a malady. Nine more were stricken within a week.

Every night in the yard the assistants talked with one another about this visitation. Some called it cholera, some black death, and some yellow fever. But none knew its cause or its name, for the management had made no pronouncement. The most rebellious uttered their judgment openly and without fear.

'They daren't sack us just now.'

'With Fowler it couldn't happen. When last were the drains up?'

'The profits are up all right.'

'Ha! The drains done it.'

'Somebody ought to be hung for this.'

'Talk sense. Who can you hang?'

'Old Mastiff, of course. He's the manager.'

'What about the bathrooms he said he'd give us?'

'Kyboshed by old Meekanmile, I bet you.'

'Water's done it, I bet. Only the teetotallers got it. Down with water.'

'What's wrong with beer – good old beer?'

'Nothing. But we don't get enough. Ought to get a couple of pints for dinner and couple of pints for tea and a couple for supper and a bellyful before going to bed. Yes, a bellyful.'

'Gentlemen, please! Remember, there are ladies.'

'It'll do them good to face horrible realities. Most of our evils are due to them. We don't get paid because they work for nothing and a latchkey.'

'Fair do's! Not in Fowler's.'

'Perhaps not. But in other shows. Anyhow they must look at what's happening here. Look at the bogs. Old Cutitshort cuts us short in them. As if we want to bask in them? You know how crusty they are. They're only free from flies and bluebottles at dinner times when they fly to the dining-room.'

That was the tenor of their talk.

Faint hearts gave a moment's notice. Buyers and shop-walkers and even porters became assistants, yet they could not deal with all the customers, and there was much pilfering.

Of the assistants in the laces, two were ill and Amos was left with Norman. The fear of death was not in him; and he served more customers and made more spiffs. He caught a woman in theft and her he pointed out to Mastiff, and Mastiff growled at the Beefeaters: 'Surely to God you can stop them from pinching.' But the Beefeaters were scared and they could

184

not keep still or their tongues from the mirrors. One day Navels quaked and stamped his feet. 'I got it,' he puled; and he compared his head with a furnace and his body with an ice cart.

'Here,' he faltered, 'you, Cutitshort, count my heart, and Fitz the seconds on your watch and I'll do the pulse.'

They addressed themselves accordingly, and when they were ready Fitz cried:

'One, two, three! Heave-o!'

At the end of a minute Fitz said, 'Sixty-three,' and Cutitshort said, 'Hundred and fifty,' and Navels said, 'Fifteen.'

'This proves,' said Fitz, 'whoever's right you got it.'

'We can't all be wrong, you see,' said Cutitshort.

'Better go and have one,' said Fitz.

'We better,' said Navels. 'I want some buck in me.'

The eight rooms, each with six single beds, in the house in Heather Lane were set apart for the afflicted; and they were in the charge of a nurse by day and a nurse by night; hence the buyers and shopwalkers could say truthfully to customers: 'There's no fever on these premises, madam.'

It was noised that Dismal Jim was found by the night nurse placing tracts on the beds.

'Hush,' he said, with Messianic import. 'I am here in the cause of my father.'

By the morning he was laid low. Meekanmile wanted to have him sent away in punishment for defaming the name of Fowler.

'I shouldn't,' said Capel Clark, who had become Miss Fowler's reporter. 'If anything happens to him perhaps there will be a scandal. We must save Miss Fowler at all costs.'

'Poor Miss Fowler!' exclaimed Meekanmile.

'Poor lady,' said Clark.

'Dismal Jim's a bit of Fowler too,' declared Mastiff, gruntingly. 'If we'd spent a little money there would be no need to poor Miss Fowler.'

'There wouldn't have,' said Meekanmile. 'Everybody knows I've done my best. But then I'm not the general manager. The fellow's a no-gooder.'

A child sleeping on its mother's breast awakes with a sudden cry at the moment death takes its mother. So Dismal Jim – went the noise – awoke with a cry when one of Fowler's people died. When he was nearing the notch which death had cut for him in the pole of his scythe, he made loud lamentations that he had not absolved his father's guilt.

'Of course you have,' said the nurse; and she read to him the Parable of the Grain of Mustard Seed, but he replied that the soul of a seed is God's from first to last, whereas man breaks loose from God and becomes tainted; and the nurse read the Parable of the Sower, and she said that for every ten tracts which were cast away one fell into a contrite heart and bore fruit without end; and she made a sum on a piece of paper and lo, he had led to Jesus not a hundred thousand sinners, but a million.

None knew, other than the directors, the number that died, for the bodies of the dead were taken away betwixt midnight and dawn and the cost of conveying them to whatsoever places they belonged to was paid by Fowler's. Fowler's also sent to his people the wage of each person, from the day of his sickness to the day of his death, together of course with his clothes and other monies that might be due to him. But those who recovered were not paid for the period of their sickness. The drains were cleaned. Two bathrooms, each with hot and cold water, were built, one for the women and one for the men. A closet was added to the two in the women's sleeping quarters and also to the two in the men's. The closets in the basements were cleared of their foulness and peepholes were made in the doors so that offenders could be marked and docketed. The fever was spent, but every morning a doctor came to look at the sick at Fowler's and the unfit were put in a room which was called sickroom and a nurse attended them; and the meals were made as they were in former times. These things Mastiff accomplished, saying: 'I'd rather die than go through it all again.' But he did not abate his harshness: from the hour it was said that the fever was spent he slackened not his hand from the buyers, or the shopwalkers, or the assistants. 'We got to make up our losses,' he said.

'Old Fowler's come back to life,' they said. 'But we know when he barks he bites.'

The old year perished, with Fowler's Welsh praying at midnight services and with Fowler's Scots drinking whisky at St Paul's; and the earth awoke and unfolded her petals and it was spring; and *The Drapers' Record* announced the coming marriage of Miss Fowler to Capel Clark. Before it was said that Miss Fowler was in Meekanmile's pocket; now that Meekanmile was in Clark's pocket. Whenever Clark was in the shop, Meekanmile was with him; and they two, the rumour was, were conspiring against Mastiff.

Miss Fowler came for laces for her wedding garments and Clark was with her and Norman placed before them real laces.

'Imitation, please, Mr Norman,' said Clark.

'O very well,' said Norman peevishly; he went to the lace stockroom downstairs, calling upon Amos to attend to them.

The next day Clark and Meekanmile paused at the counter.

'Where's madam?' Clark asked jocosely.

Amos, to gain favour, smiled with an evil meaning.

'Her ladyship is missing,' said Clark to Meekanmile. 'With her sweetheart, I suppose?'

They looked towards the cash desk.

'I wonder,' said Clark, 'what his mother would say if she knew.'

'If,' said Meekanmile, 'she knew.'

'She ought to know.'

'Who's to tell her? You see, I'm not the manager.'

'We can't have a scandal, you know.'

Meekanmile stroked his goat's beard.

'I know what the wife would do. But I'm nobody here.'

At closing time about a week later Meekanmile was with a woman and Tawny in the yard and as Norman came up Meekanmile went away with Tawny and the woman fell upon Norman, screaming: 'What you've been doing to my son? You've ruined him! You won't see him any more. You filthy hound!' She beat him and tore his hair and his clothes; in the

187

midst of it she fell into a fit and Norman ran back to his bedroom. In the night several men broke into his room and they hung his underclothes, which were those of a woman, outside the door so that all could see what manner of man he was. He did not eat any breakfast, but went straight to the stockroom and strangled himself with a rope, the coils of which were real laces.

Mastiff was like a madman, running to and fro and smiting his hands as though upon him there was a spell against which there was no charm. He docketed every mannish woman and pretty youth and many an innocent, and he docketed Misery because as overseer of the bedrooms he had allowed this curse to come upon Fowler's. Amos went to his office to ask for Norman's berth, and he unburdened his mind in his presence; Mastiff was in a chair, his wrists between his knees, his hands clasped, and his eyebrows drooping like a heavy moustache. Is not the life of Mastiff written in *The Drapers' Record*?

Meekanmile appointed himself manager, keeping also his office of linen buyer. He gathered money from the staff and with it made a wedding present of a grand piano to Miss Fowler and the present he made in his name. He closed the sickroom; charged the assistants a penny for each bath and levied upon them the doctor's salary; the food which Mastiff had restored he took away and the beer also he stopped, saying: 'The water's all right now and it's cost us a nice sum.'

Meekanmile reigned five weeks as manager and after him came Capel Clark; and at his coming Capel Clark shook the hand of every buyer and shopwalker and the hand of every assistant in the presence of his buyer. He called himself a hewer of wood and a drawer of water; he was but a servant at Fowler's – the great Metropolitan House of Fowler's. He had the private letter notices covered with the face of Fowler and the words: 'Our Revered Founder.' He had notices on the doors of the lavatories: 'One speck of Dirt May Turn the Whole Store Sick.' He put mottoes in the bedrooms and the corridors: 'Your Turn is Not Next – it is NOW.' 'The Success of This House is – YOUR Success.' 'Don't Deserve Dismissal – Do

YOU?' 'Slackers are Soon Sacked – are YOU a Slacker?' 'No jobs here for Clockers – are YOU a Clocker?' 'Good Service Pays a Good profit – is your name MR PROFIT?' 'A Cheerful Salesman makes a Ready Spender – Are You MR CHEER-FUL?' He caused to be destroyed all billheads and bags and boxes which bore the word Fowler's and had others printed with the words Metropolitan House. Then on the twenty-first day of his reign men pulled down from the outer walls of the building the grey letters which spelt Fowler's and in their place they put Metropolitan House; that day also he docketed the legacies.

Amos sought him and found him and told him how Mastiff had promised him advancement.

'Laces, aren't you?'

'Yes, sir.'

'Age?'

'Thirty-three, sir.'

'Good gracious! I'm only three years older myself. What have you been doing all these years?'

'That's quite it, sir. They keep me down.'

'I'll think about it. Come and see me in a fortnight.'

But before the end of the fortnight the great war had begun and to each male assistant was given a pamphlet which read: 'Your country needs us. It is your duty to present yourself at the nearest recruiting station and offer our King your good right arm and that he will accept it to help drive the Germans back to Berlin is the sincere wish of your friend – CAPEL CLARK.

'P.S. Army rejection forms must be produced in each and all circumstances and shown to the General Manager – C.C.'

Amos offered himself and when he was stripped to his waist of his clothes, the doctor said to him:

'Your ribs are thin enough to sharpen a pencil on. Get a job in the open if you want to live a few more months.'

CHAPTER XXXI

THE men of Fowler's who were refused by the Army were examined by Fowler's doctor and he reported on them to Capel Clark; and Capel Clark ridded Fowler's of such as were suffering from diseases and Amos was among them.

When a Welshman is harshly used he blames his God, and on the Day of Reckoning he will demand the meaning of the deeds and acts that wearied his flesh. There is no purpose in prayer and hymn and sermon if God fails you in your hour of need. God is on high that He can watch over you and prevent harm falling upon you. Amos had asked many gifts of God and had received much, but he never returned thanks. Why had he been docketed? He was as good as any man at Fowler's. He could endure affronts and the endurance of affronts makes the perfect draper; he could adore the tongue that scolded him and kiss the foot that kicked him. He had been on the side of the righteous, ignoring the talks of Trade Union men, hanging Norman's clothes on the door, acquainting Mastiff with misdemeanours, fawning in the face of Meekanmile, bowing and cringing in the way of Capel Clark. A man bearing such a name as Capel should be religious. Amos lamented his misery and bleated his woes in solitude.

He was alone at the Hotel. Most of the battered cribbers had found jobs and they strode about with the pride of men. The restaurant had been closed, and Miss Larney was become 'Our Florrie – Character Comedienne,' and pictures showing her as a Welsh landlady, a London charwoman, a Piccadilly flower girl, and so forth, were outside music halls and on hoardings.

Miss Temple was become 'Temple Bells – the Belle with a Bell in her Throat.' 'They are pocketing fortunes,' Picton said. The stewed fruit trade was no more, the young men having joined the soldiers, but Slim boasted that his stock of small groceries was worth treble its former price and that he was holding it until the price was again doubled. 'I shouldn't sell the goodwill for a couple of hundred,' he said.

Maggie Cowslip his wife was in the family way and he was proud of her condition, and such was his care that no hurt should befall her that he performed every household duty himself. 'No work for my lady. No capel-going.' That was his talk. Maggie too was proud. Her eyes shone with blessed expectancy. The sight of her body tormented Amos and caused Picton to sing loudly:

> 'Wass you ever see,
> Wass you ever see
> Such a belly before?'

How the wicked and the waster prosper! They were exalted and Amos was brought low. Even Slim who had been broken out of Tabernacle for that he went into the chapel drunk with beer and shouted: 'Shut up, Hampton! If you don't, God will spew on you.' None said to Amos: 'I got a crib for you.' All asked him: 'Why aren't you in the war, man? Too afraid you are.' The Rev. Windsor-Daniel to the congregation: 'This is a war between good and evil. I hear a call to arms: who calls? Listen. It is the voice of Jesus. O had I the sinews of youth! Do your bit.' The young men of Tabernacle left their fathers' shops and counting houses and offices and hurled themselves into the offices of the Government.

As a man with a crust of bread begets comfort from the thought of the man with nothing, so Amos begat comfort from the German baker, who was forsaken by men and vilified by children.

Picton was allowed two pounds a week and was brave in speech. Of the baker he declared:

'That Sherman should be hung at once.'

'Every jack of them should be hung,' said Slim.

'We allow him to coin cash,' said Picton, 'while our friend here – one of the Motherland – can't get jobs. Yes. One of the one and only Motherland.'

'It isn't o-rait, you know,' said Amos.

He went on to tell how in Ceri they broke the windows of the parish parson who sent a bum-bailiff to seize cattle for his tithes.

Picton churned his spittle and splashed it on the ground.

'I may spit ice every time I see him,' he said.

Slim said:

'Pity the stones didn't break his head.'

'He was knocked on the head,' Amos added. 'There was a plentiful boomp there.'

'That Sherman ought to be knocked into a bump too,' said Slim.

'And we pay him rent,' said Picton. 'The cash is for Sher-many. I won't pay any more for my Hotel. Who's fighting? Who are we fighting with? No money for the Sherman is the motto.'

'Diawl!' cried Slim. 'I'm off to cook the sticks and ships for supper.'

'It's early,' said Picton.

'I want to get things over. The Sherman cat is going to be turned in the pan tonight. So long.'

Amos and Picton remained at the door of the Hotel. Amos was gazing at two empty houses, with their tumbling basement walls; and a thought was born unto him.

'Why do birds speak?' he asked.

'They don't and they do,' replied Picton.

'I hear one cawing, "Take two cows, Taffy".'

'Very bad advice,' said Picton. 'It shows what He above thinks of the English to give their language to the birds. You never hear a bird talking Welsh.'

Amos walked abroad, the thought warming his fancy and enchanting his mind. Maybe he would start with groceries and milk. He was smarter than Slim, and Cowslip would soon be in bed with child and a mother and a baby cannot always be in the shop. Slim was wasteful: steaks and chip potatoes for supper. Fancy-mongering he roamed and night found him in Wardour Street; and he saw Slim running toward him like a bum-bailiff, being pursued by a great number of people; the fleetest overtook him and turned upon him and then they all rounded upon him and drove him into Byway Passage; and he could not escape from them, a wall being at the back of him and a wall on each side of him and the people stood in the outgoing path, shouting: 'Hun!' 'German!' 'Spy!'

'I'm not a Sherman!' Slim cried to them. 'I am a shop assistant. But I'm now in the milk trade.'

'With that accent!'

One caught him by the throat and struck his face and thumped his head upon the wall, and this made Slim reel as if his eyes were dazzled.

'Watyourunforifyounospy?'

'Yes. Watyourunfor?'

Slim smiled for the trust of his persecutors.

'I –' he said, 'I threw the first stone.'

'Spy-like that was! Putting us off the scent.'

He saw Amos and cried:

'He knows me. Me and he were in school together.'

'You mean in Berlin!'

'Another of them spies!'

Amos did not speak.

'Tell them I am the Welsh,' Slim pleaded. 'Aren't I Welsh?'

Amos did not answer.

As a man at the brim of a fiery pit chancing a leap into safety or death was Slim's leap. Amos stayed until the cries of 'Hun!' and 'Spy!' died away. When he came to the German's shop there was a crowd of people assembled thereat, and they too were crying: 'Spy!' 'Huns!' 'German sausages!' 'We'll learn you!' They tore the bricks from the crumbling walls, broke all the windows of the house; and by and by one threw a stone at a window of the Hotel. Picton appeared at it.

'Friends and brothers,' he cried, 'you know not what you

do. I'm not a dirty Sherman. O no. I'm for war till there is not one Sherman left.'

Talk English.'

'I hate the Sherman and his bakerings. He is only my land-lord and that won't be for long. He owns my Hotel and the milkshop.'

'Regular nest of spies!'

'German property! Let's at them!'

The moment that Picton was howled into sheepish terror was the moment that Amos's eyes were opened with the glad relief of a sinner receiving the gift of salvation. Though he stoned, he did not speak lest he was manhandled.

Cowslip stood at a window. She was clothed in a nightgown and her fair hair was loosened.

'Blonde beasts!'

The crowd was large and angry when Miss Larney came from her work and seeing that which was done, her anger brewed stormily and she delivered herself of phrases from many plays:

'What venom did you suckle at your mother's breast? How shall this profit your savagery? You roar like a giant whose feet are on shifting sands. You malevolent monsters with the guts of pigmies.'

'It's Our Florrie!' one cried.

The people were pacified.

'Good Old Florrie!'

'Go on, Florrie! Give us the Piccadilly flower girl!'

'Scum of the earth and pests of the air. You think you're gods to wreck the homes of the innocents. May your masters make toys of your daughters and abandon them and may they tear you from your wives and your mothers and your children and give you to the sword.'

So the people were subdued and shamed and their voices waned and their hands feebled, and they repaired to their several places.

Amos went into his bed and slept confidently and in the morning he made a treaty whereby he obtained the German's

194

houses for three hundred and fifty pounds.

'I've purchased the Hotel,' he announced to Picton. 'I'm the boss. I need the place for my private particulars. You got to go.'

Picton was dressed for a journey and there was a bag at his feet: and he answered and said:

'I'm flying from this wickedness to the rightful but lawful wife. Better the lumpy mattress of marriage than the feather bed of sin.'

Amos went to Mother Griff's. Miss Larney was at a bed, upon which were the bodies of Cowslip and her child, declaiming:

'Heaven hath a breast for the tiny babe. And the wail of the stricken mother is as powerful a prayer to the throne of grace as the eloquent effusions of the most learned and ardent divine.'

Amos spoke as he had spoken to Picton. His manner was resolute. He who had been humble was arrogant; he whose tongue had stumbled was fluent. So man's ways change with his fortune.

Miss Larney continued:

'Merciful heaven, has not my aching heart sufficient misery without being galled by this? Avaunt, rash man! Steep not your reeking hands still deeper in the blood of the innocent. Remember that He who shatters the mighty oak is quick to revenge the sparrow's slayer.'

She washed away the blood from Cowslip's forehead and covered the mother and child. Then she seized Amos and thrust him out of the room. She closed the door upon the dead and stood up before Amos as if she were defying a sottish tyrant.

'You blithering angel face!' she cried. 'If your neck wasn't so lean and scraggy, I'd twist it and put your head on the doorstep as a lesson.'

CHAPTER XXXII

THE windows of Mother Griff's were put in order and 'A. Kent-Morgan' was printed over the door and the business was a going concern, Amos having set himself therein immediately. The German had gone none knew where. Miss Larney took Miss Johnson with her and had the bodies of Maggie and her child buried with pomp. Slim had returned after many weeks, he having been maltreated and in a hospital, and Amos told him every whit of what had befallen Maggie; also that he had provided for her a tidy funeral.

Slim was smitten with grief. The ways of man are as mysterious as God's, but man is not endowed with the power of knowing whither his ways lead. Even so Slim. He moaned like the sad old woman whose son had been hanged and the theme of his moaning was his Cowslip fach, and he blamed old Griff that his forehead was not there to receive the stone.

'Diawl!' he exclaimed.

Amos rebuked him with the authority of a master.

'Why for you call on Satan, man?' he said in Welsh. 'Be you solemn and if you can't be solemn be religious.'

Slim babbled praises of Cowslip, plucking up memories of her kindness and her sweetness. Sooner will Mary forgive Caiaphas than he his Maggie's slayer.

'The old Sherman killed her,' said Amos. 'I see him pelting to put persons off his smell.'

At a word she would have gone forth to pick for him red berries from the flaming walls of hell.

Slim groaned and blubbered and Amos tried to comfort him with ridicule:

'Quieten up, Slim bach. You are like a mongrel with mixed parents.'

'Mongrels are fighters. I'll fight for her.'

'Fight for the country, man. And good luck all round. There was the bastard from Eben.'

But Slim would not be comforted, such was the bitterness of his soul and the fulness of his grief. He raised his shoulders, even his lower shoulder he raised, and he stood as if he were in array against the enemy and he said:

'I'll make the Shermans pay for this.'

Before he went away Amos gave him fifteen pounds for the business, forgiving what money was owed for rent. Slim departed with the jaunty stride of the man who has been taken from the dust to fight for God.

Amos hired four lusty women, one after the other, and each he sent off after knowing her, because he was sure that she was a thief. The fifth he hired because she was not like the others, being frail and bashful, and she had come to dwell in one of the two houses which he was in a mind to open as a shop with the intent of taking away Slim's custom. He did with her as he had done with the others, whereupon she shed her bashfulness and was continually at his door slandering him, and in all he gave her three shillings; and as he got no peace he bought the two houses for two hundred and fifty pounds and had her removed. He made up his mind to marry Miss Owen: a wife needs no salary, she does not defraud her husband, she is always at her husband's call; for a wife there is nothing to pay. He sent a letter to Miss Owen and she demurred at the cost of lodgings in the interval before marriage. He said: 'Abide with me,' and she said that it is not religious to sleep with a man before wedlock. He said that she could go into a berth. Sara Owen sold her belongings, but the harmonium and the portraits of preachers and that of Jesus she brought with her, and the picture of Jesus she hung in the parlour so that, said she, the customers will know that they are dealing with religious people; and she went to Hampton's and remained there until the eve of her marriage.

They married on a Sunday, trade being slack on that day; and when they were together he asked, speaking in Welsh-English:

'How much you have?'

'How much you have?' she also asked.

'Well now, one hundred or two? Now say.'

'Just like that!'

'There's close you are! Why are you so Welshy?'

He pressed her and she told him that she had two hundred and seventy-five pounds and he feigned surprise and unbelief at the vastness of the amount, and his earnestness cheated her into showing him her savings' book.

'You have wasted quite a lot,' he then said.

That was how he began to repent his bargain. The woman was a squanderer and day by day he watched her and reproved her and nagged her, and some of her acts stopped his words with despair.... She gives to a cat a portion of herring which was sufficient for a threepenny sandwich. She throws on the ground cake crumbs and mouldy pieces of cheese and bacon and the dogs come for them and after them the mice, and wherever there are cats and dogs and mice there is a loss. Her measures are the same whether the customer is a child or a blind man or an attentive woman. She puts jam on her margarine-scraped bread or eats cheese with it. He who eats relish with relish shall want; so shall he who eats meat more than once a day, and a sardine is counted meat, and fish-paste, a sausage, tinned salmon, or a slice of corned-beef....

'There's the Final Supper, Saran,' said Amos. 'Bread and one relish, and the wine was vinegar and who enjoys vinegar?'

Sara listened.

'We must narrow down, Saran. If you don't nothing will I have to live on after you have died.'

'I'll narrow down,' she said, gazing at him through eyes the beds of which were like holes burnt into the bark of a tree; and she made her ways as frugal as the scraps of flesh around his neck.

Amos sought a side-line by the profit of which they could

live, and he thought out a sort of pudding made from bacon-rinds, ground bacon bones, moulded cheese, mildewy jams, soured lard, and what not. Sara made such a mess, and he counted the cost and tasted it and said:

'O-rait. Twopence per slab.'

The pudding money was placed in a cup as they received it and by the profit of it they ate, and every morsel they took up on the tip of their knives they eyed with the infinite sorrow of a fond father burying his first-born child. Amos's jubilation was made whole when in the Tabernacle he heard that Slim had been killed in an act which was worthy of the Victoria Cross.

'He can't make a muster in the shop now.'

Windsor-Daniel preached from the text: 'The Lord killeth, the Lord maketh alive.' Amos joined the young Welshmen in the congregation in shouting the song: 'March of the Men of Harlech', and before he left he had devised words to put in his window, these being the words: 'Bereaved owner was deceased proprietor and gets V.C.'

He sold two of his houses at a profit of one hundred and fifty pounds and when he saw these opening as a factory for aeroplane wings, he repined that he had been cheated and marked down his loss at five hundred pounds.... The man was a rascal and though he made a million wings he would never go heavenwards.... An Italian offered him eighty pounds a year for the Hotel and the bakery shop, for the purpose of a hostel for women workers. Amos haggled. The Italian said that his hostel would bring custom into the shop and brighten the meanness of the street. He smiled and whispered in Amos's ears:

'There will be lots of pretty girls, Mr Morgan.'

Amos stopped haggling.

'Three hundred,' he said, 'is the rock price top or bottom.'

The gloom was rising from Corsica Street; and Amos's counter rang with the money of factory workers and hostel harlots, and the publican's wife who had been drab was clothed in finery.

CHAPTER XXXIII

'SEND my money in haste and earn the Big Man's mercy till they do Germans are on London marching a mile every minute to pillage my money beware the fire of hell Amos it is hotter than the fire of the bones of Church parsons write on the box of money "eggs with care" for to cheat the postmen console the grey whiskers of your father in flesh and he is your father in the Lord and honour your father Ianto as says Bible.'

Thus Ianto to his son Amos.

Amos remembered his father; yea, he was of the temple of his flesh and the subtleness of his mind. He ordered Sara to be sparing of the things that cost money and to charge her feet with nimbleness and her mind with cunning, she being a toopess, and he made for Tyrhos his father's house. As he walked from Station Castle Owain he refused a ride from a cartman: man gives away nothing. He descended towards Ceri. The sun was going down and the cows lowed and the birds dirged. He came to Capel Moriah. All men end in Moriah. The white walls of Moriah were like the shoulders of God. The sadness of decay was upon Amos, for the fainting light was heavy with menace.

Katrin his father's stepmother was on Pont Ceri just by her house. She hooted:

'Drato, Amos bach! Your hat bowler is wider than your body. Is that the fashion now?'

He smiled as the townsman smiles at a peasant's jest.

'Jawch!' she continued. 'You won't find the soverens. Afraid he is to loosen his britches lest he lets down a soveren.'

Ben Shop questioned him about affairs in the great and

sinful City, Carpenter examined him with the eye of a foot-rule, Schoolin made a sum of the hours of his life, Gravedigger told him that there was space at the side of his perished mother, and Catti said that Ianto was a mess of sludge.

He panted from hedge to hedge up Road Saints and as the darkness deepened so his spirit brightened.

Ianto was sitting on the coffin which he had made to contain his body and the life-giving stones and he raised his head and rejoiced. He ran to his son, his arms stretched out and his hands were like huge spoons at the end of long handles, and his trousers and his long beard were like the crust of a dunghill; and he stood before Amos dumbly.

'Here's awful, father bach,' said Amos, his tone apprehensive of evil. 'Shermans will find your soverens quite soon.'

Ianto did not move. He with a giant's beard and the limbs of a Samson, had a heart which fluttered like a wounded sea-gull's.

'Woe for you,' said Amos.

'How you speak like that then?' Ianto stammered.

'Shermans are sailing for Cardigan Bay. Did I hear the pounce of a gun?'

'Perhaps Deio Blacksmith is pretending to shoot rabbits and trying to find my soverens.'

'Father bach, hope I do the soverens are in a very secret hiding place.'

Ianto answered in the guileless voice of a simple:

'What soverens can a poor piece like me have? Give me what is mine.'

'Bring them I would had you a safe hiding place.'

'Even my heart is a mirror. Look you into her.'

Amos looked at his father and he saw himself.

'Shermans will hear I give you the soverens and spoil you.'

'My bits of gold now, boy bach. At the sound of Shermans stretched I'll be in the coffin and the soverens under me. And go off they will, for dead men are at once robbed to their skin.'

'In far distant France,' said Amos, 'they took a perished corpse in his coffin and boiled him for to make grease for the axles of guns. What of your soverens then?'

'Poof-poof.'

'Father bach, go you not into the old coffin. Why will you drown your son in sorrow? Hap you stay in him three days and three nights. Hoo–hoo!'

'Poof-poof! Say I am in him thirty days and three times thirty nights. Shake the little stones they will in the carrying and jolt me into life. A great shout I'll make. All men run when a dead man speaks.'

Amos put his fingers in his ears, and cried:

'Why for you make me weep? Find a hiding for your soverens. How say you to holes in the moor?'

'No–no! Every night, be the Big Man's lamp never so wanly lit, blacks of men will search them.'

'How now the mattress of the bed?'

'There an old rat has made her bed. Stealers are rats.'

'In the wall of the stable, father bach?'

'Maybe I have an ass and he eats them for carrots.'

'Safe I hope are your few shillings.'

'I have no white money. As true as the eye of the well.' He brought the Box-Bible from the coffin and he put it against his lips as a holy man his crucifix. 'This is my only possession. It is the Word to the Life and the Law of the Life. It is the maker of the Earth.'

Father and son laid themselves down to sleep, and the father said: 'Feast will I on the morrow with the Big Man in Moriah.' His head was on the Bible and a hand rested on Amos's shoulder; and upon Amos complaining that the hand was heavy, he said: 'Is my son also among my enemies?' In the morning they were in Moriah, Ianto in the Big Seat and Amos in the ninth pew therefrom. Preacher discovered the bread and wine and while he said the words of the ritual he separated the bread into four portions and each portion he put on a dish and he poured the wine into four cups; and four Big Heads received the bread and the wine for to serve the four quarters of the congregation. Ianto took a dish of bread and a cup of wine and he drank all the wine and ate all the bread, and then he cried in English: 'God save the King!' He looked at Amos and he saw himself; and he began to climb over the pews to go to him, but he was prevented by men. Then he rose and went forth and came back with a headstone from a grave and he held it before him as if it were a school-child's slate and he named himself Moses, saying: 'The Law, persons, am I.'

The people were alarmed and like frightened half-wits they stole from Moriah and he chased them to Pont Ceri; and on the bridge men waited for him with ropes, but none could seize him. Amos knew his father's disorder and being afraid for his life, he ran for sanctuary toward Katrin's house; as he ran Ianto threw the stone after him and it fell aside of him. Katrin then gave him a hay-fork to guard himself, and Ianto fell upon the prongs and the pole broke therewith, for he was a very heavy man.

Katrin spoke, and said:

'Be you sure, Amos, you clip his whiskers. If you don't hap they mistake him in the Mansion for a saint.'

The men were astonished that such wisdom should come from the mouth of a woman.

CHAPTER XXXIV

THE money that Amos brought with him from Tyrhos was over four hundred pounds, counting the nineteen pounds he got for Tyrhos and not counting the cost of his father's funeral. He hid this money in his house, for if the Germans came to London they would of a surety rob the banks. But he was constantly uneasy that thieves armed with guns would come and steal it. So whenever he was at worship in Tabernacle or abroad at some business, Sara remained in the shop; and she did not know that she was the guardian of wealth, Amos telling her not a whit about his affairs.

He wore grief clothes for his father in Tabernacle and his eyes spoke his anguish. People Tabernacle said that he had inherited a great fortune and that he was doing great business; his air, said they, having been bowed was lofty. 'How a boy bach with nothing got on!' Hence they esteemed him. He paraded his father's Box-Bible and showed the written words which were in it. 'You can have only one father,' he lamented.

Said Windsor-Daniel:

'Bible and hymn book in one. Complete. A treasure over all treasures. He who fashioned it – he who lovingly fashioned it in the flickering light of a rushlight in his humble dwelling on an ancient hillside of our beloved Wales – the land where the harp is never tired of singing praises unto the God of our fathers – he who put page with page and lock on cover is departed but his fragrance remains in his son – his only begotten son – and he this day is treading the milky way of Tabernacle. Every page in his book is a cheque which he can fill for any amount and the Big Banker will honour it.'

'So be it!' milkmen and drapers exclaimed. 'Hosanna to the Big Banker!'

Still at that evening service Amos was a sorrowful young man. Why cannot money, the allayer of ill and the giver of hope, scatter the gloom that oppresses the heart and plunges the spirit in woe? Sara was a burden. Her voice was like a beggar's voice whining a tale and her upper lip drooped like the edge of a mushroom. On the occasions that he addressed her sharply, she puckered her forehead as if she were a captive knowing that her hour of deliverance was at hand.

One night he awoke in his sweat and railed at her.

'You riot away my money,' he said.

'Indeed,' she protested, 'I can't be narrower.'

'Shut your head, toopess.'

'Oh, wedded to a dolt you are for not long.'

'After you go I won't have one red penny.'

She made weeping noises.

'You even waste your tears!' he said. 'Drop them in the vinegar for to make it more.'

They were too much alike to make good company. Both were close. They separated the grain from the chaff, but they did not throw away the chaff. She falsified everything which could be falsified: butter and margarine, milk and cream, jam and treacle. There was nothing in her house for dog or cat or sparrow. She rinsed greasy dishes in cold water and brewed tea in singing water, and she and Amos went to their bed in the dark, the electric light having been disconnected in every room other than the parlour and shop.

The height of day was the height of Amos's spirits. Then he planned Corsica Street from end to end and side to side into a shop bigger than Fowler's and he would marry a buxom woman who had money and who always would be kindling his amour. Sara's trunk was like a meagre sapling set in briny soil and in love she was a martyr. Why was she not as full and rosy-red and loud and blooming as the publican's wife? She was worth clothing for the sake of the stripping. Sara would not last for ever. The hue of cancer is the hue of fungus gathering on a tree: that was Sara's hue. She was walking toward the tanner's yard. He left over wearing his grief suit on Sundays.

'Dear me,' said Sara, 'you should show your mourning for a year.'

'The grief suit,' he announced, 'I keep fresh for a certain funeral.'

Sara tantalized him with a pitying smile.

'A shroud they have for the dead, Amos.'

'Ho, yes, for you a shroud.'

So each bore the troubles of the day in the belief of the other's early death.

The sun continued to shine on Amos. A Jew said that he wanted to buy the Hotel and bakery shop and Amos answered: 'How shall I sack the ingoing tenant? Let live is the motto.' The Jew offered him a thousand pounds, and Amos said: 'What you think am I, man? Thanks and much obliged.' The Jew offered him fifteen hundred pounds, and Amos said: 'The property is very precious to me.' The Jew declared that he would give no more, and Amos said: 'Half one mo.' The Jew could not wait, and Amos said: 'Stop three mos. You're in a big push.' Within three days he consented to the Jew's price of two thousand pounds, and he said: 'I'll pack him off.' Amos gave the Italian notice to go but he would not go. Then he meditated in wisdom for an hour. He would say to him: 'Fly, Italian! Put wings on you! Polisses are haunting you!' But as he was about to utter those phrases, he altered his solemn countenance into that of shamed honesty, saying: 'The prostrate fact I am short length in the money I owe. Bum-bailiff is going to have me. Pay me a year's rent beforehand and no more I'll speak about this.' Even so the Italian. Even so God helps in time of need. Then Amos made a complaint to the police and the man was sent to prison. The Big Banker honours the cheques of His children.

'Saran,' he cried, 'give me pins.'

Sara found two pins.

'Here's a pinless house!' he cried. 'Why don't you own pins?

206

You squander on the belly but not on pins.'

'What for I want pins?'

'I'll buy pins – millions.'

The huge quantity that he bought nonplussed Sara and moved her into asking:

'Opening a shop?'

He was silent.

'Say and tell me.'

He licked his dry lips and mouthed provoking sounds.

He exchanged at his bank the Jew's cheque and his father's sovereigns and the sum that was lodged in his name for paper money, but the Tyrhos pounds he left in his name. He was on his way home, at the place where Wardour Street begins in Oxford Street, when Drake 48 came upon him.

Drake leant against the wall like a man before he faints from hunger. His nose was smudgy and dribbly and it looked like an over-used and battered poker, and he could not keep it from trembling or make his tongue to speak. Presently he stammered:

'It's a vrosty morning.'

'What you want to say?' asked Amos.

'It didn't ought to be. It's like this –'

'Hampton will give you a ref. But you must smarten up. Good da.'

But he followed him.

'The police are after me and they didn't ought to be neither.'

'You stole money then.'

Then Drake blurted out:

'I only took Miss Brooks to Mrs Richardson. I didn't do no more and no further. And she died there. Lend me two pounds and I'll take the train and the police won't know where I am. I'll pay you back as I can.'

'I haven't any money at all,' said Amos. 'Not one coin.'

He felt as if he were the heir of the sun's gold. 'The Lord maketh alive.' Money came to him easily and there was nothing to pay. He would not buy Corsica Street; he would buy a bit of Kensington or of Holborn. He pinned on his door:

'Premises for Sale', which made Sara weep bitterly and in earnest, and he tried to save her tears in a cup. He closeted himself for a long time and then he sat in the parlour with his father's Box-Bible on his knees, and having purposely placed the book of his account with the bank on a table, he went into a dogsleep. Sara entered and she peeped into the book, and as he watched her lips screwing with balked hopes his soul floated in ecstatic joy. But it sank. There were symbols of religion about him: the harmonium, a hymn book, the picture of Jesus; and religion is preparation for death.

The shop was closed for the day; and Sara sang at the harmonium:

> Sweet soul, the cold and swollen waves
>> Of the deep Jordan are at hand,
> And Sion, holy city, now
>> Rises upon the farther strand.

Like a peevish child he bade her to still her voice and to turn the face of Jesus to the wall.

CHAPTER XXXV

Amos sold the harmonium, the picture of Jesus, and the portraits of the preachers, and with the pages of Sara's hymn-book
he wrapped purchases. He removed all symbols of religion
from his sight. Though these things made him sad, the cooing
eloquence of Windsor-Daniel allured him to Tabernacle and
aroused his passion.

Great was Windsor-Daniel, but greater – so they told – was
Eben L. Pembroke. Once a year in the month November
Tabernacle sets apart a Sunday for a preaching feast, when the
pulpit is occupied by the sweetest preacher that money can
bring to it. Welsh is the speech of the Sunday morning sermon
but English is the evening's, because at the evening sermon
feast sit many honourable Welsh who have forgotten their
language. On such a Sunday the preacher was Eben L. Pembroke, who had fame in America for his lovely sermons and
was called 'God's Lovemonger', and all his sermons were on
the text 'God is Love'. Tabernacle could not contain all the
people who came to its door, but for the more honourable
room was made in the Big Seat, chairs having been borrowed
from the Crown and Anchor. Amos, his Box-Bible on the
ledge before him, vowed that soon he would be as genteel as
the most honourable. Perhaps next year or the year after he
would be among them, enjoying the obscene photographs of
Duke-Dan Grocer, the lewd matchbox of Sir Devon-Davies,
the imitation cigarettes of Sam Lawyer, the fountain pen of
Williams Contractor, and the ornamented marbles of Goliath
Jones Parliament.

Eben came in from the vestry. He had on him a black silk

hood and a purple sash, which was also of silk, was drawn from his left shoulder to the right of his waist. He held his hands aloft and prayed. Then he stepped into the pulpit and threw the Bible and the hymn book on the floor. The Bible cushion he threw into the Big Seat. He said in English: 'Somebody sit on it. That's what it's made for. God doesn't want soft places. He wants freedom in the pulpit. I – not the Bible – am the mouth-organ of God. I speak as He speaks. What comes from my lips comes from His lips. The message is a simple message – the message that was spoken to the first man – not the first monkey – God is love.' To deliver that message he had travelled over the broad Atlantic. He spoke it to the waves, he whispered it in the solitude of his first-class cabin, he breathed it to the men and dames in the first-class swimming pool, and his secretary made her typewriter sing it. He would go through any hardship for God. He was never too busy for God. 'Don't keep God waiting on the doormat. It's up to you to keep in with God. His stock is always soaring and there's always a dividend.' He told how as a young man in Carmarthen he sold his hat to travel to his dying mother in far-off Milford Haven. Her humble cottage was in the midst of a wilderness, but it was kept as clean as a new pin. 'The Welsh are the cleanest people in the world.' He saw a light in the window. 'A blazing beacon in the open fields.' He reached it sweaty and dusty and cooled the fevered brow with his cold hands, and he cried unto the Lord in her behalf. 'O mother o' mine, you are the most shining saint that was ever born of woman or came from the loins of man. Men, honour your mothers. Dames, honour your sex for the sake of her sublime sex. Mother o' mine, give your son counsel before you go to the throne. The counsel of the dying is the counsel of God. "What shall I say to you, dear son? You have not hurt me with one pang." Speak mother o' mine, my breast hungers for news. "Dear son, labour for Him diligently and you shall be rewarded with a crown." That is how I a sinner was converted and from that day my feet have never wandered from the agonizing path to Calvary nor my eyes from the Spirit on the Cross. In far-distant Phildelphia I founded Christ's Crusaders – Christ's boys – and we clear the boozing saloons, the boxing booths, the houses of ill fame – we sweep the city of its hell-broth. Why do I do it? Mothers in Tabernacle, when mother o' mine ascended to the arms of her Lover, I saw in her eyes a photo. It was a snap of Him she had seen – Jesus the Son of the Virgin.'

The preacher made himself into a beacon, he shaded his eyes as if he were a lost wanderer, ploughed the air with his hands, spread his arms like a swimmer, wept like a man in sorrow, and assumed the teasing eyes of a harlot.

Amos drew his fingers over the edge of his Box-Bible.

The preacher sang in a tenor voice:

> Let us sweep
> In a cloud.
> In a cloud
> Let us sweep.
> Let us sweep in a cloud
> To plague old Phar-a-oh!
> A-oh! A-oh! A-oh!

'I want that mother o' mine to hear you plugging that number. She's heard me putting it over in every city in the States. But I want her to hear my very own people doing it. Now all you folk that love Jesus, sing.'

After the congregation had sung the verse several times he eloquented in the incantating manner 'The Story of the Virgin and her Lover':

There lived a maid in the vale of the Rheidol and her name was Ann Elen. When she was grown into young womanhood, her beauty made every man in the neighbourhood want to marry her, but she would not have anything to do with anybody, saying: 'I shall become betrothed to an angel.' The parson's son heard about her words and made up his mind to lie with her. But his flattery and his hunting crop and his whipcord leggings did not avail him. She answered him and said: 'I am now betrothed to my angel prince.' Thenceforward she

211

walked alone on the banks of the Rheidol or on the roads or in the fields. Sometimes she rested in Joseph's Cave, this being the cave in which were housed the lead miners of Joseph of Arimathea. The parson's scampish son was so often near the cave that a man with the fevered brow of Savonarola made himself her guard, sitting far on the right side as if he were the young man in the Tomb, and he witnessed several of her faintings. She also talked with herself and people crawled behind the hedges alongside of her and they said that she spoke in two voices: her own and a man's. This was the way of her talkings. 'Your beauty shames the sun, my Prince.' 'Bring your sweetness, dear Anlen, to the shelter of my arms.' 'My Prince, my love is sighings and gentle quakings.' 'Love is the promise of life.' 'My life is yours. I am yours. Let me sip of your strength.' 'We will go away, Anlen.' 'Yes. And we'll find the road that is love's aisle.' 'The Star of Mary will show us the road, darling maid.' 'Mary is compassionate and she will understand.' 'We'll make our bed in a garden where the flowers are ever in bloom. And my Princess's kisses shall come upon my lips like burning hailstones.' When she went towards the cave her arm was as if it was in her lover's arm and her eyes were nearly closed in a longing prayer. A miracle happened in that cave. One day she came from it with a child in her arms and she said that the child's father was her angel lover. The people did not believe her and they searched her, but she would not say any more. The parson's son bade the people examine the disturbed earth on the right of the cave, but the young man with the fevered brow spoke out and said—

The preacher halted in his playacting.

Men and women pressed their bodies against one another; the men in the Big Seat had no women at their side and they gaped and breathed loudly. The congregation was under a spell. Amos fell forward, he having broken a blood vessel; and he was taken without.

The preacher continued his sermon.

CHAPTER XXXVI

'I'M quite a stylish gent,' said Amos. 'Laying down like a toff and a lady to serve me.'

'It's a beast of a morning,' said the publican's wife. 'You must be perishing!'

'No–no,' he replied quickly.

'I'll put a bit of coal on the fire.'

'Don't. I'm very warm, much obliged. There's dear coal is.'

'Still we must have it here. The street's knee deep in slush. I hate the place.'

'It isn't very fashionable, you know.'

'My old chap say they're going to rebuild and make offices for cinemas.'

'A cinema gent bought my next doors.'

'My old chap's holding out for a price.'

'I'll come over,' said Amos. 'I am liable do a bargain.'

'How much did you get for the shop?'

Amos hesitated, for he guarded his secrets as a heathen his idols.

'Five hundred I had. Houses are on the down, honestly.'

'The wife will miss the business. What's she going to do?'

The question was spoken in so uncommon a tone that he asked:

'What you said just then?'

'I mean what you both going to do?'

A settle had been made into a sort of bed and Amos was on it in the parlour: sick men who take off their clothes and go to bed soon die. His Box-Bible was under the blanket and made a small mound. The door which led into the shop was

213

kept open that he could see the happenings therein and be sure that Sara was not defrauding him; and Sara brought him every penny she received as she received it. The publican's wife came to see him now and again and his mind was never weary of dwelling upon her body. He had the horrid gaiety of the doomed man.

'You ought to get babies,' he said, leading her to the subject of his heart.

'Lord!' she laughed. 'The guv is quite enough for me to handle.'

'A box of tricks he is. Does he do much courting, shall I ask?'

'I'm sure you're getting better!'

'Well, does he then?'

The woman resigned herself to his mood.

'Hubbies,' she said, 'are never up to their courting days.'

'Not up to standard! Of course I'd give you a time.'

'I'm past funny business.'

'O dash!' Amos exclaimed. 'And I was thinking too.'

'I've had two husbands. Consumption took them off.'

'There's no cure for decline.'

He had a fit of coughing and his breath trembled through his fair moustache like a wind and his spittle fell like fine rain. The fit passed and he returned his gaze to the woman. Like bright lights that give no heat were the lights in his eyes and his eyes looked as if they were a child's playthings embedded in clay; and like porcelain clay cast into human mould was his face. His long fingers seethed with desire and suddenly he clutched her breast.

'You mustn't!' she said kindly and understandingly. 'You mustn't excite yourself.'

She lightly told him to make his will, and he raised his husky voice that Sara could hear him and said that he had no money to leave.

He abhorred Sara. No man can be more cruel than a sick man. Why had he burdened himself with such a meagre contrivance? She had inflamed whatever small fever had seized him. His cough would ease at her death, and he would gasp

214

and pant and twitch no more. When she brought her wizening body into the room she trod softly as if she were the sly messenger of death afraid of stirring the sleeper into life. Once upon awaking he found that she had put white paper on the table and a dish of water and a saucer of biscuits. They reminded him of the Communion service and he scolded her and ordered her to take them away.

He believed in God sufficiently to blame Him also for his affliction. But in a few days he would be about, looking at empty houses and gossiping with the publican's wife. At the turn of the year his malady would turn, and then he would take a jaunt to Ceri and lord it about the place.

'Saran! Saran! What's the matter with you, toop wench? Your ear you can't hear with?'

'Here am I, Amos.'

'When is the turn?'

'The third day is the New Year.'

'Get the grief clothes ready. Why for you stand, old slit?'

In the evenings Sara brooded her misery. She sat as one at a deathbed, her upper lip, bulging as if a lozenge was under it, trembling to be free.

'If anything occurs,' she droned, 'where's the cash for expenses?'

'Is there not a fortune in the bank? Nineteen pounds. More than I've ever had.'

'Amos bach, the twelve hundred for the shop.'

'All gone for debts you made. I always pay out for you.' She sobbed.

'Nothing there is for me then. What will I do?'

'Go on the streets – for to make them miserable with hymns.'

He was on a high sunlit plain. His shops were spread before him like mansions. Cunning were to be the schemes of his business and there was to be nothing to pay for the honey of his women. Men who had been in prison were to be behind his counters, for the wage of a punished man is low and he never errs again. The lights of his shops winked at his devices.

He was glad that he had lent no money to Drake 48. It came out at his trial that 48 had been in prison before. That was Hampton's secret. Drake was in prison and he had tried to drown himself in Regent's Park Canal. Whose baby was it? Of course it was Miss Gertrude's: the other two sisters always said 'our baby'. He ought to have done a little courting with them. That was a grand profit Sara made on the hat. He would wed a lady with millinery experience and with a great body like the publican's wife. He was slipping into a valley. God would not let him die. A commercial traveller does not go on a long journey at a short notice. Calamity hung over the valley; it was a land through which man groped alone. He had never questioned God's bargains, attending His chapels and giving to His cause in accordance with his means. He would put a stone over his father's grave and also have his mother's name cut into it and pay Carpenter for his father's coffin and Gravedigger for the grave and Katrin for the hay-fork. He would give Sara her money, withholding only the cost of her keep. He moved his legs lest they stiffen unbeknown to him.

The night and its gloom passed. He moved upward, and when his doctor came he was like a dying plant which has been shut up and is put out.

The doctor, who had a bull-like neck, put his ear against his chest and said:

'You won't want to see me again for a week.'

'You pass me A 1 o-rait?' Amos said with the credence of a child.

'I leave you to my partner.'

'Pity she's not the lady of the pub.'

Amos's eyes were as sharp as the doctor's ears were acute and he saw how he had belittled Sara; her short teeth, which were as hard as those of a death-watch beetle, were pressed together.

He thought out a plan to feed her with false hopes.

'A joke I made of the twelve hundred,' he said amiably to her. 'You shall get them in the will.'

She put a pen and ink and paper before him.

'No–no,' he said. 'Tomorrow I'll make her out.'

'Do the writing now before it's –'

She bothered him, but he held his temper even.

'You are a believer?' he asked.

'Indeed, yes.'

She placed the pen in his hand.

'What's a will without a witness? Say "drop dead and blind".'

'Drop dead and blind.'

'The husband Amos shall be buried in Capel Moriah.'

'The husband Amos shall be buried in Capel Moriah.'

'At whatever price in cash.'

'At whatever price in cash.'

'I'll bury the Box–Bible in the coffin.'

'I'll bury the Box–Bible in the coffin.'

'In the coffin of the husband Amos Morgan.'

'In the coffin of the husband Amos Morgan.'

'Drop dead and blind.'

'Drop dead and blind.'

He made her put her hands on the Bible and repeat the promises, and she did so.

The minutes followed one another and the night wore on and the year marched towards the end of its journey.

Sara wrote on paper: 'I leave money furniture shop stock to the dearly memorialled wife Sara Morgan,' and she placed the pen in Amos's hand and he wrote his name below the writing. Then she went to the publican's wife.

Amos was up and down the hill. He threw the key of his Bible into the fire and his face glimmered with the triumph that stings in life and in death.

Mastiff died on a sudden and also his father Ianto and Maggie Cowslip. There was in Gray's Inn Road a shop where one could buy second-hand counters, and he would go thereto. People were singing in the streets. He wished that he had a box other than the Box-Bible, for the Bible is religion and religion is death. Queen used silk handkerchiefs. What was the name of the Queen? She had a silk handkerchief. Silks, forward. Rash man, avaunt. Someone called him that. O yes, the Miss Actress. Three-eleven-eleven-three-eleven-eleven-three per yard, madam. Colour guara-guara-guara. Sign 69-78-454. Hurry up there, Mastiff. Capel goes to Clark on Sundays. No. Capel goes. Film offices in Corsica Street. How he had been robbed!

Sara was returned, her gaping teeth shining with pleasure.

He opened his eyes.

'What's the old row?'

'Singing they are the old year out,' she answered.

He groaned noisily.

'Miss Temple. The temple bells are ringing.'

She bent down to him.

'What you mean?'

He groaned as if he were parting from money and his body twitched as if his feet were on the brim of some hideous sea. He mumbled loosely.

'It's o-rait,' said Sara. 'There's nothing to pay for death.'

Amos thanked God for the first time in his life. Then his head inclined and the year stopped and as it turned the doctor's partner took charge of him.

Sara became aware that the electric light was burning, and she hastened to put it out. In the morning she was as if sleep had made her another woman. She searched for money and found none; and the old toiler within her stirred with hatred of the man who had made her back bent and her fingers crooked. She looked upon the tyrant who had had his day with the contempt of the conqueror and the pride of the living. She cast the Box-Bible on the floor. He should go to his Judge with nothing in his hands. Her rage was beyond reason. She battered the Bible with the heel of his shoe, lest she repent into obeying his command. The covers of the book parted and paper money was pinned to many of the leaves. She counted the money and in all there was nearly five thousand pounds.

She had him buried in London, and then she went to live in a little house foreby St Peter's Church in Carmarthen. On

market days and fair days and high days she sits in her doorway at a tray of pins and needles and reels of cotton, beseeching
passers-by:

'Do you buy something from a very poor little widow.'

'GAZING AT AN INFERNO':
AN AFTERWORD

Nothing to Pay came at a significant moment for Caradoc Evans. 1930, the year of publication, marked the close of his Fleet Street career and a move away with Marguerite Barcinsky, the popular romantic novelist who wrote under the name of Countess Barcynska and Oliver Sandys. Some years previously Evans had established his literary reputation with *My People* (1915), a striking collection of short stories which, drawing on grim incident from his native south Cardiganshire, pointed to the iniquities and oppression at the heart of rural Wales; to injustices practised by community leaders and, so Evans believed, sanctioned by a debased religion. The book was received as a frontal attack on the Welsh establishment and, while English critics might praise it as 'austere in form and precise in psychology', in Wales it stank of treachery.[1] Evans had sold his country for English gold. Welsh hatred pursued him: in 1923 and 1925 jeering exiles wrecked performances of his play *Taffy*, as anger now exploded in London's West End. All at once Caradoc Evans had become something of a celebrity: Mrs Asquith invited him to lunch, a series of speaking engagements followed, and the *Sunday Express* offered him a guest column.

Journalism had been Evans's occupation for almost twenty years. He had edited a popular weekly, subbed for the *Daily Mirror*, and in 1923 joined the staff of *T.P.'s and Cassell's Weekly*. By 1927 he had risen to be effective editor of the literary paper founded by T.P. O'Connor. His den at Ludgate Hill (once occupied by Oscar Wilde) held a plain table flanked by two hard chairs and a cupboard of review books: one contributor recalls him on a chilly November morning, windows wide open, the coal fire almost dead, sitting in a bright yellow shirt. 'He had shaggy grey-black goat's hair and violent features and the eyes of a squirrel.'

Evans stood out as a Fleet Street personality. 'He goes about with spurts and dashes,' wrote Thomas Burke, 'bursting into a place and bursting out before you know he has been there. He talks in cascades, words tumbling over each other, precisely the opposite to the caustic manner of his work.' Fellow journalist George Blake described his appearance: 'Imagine a hollow strong face, the mouth large, the eyes small and piercing, beneath a black felt hat, of which the turned-down brim keeps even the high cheek-bones of the creature in shadow.' Blake also recalls Evans's talk, 'invariably violent and violently phrased':

> I always remember a moving story he told me of an old Welsh peasant setting out to meet at Holyhead a son who had prospered in the States. He was a poor man and he had walked all the way, and the road to Holyhead was one of those smooth, straight, oppressive high roads we have built for our motorists; and, according to Caradoc, "there was this poor old man, trudging that great *arrogant* road..." I shall never forget the intensely dramatic effect of the word as Evans used it.

The word and incident recur in the eighth chapter of *Nothing to Pay*, the novel upon which Evans had been working whilst at *T.P.'s Weekly* and part of which he offered Frank Morley, a director of Faber & Faber and Fleet Street acquaintance. Even though incomplete, the book struck Morley as remarkable: Faber agreed to publish, and with a generous £175 advance.

Nothing to Pay is Caradoc Evans's most autobiographical novel, drawing on a background of shop work in South Wales and London which had encompassed premises of ineffable squalor as well as fashionable West End stores. Evans mined his drapery experiences directly and in doing so he followed

222

his own literary advice: 'If you do not move among dukes, do not write about them; if you have only the outsider's knowledge of shop life, do not write about it. Amen.'[2] He entered the trade at fourteen, leaving his Cardiganshire village of Rhydlewis in 1893 for Jones Brothers, Carmarthen, a drapery store owned by distant relatives where his elder sister, Mary, was already employed. From there he moved to Barry Docks, thence to the celebrated Cardiff establishment of James Howell. By 1899 he had reached London, working first in Kentish Town, next at Wallis's of Holborn, then at the vast Bayswater premises of William Whiteley. *Nothing to Pay* has Amos Morgan, the lad of fifteen from Pont Ceri (identifiably Rhydlewis), experiencing a similar succession of berths, though not sharing his creator's reactions. Evans, in productive revolt against the slavery of the counter, abandoned shop work in 1905; Amos, by assiduous application, becomes the perfect assistant.

Young Caradoc had entered a favoured occupation, one much esteemed as traditionally allowing the rags-to-riches transformation of enterprising West Wales' sons. The eastwards progression, the conquering advance upon a city emporium, fuelled the ambitions of many an assistant in port and coalfield town. Evans knew at first hand his countrymen who had arrived in London as shopkeepers or milkmen; their origins, their methods of success, and what they had become. His apprenticeship in drapery gave him peculiar access to the London Welsh, the one or two who placed their names above a West End store and the rest who made their way in the suburbs. He could meditate on business advancement, on 'How a boy bach with nothing got on!'

Hannen Swaffer claimed that it was he who urged Caradoc Evans, following the second collection of stories, *Capel Sion* (1916), to tell the tale of a Welsh William Whiteley. In December 1916 Evans indeed promised 'a drapery novel' though, as one might expect, he was to approach his new subject matter by way of the short story. *My Neighbours*, the 1920 collection treating of London Welsh society – its drapers, milkmen, ministers and politicians – has two stories that bear particularly upon *Nothing to Pay*: 'Joseph's House', where Evans first writes about shop work, and 'According to the Pattern', which considers the making of a London Welsh preacher-politician in terms of his background, calculated assault on the city, and eventual psychological disintegration. Evans took the preoccupations of *My Neighbours* and worked them with an altogether greater imaginative power. *Nothing to Pay* considers the myths and realities of commercial success, as exemplified in the drapery trade and in the career of one such as himself, the Cardiganshire apprentice Amos Morgan. The novel gave Evans the opportunity to explore inter-related concerns: Welsh Nonconformity, as it was and as it became; decayed modern religion, manipulated for self-interest and now a weapon of social control; the emotional stultification induced by money-worship; the family as the seat of visceral antagonisms; and genetic inheritance, by which historical processes are manifested in the individual life.

The Ceri chapters consider Amos Morgan's background and the roots of his community. More than once Evans stressed the dimension of genetic inheritance and childhood imprinting:[3]

> I think that man is occupied by the army of his ancestors: the mad and bad, the wastrel and miser, the moral and immoral, the fair and foul. They are all in him from his first carnal conception; they are alive and functioning and ever at war as to which group shall rule us. It is a war between God and Satan.

'Maybe we are the victims of a carefully planned tradition,' he suggests to readers of *Ideas*. Amos's family helped shape the village: great-grandfather Bensha belongs to its mythic past, to a world of folk practice from which arises a new religious zeal. The church is alien, an English institution deeply antipathetic to the people's aspirations. Bensha resolves on his purifying mission. From a mud-and-stone cottage on the moor (historically associated with the *tŷ unnos*, or 'the one-night house' built in defiance of the lord of the manor) he

224

must preach the true gospel.

Caradoc Evans here draws upon the heroic phase of Welsh Nonconformity, grounded in its cultural and political opposition to Anglicanism. Capel Moriah is built through the skills and sacrifice of local men and women, 'hungry for spiritual refreshment and in the certainty of a God other than the God of the jocose Parson'. That idealism Evans sees as quickly betrayed, and with profoundest consequences for his people. In talks given at the time of *Nothing to Pay* he speaks passionately of a new kind of political and religious oppression, and of the spiritual inheritance of children such as himself and Amos Morgan, born into the rural Wales of the 1870s:[4]

> I write down our ill-condition to the tyranny of the preachers and the Liberal politicians. They have not only robbed us and given us a god of their own likeness – a god who imparts neither charity nor love – but they have dominated us for so many generations that they have fashioned our mind...
> The chief offender is Methodism, which of all denominations is the most anti-democratic in Wales. She is the handmaid of Liberalism. The black-garbed soldiers are on the highways and in the lanes, worrying the people into the chapels and polling booths. They have made more havoc than any army of occupation; they have deadened more spirits than a famine....
>
> Liberal-Nonconformity drove the squire from his land and set in his place the draper, grocer, lawyer, or preacher. It sought the people's help to do so by empty promises and lies. When the squire was driven away, what happened? Rents were raised, wages lowered, and field paths, which had been trodden by generations of our people were fenced in. The new squire is a businessman and every foot of his land must show a dividend.

As it happens, the Ceri chapters forgo the fierce anti-chapel sentiment noticeable in the earlier fiction. Moriah's minister is a lightweight, with tradesmen as his deacons, not the farmers of substance who govern the Manteg of *My People*. The Ceri canvas broadens outwards socially and backwards historically to present the community's religious foundations. The approach is schematic and largely by means of satiric humour; the fuller indictment of Nonconformity, the poisoned legacy of Ceri to one of its number, emerges as the novel progresses. We focus on Ianto and his son Amos. Ianto has the classic marks of a man from the Evans country: word-obsessed, given to violence, exploiting women, at war within his family. For Evans the deepest lunacies reside within the patriarchal family, where collective shortcomings are intolerably amplified. Husbands and wives, parents and children, become tormenting alter egos, recognizing in each other characteristics which they overlook in themselves. Money is usually the battleground, with biblical style and precept hypocritically appropriated for personal gain. Amos quickly learns that all money is clean. His first halfpenny, a bribe to hurry to Moriah, spells out the lesson: a shopkeeper has money to spare; sexual favours can be purchased; rewards flow naturally to a chapel-goer; and real satisfaction comes from saving, not spending. For father and son, stones struck together on the moor become as gold and diamonds, shining like angels' eyes and wings. Money is the life force, the transcendent power.

The country boy carries his family baggage to Carmarthen, where he wakens to the attractions and snares of Englishness. Welsh–English polarities, the ambivalence of the Welsh to things English, surface in the novel, particularly in the treatment of a London–Welsh establishment which sets its fabricated Wales against patent English weaknesses. ('You know what they are. Vanity, frivolity and pleasure.') Florence Larney, the libertarian actress, epitomizes these defects. She it is who initiates Amos sexually, an encounter as meaningless as all the rest. For a Ceri son cannot incorporate his sexual self into the mature emotional life; emotions are beyond him, unless capel-sparked. He needs the 'violent ardour' of the pulpit, 'the sounding lashes and sweetening honey of the perfect prayer'. Near the end of the novel, an entire Welsh congregation stirs to the aphrodisiac of religious fervour as actor-preacher

Eben Pembroke tells of Ann Elen, a young woman betrothed to Christ, her angel prince. Eben's sermon suggests aspects of Ann Griffiths (1776-1805), the Welsh hymn-writer whose passion for Christ had its distinctly physical overtones. One is reminded also of that 'ritualised form of psychic masturbation' which E.P. Thompson detects in early Methodist gatherings.[5] In one phase of the faith, Thompson argues, emotional and spiritual energies were displaced from expression in personal and social life and appropriated for the service of the church; all with marked consequences for the individual. 'These Sabbath orgasms of feeling made more possible the single-minded weekday direction of these energies to the consummation of productive labour . . . But so drastic a redirection of impulses could not be effected without a central disorganisation of the human personality.' *Nothing to Pay* explores this phenomenon.

Business ambition alone propels Amos, journeying eastwards into his commercial hell. Manchester House, Carmarthen, is a tempered portrait; a nearly blind Boss takes in as much as allows him to prosper; emotionally unencumbered (he is unmarried), he also keeps his politics and religion to himself. Boss stands out as the most humane of Amos's employers: at Cardiff, Sam Samson rules by fear, his store an enclosed quasi-military world where staff bully juniors and fawn on superiors. 'We Welsh are ideal shop assistants because we are meek and mild hypocrites and born liars,' says Burns the survivor. The ordering of events at Sam's supports the contention. One passage (Ch.22, p.121), fusing individual biography and a people's history, psychological veracity and social insight, probes the origins of those amongst whom Evans worked at Cardiff: people like himself, of peasant stock, betrayed by their new political leaders and forced south to the coalfields in search of a living. At Sam's they become still more deeply enslaved, stripped of purpose and ambition. 'When I was a shop assistant I thought that I was following the densest occupation in the world. I never exercised my brain, nor was I asked to exercise my brain.'[6] For Evans the material hardship of the draper's assistant goes hand in hand with a poverty of personal interests, limited social concerns and a bare emotional life. Burns functions as a kind of social critic and Amos warms to his cheek; from their differing position both have the measure of Sam's. Yet Amos, ever the boss's man, shuns Union action against working conditions. (Evans's own socialism was defined in the radicalised Cardiff of the 1890s: at Whiteley's he teamed up with Duncan Davies, the militant Union official who became a valued political mentor.)

In the London chapters the hypocrisy of shop owners emerges as a theme. They justify living-in, a system for coining more profit, in the name of Christian guardianship. At Kentish Town, John Hampton-John presides over a mire of professional jealousy and public humiliation, sexual exploitation and moral compromise. Yet John is of the 'Apostolic Troop', his prosperity in accordance with his place amongst the elders of Holborn Tabernacle. Caradoc Evans repeatedly probes a diseased religion which equates godliness with worldly success. Lordly ministers preach thrift, labour and obedience to employers. 'Hosanna to the Big Banker!' chorus flocks of milkmen and drapers. In Amos, too, avarice and piety go hand in hand. One incident epitomises his religious universe. An encounter with the down-and-out Drake (Ch. 34) restores his ebbing sense of justice, and immediately comes the reflection, 'He felt as if he were heir of the sun's gold. "The Lord maketh alive".' The reference is to Samuel 2. 6-7: 'The Lord killeth, and maketh alive: he bringeth down to the grave, and bringeth up.' The Nonconformist strain which sees wealth as a reward for blind industry and chapel conformity sets Amos chillingly apart. He is the dullest of misers. Money for him has no vital power, expressing neither will nor imagination; it is a self-denying commodity, the intransitive bedrock of a drab identity. Amos fights his way through regimes calculated to brutalize better men than he. Hard work, cold opportunism, the obliteration of all sentiment and self-respect, these are weapons; these and the protective shield of money.

Asked to point the way to heaven, Caradoc Evans replied: 'through religion, charity and loyalty'.[7] A false religion which cynically reinforces the norms of Amos's world now holds sway. 'Poor saints are out of date...Poor saints laboured in vain and their wisdom is in the strong room of oblivion.'[8]

The classic Sunday school prize book is Samuel Smiles' *Self-Help*. The modern saint expounds his gospel of love and sacrifice at the banquet table and he is at his best in a prayer meeting of millionaires. His patron saint is Daniel who was rewarded for his prophetic services by being made "ruler of the whole province of Babylon".

'You cannot dish Christian ethics into the devil's decanter'; Evans holds to the doctrine of original sin in which humankind moves painfully from birth to death ('a land through which man groped alone'). With Swiftian logic he points the rules for survival: 'The New Testament maxims make bankrupts... The precept that should be engraved on every heart is: "If your religion interferes with your business, chuck your religion." Man has no obligation to his neighbour. Man's obligation is to himself.' Amos lives out this tenet, not as a buccaneering eccentric, but as a dutiful counter-assistant. He is all the more appalling because he is representative. And in his deadened sympathies and dull application to business, in his belief in a creed that pharisaically brands as inferior the poor and unsuccessful, Amos stands as the perfect servant of totalitarianism. He accumulates his gold and must endure the hell of success. If Evans cannot condemn, he denies the means of redemption. Amos dies as he lives, imagining shops spread as mansions, a slave-labour force and the honey of women. Agitated by lust, believing that his wife's death alone can restore him, preoccupied with second-hand counters in Grays Inn Road, Amos suggests a yet deeper hell. We acknowledge the infinite, futile pursuit of money; 'that her hiding place is among the secret recesses beyond the horizon, that the quest for her has no end.'

Augustus John thought Caradoc Evans 'a far more conscientious historian' than Dylan Thomas.[9] This calls attention to an element in Evans often overlooked: he needs to work from recorded or remembered fact, whether the social life of West Wales or the condition of shop workers at the turn of the century. *Nothing to Pay* offers evidence generally suppressed, and troubling insights into both employers and workers. This is what impressed H.G. Wells when he recommended the book to the 1931 conference of the Shop Assistants' Union:[10]

> ...there are a great many writers who were formerly shop assistants. The curious thing is that not one of them, with one brilliant exception, has written about the shop and what it means to be in a shop as an assistant. There was one, who is too little esteemed, who has done the thing with a certain brutal thoroughness, and he tells a great deal of truth. That is Caradoc Evans in his book *Nothing to Pay*.

The compliment would have pleased Evans, for *Nothing to Pay* he regarded as his exposé of the drapery underworld, a subject seldom documented in or outside fiction. Though at the beginning of the century shop–workers numbered a million or more, an assumed middle–class reticence made them reluctant to speak out on their circumstances. Conditions within the trade were such as no artisan would endure. Joseph Hallsworth and Rhys J. Davies, in their *The Working Life of Shop Assistants* (1910), constructed a painful picture; *Nothing to Pay* renders it with graphic immediacy.

Amos Morgan's consumption has its symbolic side, but we need to remember that it arises directly from his occupation. Young Caradoc entered drapery partly for the sake of his health. In urging the calling upon Amos, Catti repeats advice that Evans's own grandmother had given. 'In the shop the coat is ever dry. And the little feet are never wet.' To genteel parents, shop work was a suitable haven for their more delicate offspring. The facts speak otherwise. Unbelievably long hours, poor food, bodies packed together in unhygienic living quarters, all took a dreadful toll. In these years the death rate from tuberculosis amongst shop assistants exceeded those for quarrymen and coalminers. 'Get a job in the open if you want to live a few more months,' suggests the military doctor.

The sustained assault on the bosses unleashed in *Nothing to Pay* might imply an easy sympathy for the workers. But Caradoc Evans has no heroes. The novel shows shop-workers systematically reduced, made creatures of low cunning, lacking in backbone, but this is much of their own making. Amos defines success in the trade: '... endurance of affronts makes the perfect draper; he could adore the tongue that scolded him and kiss the foot that kicked him.' Evans's socialism is not grounded in a sense of man's innate perfectibility; the rich may oppress the poor, but both are vessels of sin and have fallen short of the glory.

Returning in his autobiography to the subject of shop work, Wells again commended *Nothing to Pay*.[11]

> [It] tells of the perpetual nagging and mutual irritation, the petty "spiffs" and fines, the intrigues and toadyism, the long tedious hours, the wretched dormitories, the insufficient "economized" food, the sudden dismissals, the dreadful interludes of unemployment with clothing growing shabby and money leaking away.

He had himself written about drapery, most notably in chapter 2 of *Kipps* (1905). Its picture of shop life resembles Evans's: the drudgery, petty rules and punitive fines, cold overcrowded bedrooms, inflamed ankles and sore feet, and assistants vying in obsequiousness. 'I tell you we're in a blessed drain-pipe, and we've got to crawl along it till we die,' as the apprentice Minton says. Kipps becomes restlessly aware of the deficiencies of his occupation, and is further distanced from Amos by a romanticism which makes bearable his drapery years. Kipps the assistant is made likeable; and Wells's picture of the shop owner lacks the savagery of Evans's portrayals. Shalford is a task master dedicated to 'Fishency' and 'System', but without the elements of lust, sadism, and religious hypocrisy that mark the Welshman's despots. Though the church's position is hinted at (a 'large, fat, sun-red clergyman' reminds Kipps 'to do his duty in that state of life into which it has pleased God to call him'), the link between religion and the commercial ethic Wells does not develop; class attitudes to work and money interest him more. 'Mr Wells knows what he is writing about, for he began life behind a drapery counter,' said Evans of *Kipps*.[12] Wells praised *Nothing to Pay* in much the same way. Its darker aspects he found convincing; the trade's full sordidness he had thankfully escaped but someone had at last revealed it. 'Caradoc Evans, like myself, has been a draper, and the scene he draws of a draper's existence in the meaner shops of London in *Nothing to Pay* is, I know, true in all substantial particulars.'

In speaking of this 'mature, completely honest narrative' as offering 'stories within the story', the Faber blurb acknowledged its unconventional structure, whereby a series of self-contained episodes are grouped into larger geographically-related sections, all linked by the central character of Amos Morgan. Authorial detachment characterizes the book, developing the approach of Evans's early fiction, where the author's standpoint emerges obliquely through action and dialogue. Evans can intervene directly (never more passionately than on the plight of fellow West Walians driven into Sam's emporium), but he prefers shifting the perspectives, working ironically through a narrator (generally aligned with Amos) whose opinions cannot possibly be sustained as events unfold. The technique goes to the heart of *Nothing to Pay*. Every claim made on behalf of Amos will be qualified or rejected by the reader.

The language of *Nothing to Pay* is a distinctive achievement. No Anglo-Welsh writer seems less English than Caradoc Evans, though he draws on native modes: a measured biblical tone for narrative (here salted with irony), and a vernacular dialogue set arrestingly against it. The opening of Chapter 14 illustrates the biblical manner, with its repetition and balance, and the power of abstract generalisation:

Slim Jones was a rip. He straddled beneath Coffee Pot, telling lies that he had courted Florence Larney in bed. Apprentices listened to him with wonder-hungry ears. Although they were from cottage and farmhouse and as children had heard man's commerce with woman talked about in plain words, they knew nothing of man's desire which is born of the flesh and is stilled by the flesh; and the knowledge, as Slim bared it with coarse jest and clownish gesture, tingled their senses and enlivened their imaginings.

The Old Testament habit of not subordinating clauses, but of linking them by 'and' as parallel and equivalent, allows Evans a tone which treats events of varying importance with a seemingly like degree of emphasis. It gives rise to particular hallmarks: his neutral way with violence and the quiet horror of his deaths. A sharply contrasting dialogue incorporates Welsh and Welsh-derived words, dialect and colloquialism, archaisms and neologisms, moving on occasions into an almost private language. 'Just as Gerard Manley Hopkins,' writes a recent critic, 'devised an elaborately artificial language to capture the inscape, the indwelling beauty of spiritual form of creatures and of people, so Caradoc Evans developed a correspondingly baroque language to convey the inscape, the indwelling ugliness of a perverted spiritual shape, of *his* people.'[13]

This distinctive moulding of material raises the question of Evans's 'realism' and those unremitting Welsh attacks upon him. He is at once realistic in facing grim circumstance, conscientious over fact, and yet powerfully imaginative in transmitting the inner experience of historical processes (family inheritance, religious practice, capitalist enterprise). He is a detached moral satirist, tightly controlling his material (though relaxing into humour: the broad farce of Eben Pembroke, the black comedy of Ianto and son), but also a man temperamentally obsessed, driven by his daemon.

The reviewers saw the novel variously as a sober insight into the lower depths of drapery, a virulent attack on the

Welsh, a study in negation and an allegory of evil, and a journey into a private heart of darkness, one author's fantasy of despair. H.G. Wells believed that *Nothing to Pay* 'was badly treated by the critics and did not get a proper run'. Many reviewers played down the context of drapery, seeing Evans's world as psychological or emotional rather than a physical environment. None, though, denied the book's impact, its deep imaginative hold. 'The corrosive etching is done with remarkable power' (*TLS*); 'Many of our novelists nowadays square their jaws in an awful determination to appear "powerful"; Caradoc Evans succeeds in being powerful simply and without effort' (*Everyman*); 'a terrible picture, yet so deftly limned that it commands attention' (*Sunday Times*). The American *Saturday Review of Literature* contrasted the serious concerns of *Nothing to Pay* and the trivial preoccupations of more 'sophisticated' writers. Evans's characters are fighting for their very lives and Amos 'has cultivated avarice as the best means of keeping himself fit and steady for this battle, as it goes on in the lower middle classes and lower'. The reviewer saw Swift's Yahoos in these appalling presentments of human nature; and 'It is not taking Dean Swift's name in vain to say so.'

Discussion of the novel inevitably touched on the quality of its realism. The *National Review* was quite decided:

> *Nothing to Pay* is not a realistic book; it is a fantasy – a fantasy of evil... You cannot call a work where the magnifying-glass is brought to bear on certain aspects while others are ignored, a realistic book... It is a bitter, mordant satire, not on the Welsh alone, for the things of which he writes, though clothed in Welsh detail, are really universal. The book is a savage sardonic exposure of the miserly life; Amos in this book can rank with Harpagon or Balzac's skinflint.

V.S. Pritchett (*Spectator*) agreed on the novel's mode: 'It is a fantasy that Mr Evans, with considerable and scalding art, emits. Mr Evans is no more a realist than Mr T.F. Powys. One accepts neither Mr Powys on Dorsetshire nor Mr Evans on Wales.' For Pritchett 'there is a wild sardonic humour about Mr Evans's hatred, something which whips the narrative off realism's earth'.

Less favourable reviews stressed the demands *Nothing to Pay* makes upon the reader: through its gallery of unattractive characters, its bitter censorious attitude ('a spark of sympathy would be as strange as an iceberg in the Sahara, and as welcome'), and through the disconcerting nature of the prose. In fact the novel achieved a modest success; initial interest was high and within a month of publication a second impression (2,000 copies) appeared.

The English reviews generally got the measure of the book's relationship to Wales. Judging it a satire on the futility of success, *John O'London*, for example, commented that the book 'compels attention by the author's own intensity, which has moulded the style and has driven him to create a rugged barren world and to people it with lost souls whom, for need of a name, he calls the Welsh... It is not a transcription from life... but the comments of genius upon life. He required that kind of world for artistic reasons.' Such aesthetic detachment was beyond Welsh reviewers, for whom the book was about Wales and Wales alone. On the day of publication (28 August) the *Western Mail*, the national paper of the Principality, launched a comprehensive attack. 'Mr Evans does not depict Wales as it is. His method is to eliminate space and time and to give, regardless of history and justice, a synthesis of everything he has heard or seen or imagined detrimental to his country.' For this pandering to English tastes, 'he will receive his pieces of silver'. The novel was 'filth masquerading as truth' and abounded with 'lewd imagery and frank obscenity'. An accompanying editorial urged the book's suppression: 'It is called "realism" in the jargon of the modern school. We prefer to call it filth. *Nothing to Pay* is a dirty book and we are surprised by its publication.' The ensuing correspondence revealed how correctly the paper had assessed national feeling. Not a single Welsh writer spoke out in defence of *Nothing to Pay* (though soon afterwards Dylan Thomas did his bit privately, through 'uninterrupted praise' of Caradoc's work).[14]

The *Western Mail* attack was as harsh as its onslaughts against *My People*, but this time the author remained silent. He had other things on his mind. To begin with, he was out of a job. A circulation of 72,000 could not convince its owners that *T.P.'s Weekly* had any settled future and in November 1929 it ceased publication. These were difficult times in Fleet Street and the chances of another post in literary journalism must have been slim. Not that Evans wholeheartedly set about finding one; he had a year's gratuity to live on and had met a person who believed that his future lay outside London. A year before, Marguerite Barcynsky entered the office in connection with an article commissioned by *T.P.'s Weekly*. Almost immediately she and the editor began a tempestuous affair. The pressures of this new involvement exacerbated a need for alcohol which had grown alarmingly during Evans's latter years on the paper. Fleet Street camaraderie depended on steady lunchtime drinking and after flare-ups with Marguerite, or with his wife Rose, Evans would career through his journalistic haunts. Disarray marked his literary relations also. Despite Frank Morley's eagerness to conclude a deal over projected Faber reprints of *My People* and *Capel Sion*, no agreement could be reached regarding the advance. Sooner than accept what he deemed 'riotously inadequate' terms, Evans severed links with his new publishers. The action pained him: 'Goodness knows I never wanted to wander away from Faber and Faber,' he begins his last letter on the subject. Marguerite now determined that together they should leave London for good; all at once Caradoc turned his back upon a wife and home, his many friends, his publisher, and any prospect of employment in the business that had sustained him. He would attempt to survive as a full-time writer.

JOHN HARRIS

Notes

1 *My People*, edited and introduced by John Harris, was republished in 1987 (Seren Books).

2 *Ideas*, 5 May 1916, p.24.

3 The quotation is from a typescript of a talk given in 1924 (Caradoc Evans Papers, in possession of Gwyn Jones).

4 From the text of a talk to the Hounslow Science and Arts Club, partly printed in *Western Mail*, 15 January 1930, p.9.

5 *The Making of the English Working Class* (Penguin Books, 1968), p.405. Chapter 11, 'The transforming power of the cross', is an illuminating background to Evans's portrayal of Welsh Nonconformity.

6 'Downtrodden actors', *Sunday Express*, 20 September 1925, p.7.

7 Interview, *Western Mail*, 22 June 1933, p.9.

8 Quotations here are from the typescript of a 1924 talk (Gwyn Jones Mss).

9 *Autobiography* (1975), p.403.

10 A text of the speech appears in *Shop Assistant*, 18 April 1931, p.325.

11 *Experiment in Autobiography*, vol.1 (1984), pp.147-8.

12 *Ideas*, 20 August 1915, p.27.

13 M. Wynn Thomas, '*My People* and the revenge of the novel', *The New Welsh Review* 1 (1988), p.20.

14 Letter to Bert Trick, December 1934, *Collected Letters of Dylan Thomas*, ed. Paul Ferris (1985), p.177.

THE SNOW BALL

Brigid Brophy

Wealthy, seal-like and much-married Anne is giving a glittering New Year's Eve costume ball. The theme is the eighteenth century, in keeping with her elegant house, and she is swathed in gold lamé – 'a solid gold orb' – to represent the queen whose name she shares. Her best friend Anna, who prefers perfection to life and is obsessed with Mozart, sex and death, is dressed as Donna Anna from the opera *Don Giovanni*.

Within the shimmering faded opulence of the great rooms an elaborate sequence of events gracefully unfolds. Anna spies a masked man in black, Don Giovanni, the heartless and impious seducer who did (or *did* he?) seduce Donna Anna. Ruth, a young Jewish girl dressed as Cherubino, sees all and frequently escapes to write it in her frenzied diary – yet she still looks an unlikely candidate for divesting a young Casanova of his virginity. Upstairs an act of 'perfect bad taste' is foiled by an act of huge and exotic normality in the warmth of a white boudoir. Yet there is a strain, as constant as the falling snow outside, of unease beneath the glitter.

The Snow Ball is a dazzling, highly-charged, erotic comedy of manners, 'deliberately constructed as a baroque monumental tomb'. It is also, like a Mozart opera, ultimately very moving.

'Very beautiful . . . brief and, taken all together or line by line, exquisitely decorated . . . What a pleasure it is to come upon a novel which so palpably enjoys itself. Not only the reader but the characters savour the deliciousness of the world which surrounds them. The superbly induced and in the best (indeed in the eighteenth century) artificial mood is sheer artistic insolence.'
Iris Murdoch *Sunday Times*

'Its verbal skill and its pervading atmosphere of fascinated disgust come out most strongly in microscopically detailed descriptions. In such passages Miss Brophy's twin obsessions with sex and mortality come together, and the result is powerful . . .'
Observer

0 7474 0580 8
CARDINAL FICTION

A FEARFUL JOY

Joyce Cary

As a child Tabitha Baskett was remarkable for nothing but a certain 'violence of ordinariness'. In impressionable young Victorian womanhood she fell prey to the most far-fetched of impudent bounders, Dick Bonser. Folly and ruin might have been her fate, had the naughty nineties not arrived – finding Tabitha's salon of decadent artists at the height of fashion. Unwittingly and with no taste for *The Yellow Book*, she founded a vanguard literary review and became the hub of the aesthetic movement.

But fortune frowned as well as smiled on Tabitha – ferociously fond mother, erstwhile lady of the manor to a crazed armaments manufacturer, prim hotelier in a new age of motor cars and public dancing and, finally, nearly forty years after their elopement, legal wife of the unrepentant Bonser.

If Tabitha Baskett hadn't had the unstoppable urge to laugh at the most important and absurd junctions of her life, none of it might have happened this way – and we might have missed one of the most enchantingly ridiculous and life-enhancing stories of modern fiction . . .

0 7474 0689 8
CARDINAL FICTION

All Cardinal books in this series are available from good bookshops, or can be ordered from the following address:

Sphere Books
Cash Sales Department
P.O. Box 11
Falmouth
Cornwall TR10 9EN

Please send cheque or postal order (no currency), and allow 60p for postage and packing for the first book plus 25p for the second book and 15p for each additional book ordered up to a maximum charge of £1.90 in the U.K.

B.F.P.O. customers please allow 60p for the first book, 25p for the second book plus 15p per copy for the next 7 books, thereafter 9p per book.

Overseas customers, including Eire, please allow £1.90 for postage and packing for the first book, 75p for the second book and 28p for each subsequent title ordered.

CARDINAL